"OUR YOUNG FOLK'S" SHILLING STORY BOOKS.

CAPTAIN RODMAN;

OR,

THE CRUISE OF THE CONQUEROR.

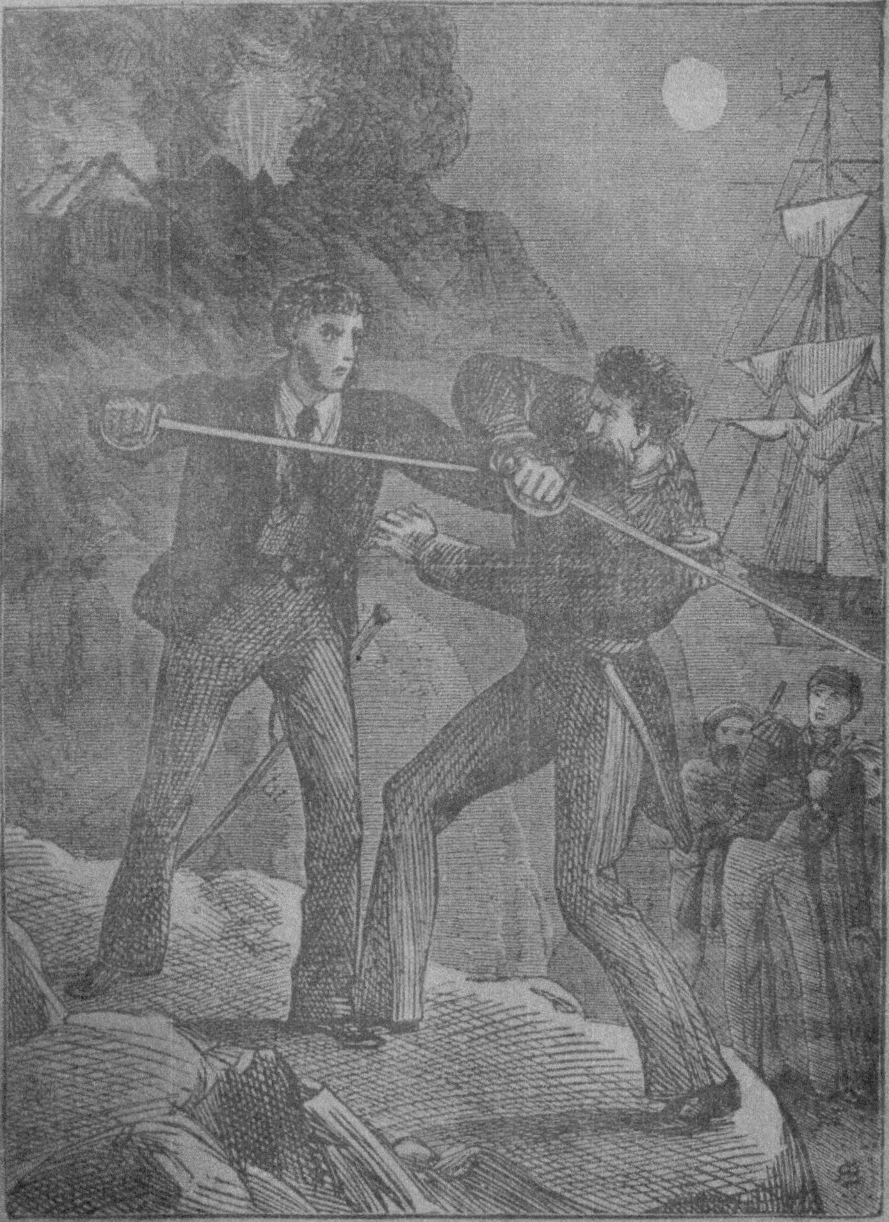

LONDON: JAMES HENDERSON, RED LION HOUSE, RED LION COURT, FLEET STREET.

"OUR YOUNG FOLKS" SHILLING STORY BOOKS.

CAPTAIN RODMAN;

OR, THE

CRUISE OF THE CONQUEROR.

A SEQUEL TO "DASHING RODMAN."

BY

J. A. MAITLAND,

Author of "Young Tom Rodman," "Tom Rodman Afloat," "Dashing Rodman, Lieutenant of the Leander,"
"Fred Hilton the Soldier-Sailor," &c., &c.

ILLUSTRATED BY W. BOUCHER.

LONDON :
JAMES HENDERSON, RED LION HOUSE, RED LION COURT, FLEET STREET.

CAPTAIN RODMAN;

OR, THE

CRUISE OF THE CONQUEROR.

CHAPTER I.

ONE fine autumn day, in the earlier portion of the present century, a large and remarkably handsome frigate—the Conqueror, carrying sixty-two guns—lay at anchor in the road of Spithead. On the shore, opposite the ship, a numerous body of seamen had congregated, who, it was easy to see from their peculiar attire, and generally clean and spruce appearance, belonged to the Royal Navy.

At this period, though England had been for many years at war with France, and through the machinations of the French Emperor, Napoleon Bonaparte, with at one time or other half the nations of Europe, peace to most people seemed to be as far distant as ever. Nay, further, for England was threatened with still more serious complications.

There was serious talk of an approaching war with America—a war which soon afterwards broke forth, and caused British seamen to meet their own countrymen as foes, and foes who fought desperately, as it were with a halter round their necks; and when, according to ignorant or prejudiced report, the "Meteor Flag of England" was not so universally triumphant on the ocean as it had been for more than a century, and as in reality it still remained.*

The sailors who were so critically examining the frigate seemed to be in doubt whether to ship on board of her, or on board some other vessel.

The question, however, was soon decided.

A young, slight-built, boyish-looking officer was presently seen approaching.

---

* In the American war of 1812-14, the war-ships of America, though generally officered by native-born Americans, were chiefly *manned* by runaway British seamen, who fought with savage desperation for the very sufficient reason that, if they were captured, they knew that they were liable to be hanged, as traitors to their king and country.

"Vast heavin' there, shipmates," said an old sailor, who had just caught sight of the youthful officer. "I think I know this gentleman as is comin' this way; and if so be, why we'll soon settle this matter;" and stepping towards the young officer, and touching his hat respectfully, he said: "Beggin' your pardon, your honour, may I ask if your name ain't Peters?"

"It is," was the reply; "and if I'm not mistaken, you are Bill Simpson, who was a quartermaster on board the Ajax?"

"The same, sir," replied the old seaman, with a gratified smile.

"I thought so," continued the young man. "I never forget the face of an old shipmate. I was a reefer when we sailed together, but I am a lieutenant now."

"So I see, sir," replied the sailor, glancing at the young gentleman's glittering epaulet. "But what I wanted to arx you, sir, if I may make so bold, is whether Cap'en Rodman, as they say is the new cap'en of the frigate lyin' off yonder, is the same genelman as was third leeftenant of the Leander, and as commanded the flotilla as was sent up the river Douro, in Portingale?"

"The very same Lieutenant Tom Rodman," replied the young officer. "He now commands one of the finest ships in the British navy; and more than that, old shipmate, I'm second lieutenant on board of her."

"That's enow, sir. That settles the question. I don't want to hear no more nor that," replied the old quartermaster. "Me and my shipmates here—most on 'em, as your honour may see, old Ajax's—volunteers for her at once. We *was* in doubt whether to ship aboard the Conqueror or the Owdacious, as is fittin' out at Plymouth. But this settles the matter. We goes aboard to-morrow mornin', every man on us; and though I says it as shouldn't, I don't think Cap'en Rodman could pick up a primer lot o' seamen if he were to search Portsmouth for a month."

"That *I* can vouch for, Simpson," said the lieutenant; "and right glad I shall be to sail with so many Ajaxes again. Don't sheer off and disappoint us though, my lads," he added, addressing the men generally.

"Never fear, sir. We'll be aboard the first thing to-morrow," the sailors replied in one voice, and the young officer passed on his way.

The next morning, greatly to the satisfaction of Mr. Bowling, the first lieutenant of the Conqueror, the volunteers made their appearance on board the frigate—Simpson, the spokesman of the party, informing the lieutenant that he and his shipmates had engaged to sail on board the Conqueror, because they had learnt from Lieutenant Peters that the ship was commanded by the same gentleman under whom most of them had served on board the boats which composed the flotilla that was sent up the River Douro. Later in the day, Peters went on board the frigate, and as he and the first lieutenant were walking the quarter-deck together, the latter complimented him upon the fine lot of men he had induced to volunteer for the frigate.

"They volunteered because I assured them that Captain Rodman was the same officer under whom they had served on the Douro," returned Peters. "By the way, Mr. Bowling," he added, "have you heard when Captain Rodman is likely to return?"

"Yes," replied the first lieutenant. "I received a letter this morning, in which he states that he will be in Portsmouth to-morrow morning. None too soon, neither, for the frigate is under orders to sail in a day or two."

"You couldn't expect to see him until the last moment, when you consider the errand he has gone upon," said Peters, with a smile.

"Well, no," replied the staid, middle-aged first-lieutenant; "when you young fellows once moor alongside your sweethearts, there's no getting you to trip your anchors till you're dragged away with the tide. For my part, I can't see what a sailor wants with a wife. I'm of the same opinion as old Admiral Lord Dundas : I consider that when an officer's married, he's spoilt for the service."

"Captain Rodman is not married yet," replied Peters ; " but to speak of other matters—how about the crew ? Are they all shipped yet ? "

"No," replied the first lieutenant ; " we want fifty more hands yet. There are so many ships fitting out, and so many men wanted by the merchant ships, that I don't know where we are to look for able seamen, nowadays. I'm afraid the frigate will be detained on that account."

For some minutes the two officers paced the deck in silence. Then the first lieutenant spoke again:

"I fear we shall have to send a pressgang on shore," he said. "I'd rather not have pressed men on board, if we can get volunteers ; and if sailors knew when they were well off, they'd join the navy without being pressed. But— ' Needs must when the old one drives '—you mind the old proverb ? I had a visit from a rascally crimp this morning, who told me that there is a fine lot of first-rate seamen, in hiding, in the town, until we have sailed, when they'll make their way to London, or to visit their friends—for most of them have just returned from a long voyage. Confound the scoundrel who seeks to betray the poor fellows, for money ! If I had *my* will, I'd have ordered the men to heave the wretch overboard. But, unfortunately, these fellows—and spies too, in time of war—are necessary evils. One must employ them, while one loathes the very sight of them."

" What did you say to the fellow ? " asked Peters.

"I told him to be off about his business. But we can't lose these men, if it can be helped. I fear we shall have to engage the rascal's services."

Again the lieutenant was silent for a while, until, once more addressing his junior officer, he said, hesitatingly :

" You sent a fine set of fellows on board this morning, Peters. What do you say to trying *your* hand with these merchant sailors ? "

" *I* lead a pressgang on shore ! " exclaimed Peters, with something like disgust. " Nay, if we must resort to impressment to procure our full complement of hands, surely you can trust one of the warrant officers to lead the party ? "

" I *can*, of course," was the lieutenant's reply ; " and if you seriously object to the duty, I will. But, my dear fellow, I've set my heart upon obtaining our full complement of seamen before Captain Rodman's return ; and if I must resort to impressment, those people now on shore are just the men I should wish to have. A warrant officer might blunder the matter. The sailors would not obey such an one as they will obey you, and "——

" Say no more," interrupted Peters. " I never *have* led a pressgang, and I don't like the idea. Still, I've been thinking it over, and though it's dirty work, unfit for a gentleman to undertake, I'll go this once ; for I like to be able to say that I've had a hand in everything."

" Thank you. I shall regard it as a favour on your part, Mr. Peters," said the first lieutenant, who forthwith acquainted his junior officer with the information he had received that morning from the crimp ; told him where he could meet the fellow, and advised him how to act under the different circumstances in which he might find himself placed.

Soon after dusk that evening, Lieutenant Peters, disguised as the young mate of a merchant ship, quitted the frigate in command of a strong party of petty officers and trusty sailors, all of whom were well armed, though *they*, too, were disguised as merchant seamen.

The rascal of a crimp was easily found at the spot he had designated; for, despite his rough reception at the hands of the first lieutenant, he guessed that he had thrown out a bait that no first lieutenant eager to complete his crew would be able to resist; and for a certain sum of money paid into his hand, the fellow led the way to the house in which the merchant seamen were in hiding.

On the way he informed Lieutenant Peters that the men—some of whom were respectable mates and second mates of ships, and all of whom, having just returned from long voyages, were flush of money—had disguised themselves in various garbs to represent themselves as tradesmen and shopkeepers, and even as professional men; some having attired themselves as lawyers, doctors, and even as clergymen, as if—under *any* disguise—it were possible to a thorough-bred seaman to conceal his real character!

The house in which the poor men had taken up their abode proved to be a respectable hotel, frequented also by commercial travellers and other guests. Here the seamen—being flush of money—had engaged several rooms; but it was their custom at night, when they believed themselves safe from the visit of a pressgang, to meet in the common room with the other guests of the hotel.*

Having stationed his men in different spots, so as to surround the hotel, and instructed them how to act, and to be prepared to make their appearance at an appointed signal, the young lieutenant, passing himself off for what his disguise represented him to be, entered the house, and, after some little difficulty, contrived to gain admission to the room in which the sailors had assembled to enjoy themselves, in company with two or three casual guests.

The sight which met the eyes of the young officer when he entered the room proved almost too much for his risible faculties, and he had much ado to restrain himself from laughing outright; but he recollected the difficult task he hoped to accomplish, and managed to compose his features, and assume an aspect of seriousness, and some alarm, as though he, too, was hiding from the pressgangs that were so often abroad.

Taking his seat amidst the company, who at first regarded him with some suspicion, he looked calmly around him, and took mental notes of his companions.

Opposite him sat a short, sturdy, red-faced man of some forty years, whose complexion was bronzed alike by tropical heats, tempestuous breezes, and the keen blasts of the frigid zone, and whose broad shoulders, and rounded back, and long arms, and comparatively short and slender nether limbs, caused him to appear almost as broad as he was high. His features, naturally of a cheerful, jovial cast, wore a forced serious aspect; for he had thought fit to attire himself in the sombre garb of a parson, and vainly struggled to look the character he wished to represent.

His hairy, bull-throat, used to exposure to all sorts of weather, was encompassed by an ample white neckcloth, in several wide folds, which evidently made him feel as uncomfortable as a Polar bear would feel in a hot-house. He wore an enormous pair of spectacles on his carbuncled nose, which, in spite of his efforts, *would* slip from their place; nor could he see through them when, after much trouble, he contrived to fix them temporarily in a proper position. His

---

* The custom of pressing men to serve in the Royal Navy has long been discontinued, though the Act of Parliament which made impressment legal has never been abolished. The better pay, the superior treatment they now receive, the easier life they lead, and the prospect of a pension for long service or if disabled by wounds, has made sailors more eager than they were formerly to enter the naval service, and has rendered compulsory service apparently unnecessary, though the question has, even of late years, been mooted in Parliament, whether it would be wise to abolish the law of impressment altogether, and whether, in case of a long and severe naval war it would be possible, without impressment, to procure a sufficient supply of seamen.

large tar-stained hands, with the fingers crooked, and the palms turned outwards, extended two inches beyond the cuffs of his wide, slop-made black coat, looking all the larger in consequence, while he seemed as if he knew not what to do with them.

Vainly the poor fellow tried to suit his voice and manner to his assumed character, and altogether he presented the most uneasy, miserable-looking object the young officer had ever beheld. Beside him sat a shipmate attired in the costume which *he* considered appropriate to a doctor. Opposite him sat another hardy, weather-beaten seaman, who fancied that he looked the very impersonification of a lawyer.

Others there were, as I have said, who endeavoured, with more or less success, though poorly at the best, to represent trades and professions of every variety, though now, believing themselves to be safe for the night, and being heartily wearied of the constraints of the day, they had generally given way to their natural habits; and, attired in the sober garments I have described, were drinking beer from large pewter pots, and smoking long churchwarden pipes, while their conversation gradually took the tone that was most familiar to them, and they had begun to discourse freely of their hardy profession, and of the voyages they had made, and the various marvellous adventures in which they had performed their several parts.

Soon after Lieutenant Peters' arrival, the other guests of the hotel had, with one solitary exception, taken their departure, and had probably gone to bed, finding little to interest or amuse them in the strange society of the commercial parlour.

He who remained was a short, stout, bald-headed man, somewhat past middle age, whose mingled pomposity and simplicity, and whose general appearance and manners, induced Peters to believe that he was some country shopkeeper, whose honest industry had raised him to comparative wealth and to influence, which gave him a high position in his native town, and had led him, while he was naturally of a kindly disposition, to entertain a somewhat high opinion of himself; though, while he looked down upon the company in which he found himself, he listened with wonder to the marvellous tales his companions told, and evidently gave them implicit credence.

He, like the rest of the company, was rather shy with Peters at first; but when the young lieutenant represented himself as the mate of a ship belonging to Bristol, which had just returned from a two years' voyage, and showed, by his conversation, that he was indeed a seaman, and professed to possess, and exhibited, a plentiful supply of money, which he averred he had received as his wages, and, moreover, insisted upon treating the company freely to whatever they chose to call for, he gradually rose in their estimation, and soon became on the most friendly terms with the stranger, who, however, while he chatted with him, implied by his manner that he considered that he was condescending in so doing.

The object of the young lieutenant was to ply his companions with drink so as to render them an easy prey to the men-of-war's men on guard, and by this means to avoid the strife and bloodshed which would probably otherwise ensue when the signal should be given, and the sailors would suddenly make their appearance; for too often it happened that the assaults of the pressgangs led to fierce and sometimes even to fatal conflicts.

With most of the merchant seamen this was an easy matter, though some among them were more wary than others. However, in a couple of hours most of the seamen were sound asleep, while those who were still awake were incapable of making any effectual resistance to an attack upon them.

Lieutenant Peters, himself, while professing good fellowship, had merely pretended to empty his glass, and was perfectly sober; while the supposed country shopkeeper, though his small eyes danced and twinkled, had drank no more than sufficient to make him jovial and friendly, and was far from intoxicated. At length the young officer thought the right moment had arrived. His men, he knew, must be tired of waiting, so, rising from his seat, he went to the door and gave the concerted signal to the men-of-war's-men, anticipating an easy victory.

In an instant the large room was filled with rough, armed men, who forthwith proceeded to drag forth and handcuff the sleeping merchant seamen, while those still awake were so confused, and had been so taken by surprise, that they too were captured and secured, after but a very slight struggle.

So far all had gone well, and Peters was pluming himself upon the praise he should receive from his superior officers for having conducted the affair in such a quiet, gentlemanlike manner, and thus secured such a fine set of seamen for the frigate.

Opposition and resistance, however, came from a quarter least suspected.

The stranger-guest, at first, looked on with amazement, unable to understand the meaning of the sudden attack, and the violent disturbance of the goodfellowship that had existed.

At length some idea of the nature of the outrage seemed to enter his mind, and rising from his seat, and steadying himself by his chair, he denounced in indignant terms the conduct of the pretended mate and his party.

The men-of-war's-men laughed, and Peters replied:

"Hold your tongue, old gentleman, or it will be the worse for you. Sit down, and mind your own business."

"I won't! I shan't!" cried the supposed shopkeeper. "I protest against such an outrage upon the liberty of Englishmen. Let these people go free, or I'll complain to the authorities and have you and your men severely punished."

"Have a care, old fellow," said Peters, laughing, "or I'll take *you* too. You'd best be silent."

"Me!—me!" cried the stranger. "You *dare* to lay hands upon *me*, you young whipper-snapper! You threadpaper apology for a brave seaman! Take care, my fine fellow. I've got more influence with your superiors than you probably suspect."

The men-of-war's-men laughed louder than before at this boast, and commenced to jeer the old gentleman; but the young lieutenant grew angry.

"By George, old fellow," he cried, "if you say another word, I will seize you, and carry you on board the frigate. Useless old landlubber that you are, you'll still be of service to swab the decks, and sweep out the cook's galley;" and, half in earnest and half in jest, he advanced to seize the old gentleman, who grew furious at the insult he had received.

"Touch me if you dare, you contemptible counter-jumper!" he cried; and snatching up his walking-stick from a corner of the room, he threw his stout person into a ludicrous attitude of defiance. "Come a step nearer, and I'll knock you down!"

A roar of laughter burst from the men-of-war's-men, while Peters felt ashamed of his own foolish passion.

"Come away, lads," he said to his men. "Lead these people down to the tender while the coast is clear, and leave that old fool to come to his senses."

The lieutenant, however, reckoned without his host. The people of the house had been alarmed by the entrance of the pressgang; but hitherto, aware of the futility of interference, the landlord and waiters had wisely kept in the background. But the violent altercation had come to the ears of the female servants in the kitchen, who immediately came to the rescue. Pressgangs were held in abhorrence by the people generally; but while the men were afraid to interfere, the women, knowing that the sailors *could* not drag them off, and that they *would* not harm them if they could avoid it, not unfrequently came to the assistance of the pressed men, falling furiously upon their assailants, and often effecting the release of some among their friends.

In the present instance, the female servants rushed into the room, led by the fat cook, who furiously brandished the long spit she carried, while the others flourished broomsticks and mops and rolling-pins, with which they laid about them bravely, calling, at the same time, upon the men-of-war's-men to release the captives, and heaping invectives upon the young lieutenant.

At first the sailors regarded the affray as a joke, and cries of, "Sheer off, Molly, my lass!" "Belay there, Sally!" "My eyes, but that was a stinger Bessy gave *you*, Bob!" and so forth.

The sailors' good humour, however, gave way at length to the provocation, and the severe blows that several of them received, and a regular battle royal ensued, in which the stranger guest took part with the females, and capered about, striking right and left with anything he could get hold of. The men-of-war's-men, however, proved the victors in the end, and the captive merchant seamen were dragged away, the old gentleman, tightly handcuffed, being also carried off, amidst a howl of execrations from the women, above which were now audible the screams of a female, who appeared to have been suddenly aroused from sleep, and who now made the house ring with lamentations for her husband, whom the "pirates"—as she termed the men of the pressgang—were tearing away from her, and with threats of dire vengeance.

By this time the people of the town had heard of the presence of the hated pressgang, and when Peters and his men reached the street, they were assailed with sticks and stones by a rabble of men and women of the lowest class. The sailors, however, laid about them, and succeeded in carrying off their captives, though not before all parties had received many severe wounds and bruises. The young lieutenant's clothes were almost torn off his back, his lips were cut, his nose was bleeding, his face swelled, and one of his eyes blackened. In this woful condition he and his party conducted their prisoners to the tender, where they were lodged for the night, to be drafted on board the frigate on the morrow.

Thus, for the time being, ended Lieutenant Peters' adventure, though he had yet to learn the result of his night's work. Still, with his customary recklessness and love of mischief, he laughed at the fun, despite the severe mauling he and his men had met with, and felt proud of his success in having secured such a fine body of seamen for his frigate.

Flushed with excitement, he put off on board his ship; and as soon as he had changed his clothes, and had his cuts and bruises seen to, he greatly amused the first lieutenant with his lively description of the affray, and of the indignation of the fussy old gentleman, whom, in the spirit of fun, he had actually pressed and carried on board the tender along with the other captives—though he vowed that he would never lead a pressgang again as long as he lived.

*　　*　　*　　*　　*　　*　　*

Change we now the scene for a while from the decks of a frigate, and the bustle and dirt of a seaport town, to a large and beautiful park in the heart of Cambridgeshire.

That same afternoon on which the two lieutenants conversed together as they paced the quarter-deck of the Conqueror, a gentleman and lady might have been seen strolling leisurely through one of the most secluded avenues of the park.

The gentleman was a young man of apparently about twenty-eight years of age, and though he was simply attired in a blue frock coat, he had the appearance of a naval officer, while his gold shoulder-straps told that, young as he still was, he had already attained to high rank in the service.

The lady, who was remarkably handsome, was, in truth, a year or two older than he, though she looked younger, for the bronzed cheeks, and the air of habitual authority that was apparent in the countenance of her companion, and that is peculiar to most naval officers of rank, gave him an appearance of greater age than he possessed.

"Then you leave us to-night, Captain Rodman?" said the lady, in a tone of regret, after a brief period of silence.

"I *must*, dear lady," was the reply. "I have already overstayed my time, for my frigate is ready for sea, and I must sail in a day or two. I should go to sea more happily," he went on, after a pause, "if you would consent to be mine before I leave you."

"It must not be, Captain Rodman," replied the lady, whose name—Lucy Sinclair—will be familiar to those who have made themselves acquainted with the gallant captain's earlier history, in "Tom Rodman's Schooldays" and "Tom Rodman Afloat."

"It must not be, for my father will not give his consent, and dearly as I love you, I would not wed without it. But time will soon pass away," she went on, after a pause, "and on your return"——

"Who can tell what may happen before my return?" interrupted the captain. "My cruise will last two years at least, probably much longer, and who can say what may occur to prevent the consummation of my happiness, ere I tread the shores of England again?"

"You have my father's word, and surely you cannot doubt *my* love, or my faith and constancy?" replied the young lady, apparently struck with something in the tone of her companion.

"No, dear Lucy, no. *You* I do not doubt, and I feel that I can trust to your father's promise that we shall be wedded on my return from my forthcoming cruise; still"——

"Still what?" said the lady. "Dear Tom, you have *some* doubt in your mind? I see—I feel that such is the case. Why hesitate to confide it to me?"

"Lucy," said the captain, "I know that I am not your equal in birth. My father has raised himself to a position of comparative wealth through his honesty and industry; but I cannot help feeling *now*—though the thought never troubled me until I had won your affection—that I am but the son of a humble shop-keeper, while you, Lucy, can boast of ancient family and high lineage; and sometimes, I fear"——

"That *I* am weak and vain enough to regard such folly? Oh, Tom, I thought you were above such weakness! I do not decry the advantages of birth and family. None do save those who have no family to boast of. But I am not so foolish and vain as to look with scorn upon those of humbler birth than I. The highest and proudest have risen from a humble origin, through their courage or skill, or sometimes through such qualities as they dare not boast of. *You* have raised yourself to a proud position, while still young, through your skill and bravery; and *who* is most to be valued and admired—he who has accomplished what *you* have done by his own merit, or he whose only merit consists in the virtues of his ancestors, which he no longer strives to emulate? Tom, banish such foolish fancies from you—they are unworthy of you. My father loves and admires you, and thinks not of your humble birth, for you are the son of honest parents, who deserve credit for the success they have achieved, and they have reason to be proud of *you*. You have sought and won my affections, and they are yours so long as life shall last. Trust in me as I trust in you, and let us both look forward to the happy day of your return, with fresh honours gained in a successful cruise, as I feel assured will be yours, and to the joy of our next meeting—I hope not to part again."

Captain Rodman took the hand of the fair speaker, and, encouraged by her words, banished the cloud of doubt and fear from his countenance. Both presently seated themselves on a rustic bench opposite an old cedar tree; and to cheer her companion, the young lady chatted of earlier days, and both laughed merrily as they recalled to mind the ludicrous adventure which had brought the captain—then a young schoolboy—an uninvited visitor to the Grange, and had led to their first acquaintance.

"Do you recollect, Tom," said the lady, "how I charged you with having hanged my favourite doll on one of the branches of that very tree before us, when, in truth, it was my own scapegrace cousin, Tom Dobson, who was the real offender, and in what a labyrinth of mystery we all of us got involved before the facts which led to your visit became known? How often since I have laughed over that visit!"

Captain Rodman laughed too, as he recalled the visit to mind; and, though both were sorrowful at the thought of soon parting for so long a period, they strove to assume an aspect of cheerfulness; and sometimes chatting merrily over the past, and sometimes talking hopefully of, and building bright *chateaux en Espagne* in the future, and sometimes intermingling their light and cheerful chat with the more earnest and serious converse of lovers secure of each other's affection, they lingered in the park until the night dews began to fall, when both —still lingering, as though loath to quit the scene—strolled leisurely towards the mansion, when Captain Rodman soon bade farewell to his kind friends, Captain and Mrs. Sinclair; and after a last parting good-bye to Lucy, sprang into the captain's carriage, which was waiting to convey him to the coach-office in the neighbouring town, and ere another hour had passed away, was well on his way to Portsmouth, to rejoin the fine frigate to which he had lately been appointed commander.

CHAPTER II.

ALTHOUGH Captain Rodman maintained strict discipline on board his ship, his friendship and regard for his old schoolfellow, Harry Peters, now appointed, through his influence, to the second lieutenancy on board the Conqueror, induced him to meet the young lieutenant on terms of perfect intimacy, and to converse with him with his old schoolboy freedom when Peters was off duty or on shore.

As I have shown, Captain Rodman, though he had raised himself to a responsible position, and acquired the favour of the Admiralty authorities, through his own strict attention to his duties from the period at which he first went to sea as a midshipman, and his utter disregard of peril or danger when deeds of daring were required from him, he was not so weak as to feel ashamed of his comparatively humble origin, or as to be guilty of that meanest of meannesses which sometimes leads people to boast of birth and family to which they can lay no claim; and though it may be said that the young captain owed his success in his profession, and his rapid promotion, in part to the interest which Captains Sinclair and Blakeley had taken in his welfare, it is certain that that interest would not have been taken in him by these gentlemen had he not merited it by his good conduct.

The father of Captain Rodman had raised himself from poverty to the possession of wealth greater than that which many who claimed to be gentlemen by birth possessed, solely by dint of his own energy, honesty, and industry, and therefore the young captain had far more reason to be proud than ashamed of his parentage.

As he concealed nothing from his most intimate friends, Lieutenant Peters and some others were aware that old Mr. Rodman was, or had been, engaged in retail trade, though, as it happened, none of the captain's friends had hitherto been introduced to, or, to their knowledge, ever seen the old gentleman.

Lieutenant Peters was again on shore the next morning after the affair of the pressgang, when Captain Rodman returned to Portsmouth from his visit to Cambridgeshire, and as soon as Peters heard of his captain's arrival he went to the hotel at which he (the captain) was accustomed to put up.

Peters had done his best to conceal all trace of the rough usage he had met with on the previous evening. He now wore his full dress uniform, in compliment to his captain, but his face still showed marks of the conflict. One eye was discoloured, he wore a strip of diachylon plaster on his lip, and his face was still swollen.

"Why, Peters, what on earth has happened to you?" said the captain, after the ordinary compliments had passed between them. "You look as if you had just come out of a smart engagement!"

"With a lot of enraged women—confound them!" replied the lieutenant, laughing at the recollection; and then, much to Captain Rodman's amusement, he related, in his own ludicrous fashion, his adventure with the pressgang, and its results.

"I led the party at the request of the first lieutenant," he said, in conclusion. "I never had seen a pressgang at work, and I thought I should like, just for once, to witness the proceedings. But I'll be hanged if you catch me at it again, if I can help it. By Jove, I'd sooner board a French frigate any day than meet a

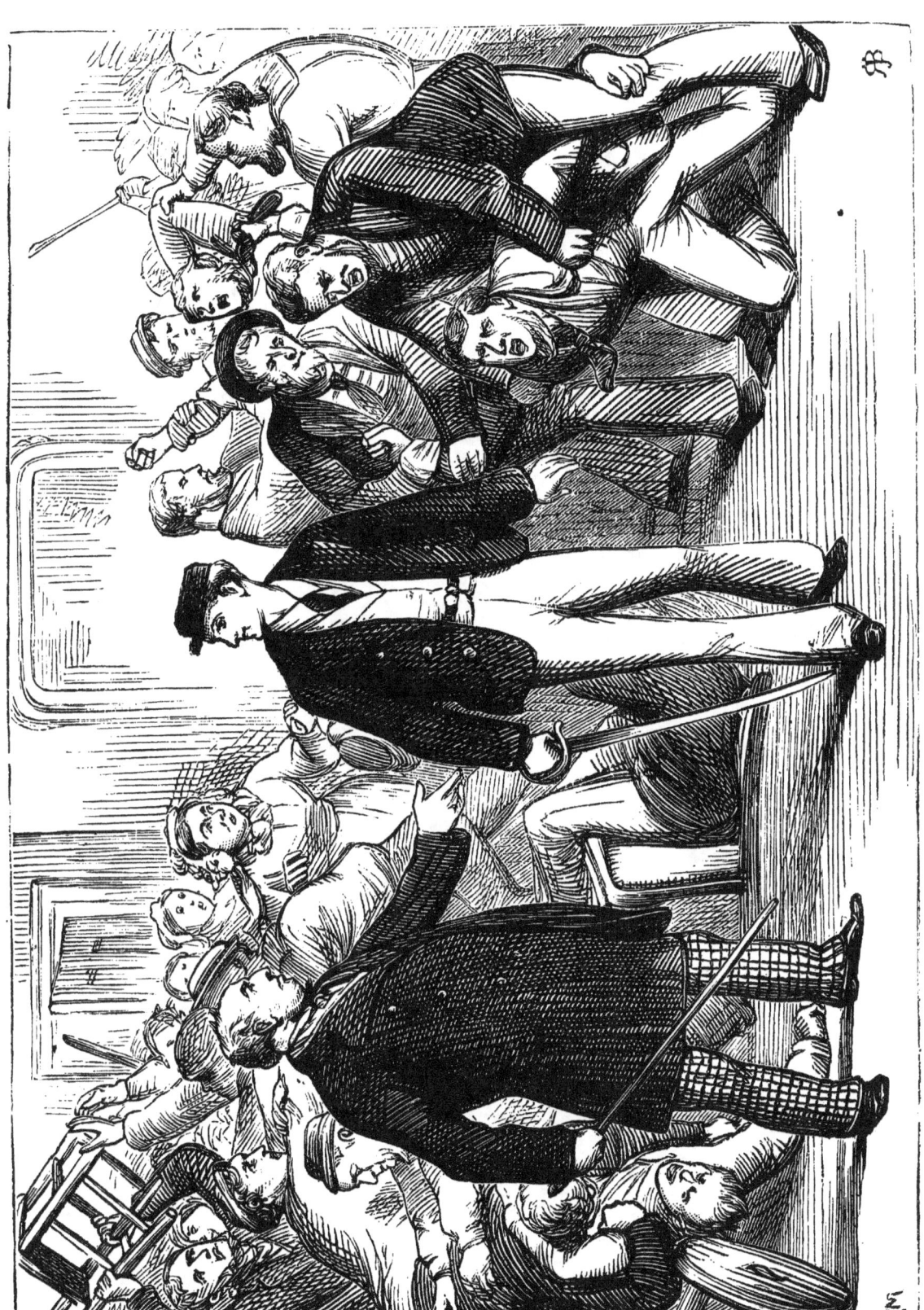

The Pressgang.—The women to the rescue.

parcel of infuriated women, whom a fellow can't strike back again! George! How the broomsticks did rattle on my poor fellows' heads! I wonder they bore it so good-humouredly as they did; and the fat old cook of the hotel was near running me through with the spit—confound her! However, I brought off a fine lot of able seamen, that's some consolation."

Captain Rodman laughed heartily, especially at Peters' description of the little stout old gentleman, who, he declared, showed plenty of pluck.

"I heartily wish," said the captain, when he had composed his countenance, "that we could do without this system of impressment. I object to it thoroughly; though, at the present time, when men are so scarce, we cannot avoid resorting to it. Not but that pressed merchant sailors, when once they get used to the routine of a ship-of-war, often turn out capital fellows, and stick to the naval service ever afterwards. It's a foolish prejudice that they have against it, which they soon get over. But I *do* object seriously to the riff-raff and rabble—the vagrants of the streets, and the scourings of gaols, that we are compelled to impress, together with better men—fellows who are never worth their salt, and, who, by their misconduct, frequently tend to attach disgrace to men-of-war's-men. But, Harry, my dear fellow, I hope you have not gone too far. You should have left the sturdy old gentleman of whom you speak alone. You had no right to impress *him*, and I fear that his arrest will get us into trouble."

"If he'd pitched into *you*, sir, as he did into me, after the women came upon the field of action," replied Peters, laughing, "you'd have pressed him too, just to teach the old fellow better behaviour another time. He made some mysterious threats, too, about some relative or friend of his, who was 'high up' in the service, to whom he was going to complain, and who would play the mischief with us for daring to lay hands upon him. I wonder what he thinks of the power of this 'high up' friend of his now?"

"I trust that he is released long before this," said the captain.

"No; he's aboard the tender with the other fellows yet," replied Peters. "I told him I'd make a swabber and bottle-washer of him, and he'll be sent on board the frigate, though I suppose the first lieutenant will soon send him on shore, and be glad to get rid of him."

"Did you not say that his wife was with him at the hotel?" asked the captain.

"I heard a female voice, apparently just aroused from sleep, screaming, and crying for her husband, as we were leaving the hotel," was the reply; "and I presume that she was the old gentleman's wife."

"I wish to heaven, Harry, you had not interfered with the old gentleman," said the captain. "Depend upon it, he'll cause us some trouble. However, what's done can't be helped. Are you going on board the frigate now?"

"Immediately, sir."

"Then tell the first lieutenant that I shall be on board by twelve o'clock, and tell him also that the port-admiral has issued orders for us to put to sea immediately after we have received our full complement of men on board."

"Ay, ay, sir," replied Peters, who then took leave of the captain, and returned on board the frigate.

* * * * * * *

Captain Rodman had already read himself into commission, and two hours after Peters' departure he went on board the frigate, where he was received with the usual honours.

The tender was alongside the ship, and the pressed men were being drafted on board from her; but Captain Rodman, who had a great deal of business to attend to, took little notice of the tender; and, almost immediately he went on board, he descended to the cabin.

Half an hour later, one of the officers made his appearance in the captain' cabin, and reported that there was a lady alongside, in a shore boat, who wished to see him.

"To see *me!*" exclaimed the captain. "What can any lady in Portsmouth want with me? I thought I had given orders, Mr. Wilton, that no one whateve: should be admitted on board save persons who have especial business with the frigate?"

"So the first lieutenant told the lady, sir. She *won't* be put off. She seems to be much agitated, and says she has an order for her admission from the port- admiral. Shall she be allowed to come on board, sir? She's quite a respectable *elderly* lady," added the young officer, as if he thought that would satisfy his captain that nothing was wrong about his strange visitor.

Captain Rodman smiled.

"Yes—yes," he said, hastily. "Tell the first lieutenant to permit her to come on board, and hear what she has to say. She comes to complain of some of the sailors owing her money or something of that sort, I suspect."

The young officer returned to the deck, and the captain had just again settled down to a letter he was writing, when he was disturbed by a great tumult in the companion-way leading to his cabin. A female voice was heard high above the rest, crying out that she *would* see the captain himself; and there was a sound as if some one was being dragged down the companion-ladder, amidst much ill-suppressed tittering and laughter, and before the captain could rise to call for order, and learn the cause of the tumult, the cabin door was burst open, and a stout female form appeared, dragging Lieutenant Peters by the collar of his coat in after her, in spite of his efforts to escape from her clutches, while her other arm was locked in that of a short, stout little man, whose swollen face was so swathed in bandages that his features could hardly be distinguished.

The surprise and consternation of Captain Rodman may, however, be easily imagined when, on looking more intently at the intruders upon his privacy, he recognized his mother in the stout, angry lady, while it was his father who appeared before him so battered and bruised that he hardly knew him!

"What does this mean?" he cried, angrily. "Leave the cabin—every one but Lieutenant Peters," he added, addressing one or two of his officers, who were following. "I will inquire into this."

"By Jove!" muttered Peters, under his breath, "it's well to say all but Lieutenant Peters! What a grip the old lady has! I *couldn't* get loose if I were to try ever so hard, unless I were to knock her down."

"*Knock her down!*" cried the old lady. who just caught Peters' last words. "Yes, you wouldn't hesitate to do *that* if your captain wasn't near. Oh, Tom, Tom," she went on, "never, never did I think things would come to this! Look at your father—ay, look at him! Did ever mortal see such a sight? He looks for all the world like the scarecrow in Farmer Jobson's fields! And this " (shaking Peters by the collar, which she still grasped) " is the little miscreant who brought all this trouble about. Tom, Tom, is this the way sailors act that you boast so much of their bravery? Is this the way we are to be treated—your father and me—when we come all the way to Portsmouth to see our brave boy, and the fine new ship he commands—all unbeknown to you, Tom? for we meant to take you by surprise, and we shouldn't have ventured to come on board unless you'd asked us; for we had no wish to demean you. But I'll be revenged. I've seen him they call the port-admiral—a fine old gentleman, though stern—and I'll have this whipper-snapper, who dared to treat my husband in this manner, severely punished."

Captain Rodman had not yet been able to get in a word, and he felt so surprised and annoyed that he hardly knew how to act. As to Mr. Rodman, he stood silent, vainly striving by signs and gestures, and nudges of his elbow, to silence his angry wife, while poor Lieutenant Peters looked uncommonly silly—the picture of confusion and dismay.

At length the captain spoke.

"Mother," said he, "pray compose yourself and sit down—and you, too, father. I am very much vexed. *I* knew nothing of this; but it shall be strictly inquired into. I am very sorry this trouble has occurred. You should have written that you were coming to Portsmouth, and I would have taken care that it should not not have happened. But, my dear mother, for *my* sake, if you would not have me appear ridiculous in the presence of my officers, cease this clamour, release this gentleman whom you have seized, and calmly acquaint me with all that has taken place."

Thus appealed to by her son, Mrs. Rodman obeyed him. She released her hold of the lieutenant, and sitting down on the well-cushioned transom-lockers—where her husband took his seat by her side—her anger and firmness both gave way, and covering her face with her hands, she burst into tears, and sobbed hysterically.

Captain Rodman and her husband both tried to console her, but for some time to no purpose. At length they partially succeeded, and then the captain heard from her own lips her version of the absurd story.

CHAPTER III.

WHEN, after a fit of hysterics, and other symptoms of feminine agitation, Mrs Rodman recovered some degree of composure, she informed the captain that sl and her husband had resolved to pay a private visit to Portsmouth, to behol their son in his pride and glory as a naval commander, and secretly to witne: the respect and honours which were paid him. They also had a great desire t see a ship-of-war; for, many years as their son had been a sailor, they had nev visited him on board ship, and indeed, Mrs. Rodman had scarcely even seen, an had never before been on board, a vessel in her life.

Captain Rodman, while serving as a midshipman, would have been gla to have received a visit from his parents; but, with a delicacy of feeling that wa hardly to be expected in persons in their condition, they had, very justl conceived the idea that their appearance among the often proud and aristocrat young gentlemen who were their boy's companions and shipmates, might tend t bring him into contempt and ridicule, or at least to subject him to muc disagreeable banter and many unpleasant jokes. To a certain extent the had acted wisely, though it would not have been well for any empty-heade coxcomb who had dared, in young Rodman's presence, or, to his knowledg to speak disrespectfully of his parents, while those among his young broth officers whose friendship and esteem were worth possessing, would have bee above any such ungenerous, and really vulgar and snobbish, behaviour.

However, Mr. Rodman knew that his son had, by his good conduct, gaine the favour and patronage of two gentlemen of wealth and influence—Captai Sinclair and Blakeley; and since such was the case, perhaps it was as we for him and his wife *not* to interfere with them, and to rest content with th son's brief visits to Fincham.

At length, however, Mrs. Rodman expressed so earnest a desire to see her s in command of his new frigate, that her husband determined to bring her Portsmouth for that purpose, and on their arrival they happened, unfortunatel to put up at the same hotel in which the merchant seamen were in hiding.

I should mention that the worthy grocer had, on his son's attaining to t rank of post-captain, retired from business, with a very snug fortune, and no inhabited a handsome villa-residence, standing in its own grounds, a few mil distant from Fincham. This property he had purchased, and he was now livi comfortably as an independent gentleman.

"And, this being the case, Tom," said the old lady, when, in a roundabo way, she had explained the motives of her and her husband's visit, "we came two days ago by the stage; but we shouldn't have ventured to come on boa this fine ship without an invitation, if so be" (with an indignant glance Peters) "things hadn't happened so outrageous."

"For to go and to press your own father, and have him knocked about in tl shameful manner, Tom!" put in Mr. Rodman, in a lugubrious tone, from amid the bandages and wrappers that almost concealed his features. "Never—i never would I have believed it of you!"

"My dear father," replied the captain, earnestly. "I had not the slight idea of the indignities to which you have been subjected until I saw you ju now"——

" To make a swabber and a bottle-washer of your poor old father !" continue
the old gentleman, giving in his turn an indignant and vindictive glance a
Lieutenant Peters.

" And you, my dear mother," the captain went on, " why *should* you hav
hesitated to visit me on board my ship ? Could you think me guilty of such
meanness as to wish to shun my own parents? Most heartily should I hav
welcomed you had you come on board in your own proper characters ; and ha
you written to *me* to say you were coming, all this unpleasantness, which I mos
sincerely regret, would not have occurred. Lieutenant Peters certainly exceede
his duty, as I told him, before I knew who it was he had pressed; but he had n
idea *who* it was he had arrested ; and I am sure that he now regrets as much as
do the course he took."

" I do, sir," put in Peters; " and feel ashamed of my conduct into th
bargain. I can only offer my humble apologies, and beg of Mr. and Mrs
Rodman, as well as you, captain, to forgive me."

The result was that forgiveness was granted, Mrs. Rodman feeling som
secret satisfaction on beholding the marks of the rough usage the lieutenant—
whom she had seized by the collar the moment he was pointed out to her by he
husband as the author of the indignities to which he had been subjected—ha
received.

All parties shook hands, and Mr. and Mrs. Rodman soon afterwards returne
to the shore, to re-visit the frigate in a day or two in a more pleasant and satis
factory manner.

Thus ended Lieutenant Peters' first and last experience as the leader o
a pressgang. He thought of it with dismay ever afterwards.

At the end of a week, the Conqueror, which was detained a few days in orde
to obtain her full complement of men, put to sea, amidst the cheers and heart
good wishes of thousands of spectators. Her farewell gun was responded to b
three rousing cheers, and one cheer more for Captain Rodman and his gallan
ship, his officers, and crew, and still the spectators lingered—Mr. and Mrs
Rodman among the rest—until the noble vessel was visible but as a mere spec
upon the water in the far distance.

The Conqueror sailed on a roving commission—the pleasantest cruise that a
adventurous captain can make, inasmuch as it leaves him free to act as h
pleases, and implies that the most perfect confidence in his courage, skill, and dis
cretion is entertained by the Board of Admiralty. He was left free to sai
wherever he thought he could render the greatest service to his king and country
and could inflict the greatest amount of injury upon their foes.

Before he was at liberty to take his own course, however, Captain Rodman ha
to undertake the most disagreeable duties that can fall to the lot of a nava
commander. He was ordered to convoy a large fleet of merchant vessels to th
West Indies.

No landsman can well understand the annoyance this duty causes to eage
and ambitious officers, and it was a duty frequently imposed upon such officer
during the long war with France. At that period the merchant service was no
nearly so well regulated as it is at present. Many of the captains and officers wer
utterly ignorant of everything save practical seamanship, and were sometime
even deficient in that respect, having been appointed through favour on the par
of the owners, or because they could be obtained cheaply ; while *now* they hav
to undergo an examination almost as severe as that to which naval officers ar
subjected.

The consequence was that, while the captain in charge of the convoy was hel answerable for the capture of any of the vessels, unless he could prove that he had exerted himself to the utmost to prevent it, many of the masters, through ignorance or obstinacy, failed constantly to obey orders. Dull sailors would lag behind, and when night closed in it would be necessary to fire a gun and heave-to till the laggers could come up to the fleet. Swift sailers *would* go ahead, despite of signals and guns fired to bring them to, and it was necessary to dispatch boats to them with peremptory orders, and sometimes even to take sharper measures with them. There was no end to the anxieties, delays, and annoyances the merchant ships occasioned, and devoutly glad were the men-of-war officers when their irksome task was ended.

The convoy, consisting of twelve vessels of different sizes, was awaiting the frigate's arrival off the Bill of Portland, and the next morning, the Conqueror leading, the fleet sailed down Channel.

All went well until the ships passed Madeira, and had run down the north-east trades, when they fell in with the usual calms, and light and variable winds, which prevail in the vicinity of the equator.

One night the frigate and her convoy were lying becalmed in these latitudes, the sails of the frigate flapping idly against the masts, and the fleet of merchantmen widely scattered, with their heads pointed in every direction. The second lieutenant was the officer of the watch, and Simpson (the quartermaster) was " conning "* the ship.

Peters having sailed as a midshipman with Simpson on board the Ajax, and the old sailor being somewhat of a favourite with him, he allowed him more freedom of speech than is usual between officers and seamen, and when they were alone on deck at night, he frequently encouraged the old man to relate some of the marvellous " yarns " for which the old fellow was famed.

" Confound it! " exclaimed the lieutenant, whistling at the same time for a breeze, " are we *never* going to see the end of this calm? How does she head, quartermaster? "

" Due west, sir. Just lies her course," answered Simpson, looking at the compass in the binnacle. " So-o, steady, my man. Don't let her yaw off. You're half asleep," he added, addressing the man at the wheel.

" Has she steerage way upon her? " said Peters, who was looking through a night telescope. " The convoy is heading in every direction."

" Just steerage way, sir, and no more," was the reply. " As to them merchantmen, the helmsmen are too lazy to heed how they steer half their time. It is strange, sir, as the winds should allers be so light and war'able in these latitudes. Do you know, sir, why they calls 'em the horse latitudes? "

" The story goes, Simpson," replied the lieutenant, " that they are so called in consequence of a large Government ship, laden with horses for the Indian army, having been so long becalmed here that the water gave out as well as the hay and corn provided for the horses, so that it was found necessary to throw the poor animals overboard rather than to let them slowly starve to death. I can't say whether this story is true, but it very probably is."

" A droll thing once happened hereaway, sir," continued the quartermaster, " which ain't hardly credible, though it's as true as gospel."

" What was that, Simpson? " inquired the second lieutenant, who saw that the seaman was itching to relate one of those marvellous " yarns " for which he was famed, and in listening to which Mr. Peters often amusingly beguiled the tedium of a midnight watch.

---

* Directing the steerage of the vessel.

"A vessel, sir, was once detained, some'eres hereaway, for three months."

"Three months! Good heavens! How came that about?"

"Why, sir," continued the quartermaster, "there was once a Yankee skipper, who hailed from Nantucket, on the coast of Ameriky, who had been in the coastin' trade, aboard schooners and other fore-and-aft-rigged vessels, all his life, until at length his owners sent him in a brig, on a v'y'ge to New Orleans.

"Well, sir, neither the skipper, nor his mate, nor any of his crew had ever sailed aboard a square-rigged vessel, and though they was good seamen in other respects, they know'd no more how to handle sich a craft nor a babby does.

"Howsomever the brig put to sea with a fair wind, and all went well until she'd run down the trades, and got into these 'ere war'ables. Then, arly one mornin', the wind fell foul all of a sudden. It was the mate's watch on deck, and down he goes to call the skipper.

"'Wind foul, d'ye say, Luke?' says the skipper. 'Wa-al, then, we must jist put the brig abeout, and bring her reound on t'other tack, my lad.'

"'All right,' says the mate; and he and the skipper went on deck together, and the mate sung out for all hands to 'bout ship.

"Now, in coorse, sir, you know that a square-rigged vessel wants a diff'rent sort o' manooverin' from a fore-and-after of any sort, when you wants for to put her about; and, as I've said, neither the mate nor the skipper had ever sailed aboard a square-rigged craft afore.

"The skipper looked aloft, and then to wind'ard, and then at the helmsman, and at last scratched his head, as though he were somewhat flusticated.

"'Put her *reound*, Luke,' says he, arter a bit, lookin' askance at the mate.

"'Hadn't *yew* best put her reound, Jonathan, it bein' the first time o' tackin'?' says the mate, who was similar flusticated, lookin' askew-like at the skipper.

"Wa-al, Luke, blest ef I kneows *ersackly* heow tew begin,' says the skipper.

"'Nor I, nather, by gum!' says the mate. 'Anyheow, I reckon we'll hev for tew brace reound the yards;' so he sings out, 'Brace reound the mainyards, boys.'

"Well, sir, the men claps on to the main-braces, and round swings the yards with a whirl, and, in coorse, the main and foresails filled different ways. The brig, in fac', were hove-to. But, instead o' puttin' the helm a lee and bracin' round the *fore*-yards, both the skipper and the mate was took aback themselves.

"'Hold hard, boys! Hold hard!' sings out the mate, glancin' aloft, and seein' as the fore and main-sails was a bellyin' out different ways. 'This is an everlastin' rum start, anyheow!' says he.

"'*Je*-rusalem!' cries the skipper, also glancin' aloft. 'This is what *I* calls *moosical!*'" (Amusing in Down East, Yankee parlance) "'Blest,' says he, 'ef the wind bean't a blowin' tew ways at once! We're reg'lar jammed up, Luke!'

"'What on airth are we tew do?' says the mate; and none o' the men know'd no more nor he or the skipper.

"'Wait a while, Luke,' says the skipper. 'Mayhap heow it's the natur' o' the weather in these furrin' parts o' the ocean! Howsomever, one o' these obstinate breezes 'll come the boss over t' other afore long and blow it back, and *then*, my boy, we shall be all right ag'in.'

"Well, sir, they waited and waited, all to no use; for, in coorse, so long as the yards was braced in different ways, the brig was kep' hove-to, no matter which way the wind blow'd. And as the crew were no wiser nor the mate and skipper, they lay hove-to day arter day, and week arter week, for nigh three months, waitin' for one wind to get the upper hand o' t' other, and writin' down every day in the logbook, 'Brig continers jammed-up 'twixt tew breezes o' ekal force,' until, at length, they got to the end o' their last bag of biscuit and to the bottom o' their last cask of water, and was in a fair way to perish from starvation; when one day the mate spied a large vessel bearin' down towards the brig, before a staggerin' breeze, with all sail set alow and aloft.

"'One o' John Bull's almighty cruisers by the looks on her,' says the skipper, when the mate p'inted out the vessel to him. '*One* of these etarnal breezes hev gi'n way whar *she* is, anyheow. Pray marsy heow she'll bring the wind 'long wi' her, so's *we* may git eout o' this everlastin' jam.'

"'Anyway we'll git some provisions eout on her, please the pigs,' says the mate, and they waited for the ship to draw near them.

"Meanwhile, sir, them on board the man-o'-war had spied out the brig, and was a wonderin' why she lay hove-to.

"'There don't seem nothin' wrong with her,' says one of the officers to the captain, 'although she's h'isted a signal of distress.'

"'At any rate,' answers the captain, 'we'll bear down to her, and learn what *is* the matter.' So they kept on steerin' towards the brig till they were almost within hail.

"Well, sir, the crew of the brig see her comin', and no sign of losin' *her* fair breeze.

"'Ef this ain't everlastin' strange!' says the skipper of the brig, lookin' up at his own sails. 'That ere craft o' John Bull's don't 'pear to lose *her* fair wind any, while we continer jammed up! The winds o' ekal force must hev met *just* in this 'ere identical spot, as we've had the misfortune to get intew! 'Twould be an act o' Christian charity to gin that 'ere vessel warnin' afore she drars *tew* nigh.'

"Meanwhile, sir, the man-o'-war came up, and rounded to, within hailin' distance of the brig, while—as vessels will do in such case—she was slowly edgin' nearer, through what they calls the force of attraction.

"'Brig, ahoy!' sings out the captain of the man-of-war, through his trumpet. "What brig's that, and what's the matter on board?'

"'We've been jammed up atwixt tew breezes o' ekal force these three months,' answers the skipper, 'and see no signs o' gettin' clear. We're eout o' perwisions and water, and are starvin'. Let us hev some food, for mercy's sake. But, lord love ye, send your boats aboard, and don't let the ship come any nearer, or *you'll* be caught as we are.'

"'What does the fool mean,' says the captain, 'by his winds of equal force? *I* can't understand, I'm sure.'

"However, sir, he sends the first leeftenant aboard, with a boat's crew, to larn what was the matter, and sends a bag of biscuit and a barrel of water at the same time.

"When the leeftenant got alongside, the skipper and the mate and the brig's crew, all a talkin' together, began to tell the story how they'd got caught atwixt two winds, and been reg'lar jammed up for well nigh three months.

"At first the leeftenant had an idea as they'd all gone loonatic together; but, at length, he see how things was, and, bustin' out a larfin', he sings out: 'Brace round your foreyards, you lubbers!'

"Well, sir, the men goes to the braces, and begins to pull on 'em, and in an instant the brig lies over to the breeze, and begins to glide away.'"

"And what said the skipper when he found out what had been the cause of his detention?" asked Peters, with a smile.

"Why, sir, he cocked his eye up towards the fore-topsail, and then he glanced with a queer look at his mate, and said:

" ' JE-rusalem !   Waal, *I'll* be busted !' and the mate, he glances back at the skipper, and then says to the crew :

" ' I say, boys, we'll hev tew keep dark 'beout this leetle mistake o' ourn when we gits back tew old Nantucket, or we'll never hear the everlastin' end on't. We'll hev the folks a' larfin' at us all our blessed lives.'

" So, sir," said the quartermaster, in conclusion, " they got some provisions on board from the man-o'-war, and havin' larnt how to put a square-rigged vessel about, went on their way rej'icin'."

" And you expect me to believe, Simpson, that this is a true story ? " said the second lieutenant, laughing.

" Well, sir," replied the quartermaster, in an offended tone of   "in course you can believe or disbelieve it, as *you* please; but I heerd it from a shipmate, as heerd it from another man, as heerd it from a man as was told the story by his *own* uncle, as was on board the man-o'-war at the time; and if *that* ain't good authority, I should like for to know what is ? "

Peters paced the quarter-deck for a short time, with his hands in his pockets, whistling for a breeze.

" There's a ripple on the water, astarn, sir," said the quartermaster, presently. " I think there's a breeze a springin' up."

" *At* last, thank heaven ! " said the lieutenant.   " We shall have a stiff breeze before long," he added, after gazing steadfastly to the eastward.   " It strikes me that the ships astern feel it already.   They seem to be overhauling us rapidly. By George ! we've got it !   The sails are filling.   Steady, my lad ! keep her full. Don't let the sails shake " (to the man at the wheel) and in a few minutes the frigate, which had so long lain almost motionless, was cleaving her way swiftly through the water.

" Hillo !   What's going on to windward ? " said the second lieutenant, after pacing the deck awhile in silence.   " Simpson, hand me my night-glass."   Peters looked long and earnestly through the telescope.   Then he called to him the midshipman of the watch.

" Mr. Neville," he said, " take this glass, and see what *you* can make of that ship farthest astern ?   Your eyes are famous for long distances at night."

The youngster took the telescope and took a long look through it, in his turn.

" There's *something* wrong about her, sir," he said, at length.   " Her yards are braced all sorts of ways, and her sails are flying loose.   It seems to me, too, that there's something on the water that looks like a boat pulling from her; but the distance is so great that I can't be certain.   It may be fancy."

" Just what *I* fancied," said the second lieutenant.   " Sentry " (to the marine on guard before the captain's cabin), " tell Captain Rodman's servant to call him immediately.   Boatswain, pipe to heave-to ; and, Mr. Neville, run up the signal lantern and dip it twice, as a signal for the convoy to heave-to also."

These orders were promptly executed.   The ships of the merchant fleet backed their mainyards and brought-to simultaneously, and in a minute Captain Rodman, in his boat-cloak, appeared on deck, and was made acquainted with what had occurred.

" Strange," said he ; " there was nothing in sight but the ships of the convoy at dusk.   I can't conceive how any privateer can have come up in the calm; and yet that ship looks as though she were boarded by an enemy.   How long has this breeze been blowing ? "

" Scarcely ten minutes, sir," replied Peters.   " Until then it was almost a dead calm."

" Possibly there may be mutiny on board the merchantman," said the captain.

"You've done quite right to heave the convoy to, Mr. Peters. This must be seen to at once. Lower the first and second cutters. Steward, bring me my sword. I'll take command of the first cutter myself."

Now, according to the rules of the service, the captain, having such a responsible charge, should not leave his ship. But there are officers in the service who disregard regulations, and sometimes even orders and signals, when there's sharp work to be done. "Nothing succeeds like success," says the French proverb; and as these officers are generally successful through their very daring, they escape reproof, and even receive praise for their disobedience, as was the case with Nelson at Copenhagen, when, putting the telescope to his blind eye, he declared that he could not see the chief admiral's signal of recall, and went on and won the battle.

Captain Rodman was one of those daring leaders who grudged his officers their share in any dashing adventure in which he did not take a part. The cutters were lowered, and then the captain, who, meanwhile, had been keenly watching the merchant ship through his glass, ordered the pinnace also to be lowered. Brass carronades were kept in these boats in readiness for any occasion in which they might be wanted.

Peters took his seat in the second cutter, and the third lieutenant commanded the pinnace. A strong party of marines entered each boat, armed with muskets and bayonets, and they were all three filled with sailors, armed with pistols and cutlasses.

The wind was still but light, and as the first cutter was pulled away, the captain shouted to the first lieutenant, who was left in command of the ship:

"Mr. Bowling, haul the frigate close to the wind, and beat up after us, and see all clear for action on board. There's more going on on board that vessel, I suspect, than we have any idea of."

The merchant vessel, still with her yards and sails in disorder, was almost hull-down, astern of the convoy; but the sailors, eager for an affray, pulled lustily, and soon began to draw near the ship. It now appeared that the boats were espied by those on board of her, for her yards were suddenly braced for'ard, as if the officer in command intended to quit the convoy; and then, as if he had taken a second thought, they were suddenly squared, and the vessel came bearing down towards the boats.

Presently, to the surprise of everybody, a boat was lowered from the ship, and pulled towards the man-of-war's boats.

"What the mischief does it all mean?" exclaimed the captain, as the boat came steadily on, pulled by four men, while two others were seated in the stern, as though they had no fear of meeting the boats of the frigate. "I can't make it out!"

Very soon the boats were within hail, and the men in the merchant boat lay on their oars, as if awaiting orders from those on board the first cutter.

"What is the meaning of this?" shouted Captain Rodman, angrily. "What boat is that?"

There was some hesitation before a reply was made, and then a voice, evidently English, answered:

"She belongs to the Martha, of Bristol, sir."

"Is the master on board of her?" cried Captain Rodman.

All the boats' crews were now resting on their oars—the merchant boat being some fifty yards distant from the boats of the frigate.

Again there was some hesitation ere the reply was made.

"No, sir; I am the chief mate."

"What's the matter on board your ship, sir?" shouted Captain Rodman, sternly.

"Nothing, sir," was the reply. "The officer and men of the watch fell asleep, and the captain came on deck and was angry. Some confusion arose; but it's all right aboard now. The captain sent me to tell you."

"Tell your captain, sir," said Captain Rodman, angry at having made such preparations to no purpose, "that I shall report his conduct to the admiral when we reach our destination, and also to his owners. How *dare* you, sir, or the master of your ship, create such an alarm on board one of his Majesty's ships, by your lubberly conduct? Return on board, sir, and let there be no more of such work. Pull round, men," he added, addressing his own boat's crew, in a vexed and angry tone. "We've had our long pull for nothing, it appears."

The men were about to obey the order, as little satisfied as their captain, and the merchant boat was already on her way back to the Martha, of Bristol, when there came from her a stifled cry, which was suddenly hushed, but immediately repeated; and then the same voice which had previously spoken, cried:

"*There's treachery—there's murder on board, sir.* I've been forced to speak falsely; but I *will* now tell the truth. We've been boarded by"——

A crushing blow was heard, followed by a loud groan from the merchant ship's boat, and then all was silent, while the boat was pulled back towards the ship as rapidly as possible.

"*After her. Give way, my lads. Bend to your oars,*" cried Captain Rodman. "Bring-to, there!" (to the men in the retreating boat). And then, addressing the marine officer, he added, "Let your men be ready to fire, sir, if those fellows don't obey."

Still the boat kept on, and was half way back to the ship, when the report of four muskets, fired simultaneously, rung out in the night air. The larboard oars were flung up aboard the boat, which instantly broached-to. In a few moments the first cutter was alongside of her, and the men grasped her gunwales. Then it was seen that she was manned by French seamen, with the exception of the wounded and dying mate, who had received a crushing blow on the forehead. The unfortunate young man had just strength to explain that the vessel had been boarded and captured, and that when it was seen by the Frenchmen that the frigate's boats were approaching, a boat had been sent to meet them, and he had been forced to enter the boat with the French sailors, and to reply—with threats of instant death if he refused—to any questions that might be put, in such a manner as, the Frenchmen hoped, would induce the frigate's officers to return to their ship, when they hoped to make off with their prize.

"But—I—I couldn't—I—couldn't see—you—leave us—to the mercy of the Frenchmen, sir," the dying mate painfully gasped forth; "so—though—I knew the fate that awaited *me*—I—cried out—and"——

The blood oozed forth in a dark crimson stream from the brave young sailor's mouth. He was unable to complete his speech, and, with a frightful gasp for breath, he fell back and expired!

The English sailors shuddered at the sight. Death occurring in such a form, to a solitary individual, appeals to the sensibilities of seamen with ten times greater force than does the fearful carnage on a vessel's deck, where scores of men have been slain in fair fight, amidst the excitement of battle.

Eager to avenge their brutally-murdered countryman, the men-of-war's-men needed not the fierce command of Captain Rodman to pull away and board the merchant ship at all hazards.

The oars bent and sprang as the men tugged at them with their utmost strength, and the heavily-laden boat seemed almost lifted out of the water by every stroke.

Perceiving, however, that their villanous *ruse* had failed, the Frenchmen on board the merchantman were not idle, and, regardless of their own boat's crew, they loaded and fired one of the carronades—which, at that period, most trading vessels were wont to carry for self-defence, and which they sometimes carry even nowadays—at the advancing boats, in the hope to sink them, and thus gain time to make off with their prize. But the ball flew over the boats, just above the men's heads, and plunged into the water far astern.

The next minute, with a loud cheer from the men-of-war's-men, the three boats ran alongside the ship.

CHAPTER IV.

A BRIEF but sanguinary struggle ensued, for although the Frenchmen who had been left on board the prize had the advantage of fighting from the ship's deck, where they were sheltered by the bulwarks, the sailors and marines on board the boats far outnumbered them.

The deck of the vessel was gained, and after another brief struggle, in which none of the men-of-war's-men were killed, though several received severe wounds, the twenty Frenchmen on board were secured, ironed, and confined between decks. Five others had been slain in the combat, while most of the remaining twenty were more or less severely wounded.

The dead bodies were ruthlessly thrown overboard to the sharks, and then Captain Rodman sought for the vessel's crew, and looked around him; for it was still a mystery to him how the ship had been boarded, in a calm, without any enemy's ship appearing in sight.

Meanwhile, the breeze had freshened, and the frigate had beat up towards the merchantman, until she was as near as it was considered safe for her to approach, while the vessels composing the convoy still lay hove-to, now nearly two leagues distant, awaiting fresh signals from the commander of the frigate—their crews unconscious of the cause of all this confusion; for, though they had seen the flash, and heard the report of the gun fired from the Martha, they had seen no strange vessel near, and the general opinion was that the Martha's crew must have mutinied.

I should have mentioned that most of the ships of the convoy were bound to different ports in the island of Jamaica. Captain Rodman had therefore kept well to the westward, intending to sail through the Windward Passage, between the islands of Hayti and Cuba, and had been caught in the "Doldrums," or "Variables," or "Horse-latitudes"—for by all these names is this portion of the Atlantic Ocean known to seamen—in the vicinity of Bahama Islands. Many of the vessels carried passengers; and the Martha, among the rest, had four or five passengers on board, who were found confined, along with the master of the vessel, in the cabin. Three of the crew had been slain fighting, before the ship surrendered; the masters was badly wounded, and the second mate had been shot dead, at the moment when the vessel was boarded by the Frenchmen. The rest of the crew were confined in the forecastle; but, as the chief mate had been brutally murdered in the boat, by the Frenchmen, the vessel had not an officer capable of duty left. The master was asleep in his cabin when the ship was boarded, and could give no explanation of the affair; but one of the passengers furnished Captain Rodman with the following information:

"The weather, as you know, sir," said he, "has been exceedingly sultry during the long calm we have experienced. I turned in, as usual, about ten o'clock, but my berth was so heated that I was unable to sleep, and I soon returned to the deck. There I found no one awake but the man at the wheel, and he, I suspect, was half dozing. It was the second mate's watch on deck, and he, poor fellow, who was the first to fall at the hands of the boarders, was sound asleep on the hen-coop. It was a lovely night; the sea was as smooth as a mirror, and the vessels of the convoy were heading in all directions. It seemed to me that the seamen had *all* taken advantage of the calm to snooze on the decks of the different ships—for all appeared to be left for the time being, to their own guidance—trusting to *you* to look after their safety.

"Well, sir, I gazed around me, and over the stern. Nothing was in sight save our own vessels and the frigate, and for a quarter of an hour I paced the decks. Then I began to feel sleepy myself, and I sat down on a hen-coop opposite the second mate, and was soon dozing. I must have heard the Frenchmen's boats approaching, for in my sleep I fancied I heard the sound of oars. However, how long I had dozed in this manner, I know not; but at length I was awakened by the sound of oars close to. I sprang to my feet to see three boats full of armed men alongside, but before I had time to give any alarm, the men were on deck. The second mate jumped up, still half asleep, and was instantly shot dead by one of the Frenchmen. The report of the pistol, and the mate's heavy fall, aroused the watch, as well as the captain and chief mate, and the men in the forecastle.

"A fierce struggle ensued; but our men, unarmed and unprepared, were soon overpowered. Some of the poor fellows were killed, and the rest, with us passengers, were ordered below and confined.

"Looking out of the cabin windows, I now saw a brig-of-war, or a large privateer, a considerable distance astern "——

"That must have been the object *we* saw from the frigate, though she was so far off that we could not make out what it was, Captain Rodman," interrupted Peters, who was standing by. "Nothing but the upper sails *could* have been visible to us," he added; "and Mr. Neville said he fancied it was a boat."

"This vessel," the passenger went on, "must have brought the breeze we afterwards caught up, with her. There was one of the vessels of the convoy astern of *us,* and having secured our ship, the Frenchmen left a few men on board, and the rest pulled away in the boats, hoping to secure a second prize. It was while this was occurring that you must have noticed our disorder, and put off in your boats; and the Frenchmen must have seen the boats approaching, for they had not got more than half-way to the second ship before they turned round and put back; and *then* they must have devised that villanous scheme to put you off your guard, and induce you to return to the frigate, which cost our gallant young first mate his life."

"What became of the French vessel, sir?" asked Captain Rodman.

"Her boats, with two men in each, hastened back to her, leaving the other men on board this ship, and the privateer—which must mount at least twenty guns—hauled close to the wind, as soon as she had taken her boats on board, and steered away westward, sailing like a witch."

"That must be the vessel that the master of the brig, that we spoke the other day, told us of," said Captain Rodman to the second lieutenant. "He said that a large French privateer that had done a great deal of mischief, was cruising in this vicinity, and that it was said that she made one of the Caicos her anchorage ground. A course due west from this would carry her to the largest of the Caicos."

For some moments Captain Rodman remained in a brown study. He had conceived a brilliant idea, if he could but carry it out.

"Mr. Peters," he said, at length, "we must capture that vessel, if possible. The frigate is too large to venture near the Caicos,* unless we had a pilot on board. Besides, I dare not leave the convoy without protection. But I'll venture in this ship. How many guns has she?"

---

* A group of rocks and sandbanks—very dangerous—off the Bahama Islands. One or two of the islets of the group, however, are capable of affording shelter to ships.

"Six four-pound carronades, sir," replied Peters.

"Which, with our brass carronades in the boats, will make twelve. *I'll venture it, by Jove!*"

Having decided how to act, Captain Rodman hailed the frigate, which, as I have said, was now close to the ship.

"Mr. Bowling," he cried, "send the launch alongside to receive the passengers and wounded men who are on board this vessel. I intend to steer for the Great Caico, which bears westward, about six miles distant. The boats and men I have with me, together with the unwounded of the ship's crew, I shall keep on board. I have good reason to believe, sir, that the Rochelle—the privateer that we heard of the other day—has seized this vessel, and has now borne away for the Great Caico. I must take her if I can. You, sir, will remain in charge of the frigate and the convoy. Keep the vessels well together, sir, and come in with the frigate as close as you can with safety, in case you may be wanted to give chase if the privateer should attempt to escape. Do you understand me, sir?"

"Ay, ay, sir," replied the lieutenant, through his trumpet. "Shall I send more men on board?"

"No. We have enough, with the ship's crew, to fight her, and to man the boats. Only be prepared to assist us should assistance be necessary."

"Ay, ay, sir," came back again, with a wave of the trumpet, and the frigate sheered off.

Presently the launch came alongside the Martha. The wounded master, and men of the ship—the wounded men-of-war's-men, and the passengers, were put on board, and she forthwith returned to the frigate; and then the Martha's yards were close-hauled, and she bore up for the Caicos—the frigate, with the ships of the convoy, followed at the distance of a league.

It was a daring scheme to venture to fight a heavily-armed and full manned privateer, or gun-brig, with the crazy guns of a merchantman; but Captain Rodman was not one to be frightened at difficulties, as those who have read his early history well know. Besides, he had twenty of the Frenchmen in irons on board the ship, for he had not had time to transfer these men to the frigate, and that was so many less men to encounter. Moreover, he hoped to take the Frenchmen by surprise, and attack them on shore. He expected—if the privateer ran into the Great Caico—that she would anchor, and perhaps land the greater portion of her crew, and events showed that he was correct.

It *was* the Rochelle, of twenty-two guns, carrying a crew of ninety men, which had so cunningly captured the Martha, only to have the ship recaptured from her immediately. Two hours' sail brought the Martha in sight of the Great Caico—an island, or rather a rock, some mile and a half in diameter, with a snug harbour, formed by a curve in the coast, which is protected by dangerous sandbanks and rocks, having only a narrow passage between them, known but to a few fishermen, and to the men on board the privateer.

However, at all hazards, Captain Rodman determined to venture to run the passage, which was not so dangerous as he had anticipated; for the privateersmen had marked it with buoys, on either side, and these buoys the bright moonlight enabled the crew of the ship to discern. Besides, as he drew near, the captain saw, through his spy-glass that a vessel was anchored in the harbour.

Not imagining that any British naval officer would be sufficiently daring and venturesome to seek for them in such a spot, the Frenchmen, after their discomfiture, had made for this, their favourite haunt, where they believed themselves to be as secure from attack as though they were in the French port of Rochelle, to which their vessel belonged, and after which she was named.

They had a magazine, and houses on the islet, in which they were accustomed to store the booty they seized, for—as I have said in " Tom Rodman Afloat"— privateersmen were but pirates in disguise; and, as Captain Rodman had anticipated, most of the men had gone on shore from the Rochelle immediately on her arrival in port, for the greater portion of them had negro *wives*, as they termed them, living on shore, among whom were a few Creoles and white women ; and in their leisure hours, privateersmen, like pirates, are fond of indulging in deep carouses.

The Martha was actually in the harbour before the lazy watch left on board the privateer—confident in their fancied security—were aware that their sanctuary was invaded ; and, Captain Rodman ordering the ship to be run on board the anchored vessel, the latter was in possession of the Englishmen without a struggle.

To carry her out of the harbour was, however, another matter; for, as is usual in such haunts, the privateersmen had planted heavy guns on the rocks, at the narrow entrance of the harbour. Besides, Captain Rodman wished to secure the person of the privateer captain—alive or dead.

The watch on board the vessel were secured, and then, with muffled oars, the man-of-war's boats pulled for the shore, from the Martha, loaded with marines and sailors.

So confident were the privateersmen in their fancied security that the boat's crew landed unseen, and the noisy carouse of the Frenchmen was distinctly audible, coming from a group of stone cottages, or huts, built in the rear of the magazine.

The armed boats' crews, led by the captain and the second and third lieutenants, landed and marched silently towards the huts, guarded by the uproarious voices and loud songs of the carousers.

The Englishmen hoped to surprise them; but just as they approached the magazine, a sentry gave the alarm.

The privateers rushed out to meet the invaders of their haunt, and a terrific conflict ensued, amidst the noise of which female voices were audible yelling with fury, or screaming with terror. The slaughter among the surprised and half-drunken Frenchmen was fearful, though they fought with savage desperation, and many of the English also fell dead or severely wounded. At length the men-of-war's-men, who were sober, and amenable to discipline, gained the victory over their more numerous foes, many of whom were half-stupefied with liquor, while those who had their senses were taken by surprise, and were ignorant of the comparatively small number of their assailants; for they fancied that no one would dare attack them unless with an overwhelming force. Night, which concealed the small force of Englishmen from sight, was favourable to the latter.

Several of the Frenchmen were made prisoners, but the majority fled with the females, and found shelter in hiding-places known only to themselves.

The English, however, after conveying their prisoners to the boats, set fire to the huts and magazine, and soon all the rude buildings, which were filled with combustibles, were in flames.

Meanwhile Captain Rodman had sought for the captain of the privateer, whom he had made up his mind to capture. It was discovered that he was not among the slain, nor the prisoners, and it was feared that he had escaped; and regardless of the persuasions of the second lieutenant, who feared for his captain's safety, Captain Rodman returned to the burning buildings. Here, on a ledge of

rock, the two captains at length encountered each other, and a fierce conflict
ensued between them. Both were determined men, and both fought for their
lives. Had there been a limner present to depict the scene, it would have made a
striking and brilliant picture.

For some time the combatants fought alone and unseen. Captain Rodman
was much the younger, and the more active and agile of the two; but the French
captain was greatly his superior in size and strength. Above their heads, as they
fought furiously, the bright tropical moon sailed majestically in the dark blue
vault of heaven, which was illumined by myriads of twinkling stars. In the
foreground was a deep and rugged precipice, rising high above the sea, into which
—over the precipice—each strove to drive the other. Deep, gloomy shadows, that
would have served as a study for a second Rembrandt, were cast upon the scene
by the surrounding rocks; while in the background the flames from the burning
huts and magazines soared high in air, in a fiery, lurid column, that served to
deepen the dark surrounding shadows; while every now and then some com-
bustible exploded with a fearful sound that seemed to shake the islet, throwing a
shower of brilliant, many-coloured sparks high in air, as though some gigantic
sky-rocket had been let off.

On the narrow ledge that I have mentioned, the two captains fought for
victory or death—now one pressing the other close to the edge of the precipice,
and now the other appearing to gain the upper hand.

For a long time the contest seemed doubtful, and if either or both had fallen,
they would have perished unseen. At length, however, guided by the loud clash
of steel, Lieutenant Peters and two seamen, who had been searching for their
captain, made their appearance, but only to witness the conflict; for the ledge
was so narrow, and the two combatants turned about so rapidly, that it had been
probably fatal to both had any one interfered with the fight.

Several times the lieutenant and the two sailors presented their pistols, but
feared to fire, lest they should injure their own captain.

At length, whether the Frenchman succumbed to the greater agility of his
youthful antagonist, or whether his attention was momentarily diverted by the
presence of the officer and seamen, can never be known; but, for some reason or
other, he left his guard open for an instant to Captain Rodman's fierce and rapid
passes. The young captain's sword was immediately sheathed in his body, and
falling back dead, he rolled over the precipice into the sea far beneath.

"So dies a brave man, at any rate, whatever else he may have been," said
Captain Rodman, gasping to recover his breath as he spoke. "Would to heaven
that I could have made him my living prisoner!"

The captain, the lieutenant, and the two sailors now hastened to the boats,
where Captain Rodman was received with cheers by the seamen and marines, who
had given him up as lost.

The privateer was towed out of the harbour, a prize to the British, and the
officers and men-of-war's-men having returned to the frigate, the convoy, still
with the prize in tow, proceeded on its way.

Four days' sail brought the frigate to Port Royal, Jamaica, where she
parted from the vessels hitherto under her protection, each of which sought her
own destined port; and thus ended the first part of the Cruise of the Conqueror.

CHAPTER V.

ON leaving Port Royal, Jamaica, after his tiresome duty of convoying a fleet of merchant ships across the Atlantic Ocean was ended, Captain Rodman sailed southward, without any very definite object in view, unless—why should the truth be concealed?—it were that he took advantage of his "roving commission" to seek after an expected letter from Lucy Sinclair. Love will sometimes cause the wisest and bravest and most conscientious men to do what they can hardly explain in a satisfactory manner; and if the Secretary of the Admiralty had written to the gallant young captain to inquire wherefore he had taken such a course, and the answer had been, "I went to look after a letter I expected from my sweetheart, sir," the Lords of the Admiralty would scarcely have been convinced of the necessity of such action on the part of a naval officer in high command!

However, Captain Rodman, as I have said, was left free to act in accordance with his own judgment, and he might easily have found other reasons to justify his procedure.

At the period of which I write, the French, who were England's only formidable enemy at sea, had been so thoroughly and completely beaten in the series of great naval battles, commencing with the battle of the Nile, and terminating with the complete rout, overthrow, and destruction of the combined naval forces of France and Spain at Cape Trafalgar, that—as I have had reason to state in the stories of "Tom Rodman Afloat," and its sequel, "Dashing Rodman, of the Leander"—they had never since dared to meet a British ship in a regular engagement. Nevertheless, with a view to injure British commerce as much as lay in their power, they had despatched vessels of war to all parts of the ocean, to cut out and capture English merchant vessels wherever they could fall in with them, and to inflict injury upon distant and ill-protected British colonies—though, even in these endeavours, they sometimes discovered that they had met their match : witness the fight in the Indian Ocean, where a squadron of East Indiamen, under the command of Commodore Dance, of the East India Company's service, actually beat off and put to flight one of the best-equipped and highest-disciplined squadrons of men-of-war, under the command of Admiral Linois, that ever sailed from France!—while instances were numerous in which French ships-of-war were beaten off when attacking some small British colonial possession, which they imagined would fall an easy prey to them.

Thus Captain Rodman could hardly do amiss in sailing southward, for the further he sailed from the great seat of war (the west coast of Europe and the Mediterranean Sea), the more likely was he to fall in with a foe worthy to be met by the Conqueror.

When Captain Rodman bade farewell to Lucy Sinclair at the Grange, in Cambridgeshire—her father's country seat—he had made the young lady promise to write to him while he was absent. But as it is difficult to arrange where letters shall be sent to find a ship, which—like Rodman's frigate—was likely to be in one part one day and in another a few days later, and whose wanderings would be guided by circumstances which none could foresee, the captain had requested Lucy to write to two or three different places.

"Let me consider," he said. "This confounded convoy that I have to conduct to Jamaica will detain me a considerable time—perhaps a couple of months.

Now, dear Lucy, suppose you write two months hence, and send a letter to—let me think—ah—to Buenos Ayres. I think I shall steer south-about after leaving Port Royal, and cruise in the Pacific, off the west coast of South America. I shall be almost certain to fall in with some French vessel thereabouts, for they will be looking out for the English specie ships which sail from that coast, and I will look in at Buenos Ayres on my way southward. Should I find no letter awaiting me there, Lucy, I shall look to find one at Valparaiso, which is the next port I shall touch at. So, dear Lucy, you will, I am sure, write to me at both ports. If I get *both* the letters, so much the better."

Lucy had faithfully promised to do this, and Captain Rodman hoped to find a letter awaiting him at Buenos Ayres on his arrival at that place.

 *   *   *   *   *   *   *

Several times had Captain Rodman crossed the equator, both as a midshipman and as a lieutenant; but though it was the almost constant practice at that period for sailors to enjoy a holiday on such occasions, and to indulge in the wild freak of "shaving" such of their unfortunate shipmates—whether officers, fellow-seamen, or passengers—who had never before sailed southward from the equinoctial line, for some reason or other the wild saturnalia had never come off on board any ship in which he had sailed. Either the captain had objected to it, or the ship had been in chase of another, or something had occurred to set it aside.

Nowadays, this wild and often savage frolic is rarely practised; but, at the time of which I write, it was supposed to renovate the spirits of the seamen, and break the monotony of a long sea voyage; and unless the weather rendered it impracticable, which in those latitudes was rarely the case, it was almost always permitted.

On the evening of the ninth day from the date on which the Conqueror had sailed from Port Royal, Captain Rodman was slowly pacing the frigate's quarter-deck by himself, when a boatswain's mate, whose duties had called him aft, touched his hat to the captain, as he was on his way for'ard, and, in a mysterious whisper, begged leave to speak a word with his honour in private.

"With *me*, my good fellow!" exclaimed the captain, rather surprised at such a request from a man in the boatswain's mate's position. "If you have any complaint to make, make it in the usual way, through the first lieutenant, and it shall be considered."

"No, please yer honour, 'taint no complaint," answered the boatswain's mate. "None on us has nothin' to complain on aboard this ship; but it is a bit of a favour as me and some o' my shipmates wants to arx of yer honour, seein' as how the first leeftenant, though a real genelman, is rayther awarse to grantin' it."

"Well, well; speak out, my man. What is it you wish for?" said the captain, still more surprised at the answer he had received.

"It's just this, yer honour," continued the man. "There's a lot o' chaps aboard the frigate as has never crossed the line. Now, I've heerd how Neptoon be comin' aboard to-morrow mornin' at four bells (six o'clock) for to inquire vy them 'ere chaps should pass his coort, which—as yer honour knows, is down under the equator—without payin' *tribute*, or bein' shaved. Belike Neptoon'll have Mrs. Neptoon—his consort, Miss Amphytrite as was, afore she got spliced—along wi' him; and, yer honour, we wants for to pay 'em proper respec'."

"Oh, I understand now," replied Captain Rodman, smiling. "And you wish to keep the matter secret from the greenhorns, until his majesty of the ocean arrives with his queen and courtiers?"

"Ersac'ly so, yer honour. That's just it," answered the sailor.

Captain Rodman was wont to allow his men every indulgence that was not subversive of discipline, or that did not interfere with the safety of the ship. He was aware that, during the frolic alluded to, all duty was, for the time being, neglected, and the respect entertained for officers was apparently, though not really, forgotten. But he knew that all was done merely in joke, and the wild saturnalia had been permitted from time immemorial, though *he* had never witnessed it. Moreover, he really wished to witness a scene he had frequently heard described, so he replied:

"Certainly, my good fellow. *I*, as commander of one of his Britannic Majesty's ships, and representing my king upon the seas, shall be most happy to receive on board Neptune, the great Monarch of the Ocean, with all due respect; and, that you and your shipmates may receive him with the usual honours, my steward shall supply all hands with an extra ration of spirits.

"But mark this, my man. While I am willing to permit you to enjoy yourselves, according to custom, and set all ordinary discipline aside for the time being, I expect that, should any emergency occur, every man will return to his duty in an instant. Also, that you will allow the usual privileges to officers who have not yet visited the Court of Neptune, and that there will be no foul play, and no wanton exhibition of cruelty. Keep within proper bounds, and I shall be satisfied. If you act otherwise, I shall keep my eye upon the offenders, and punish them severely. Now go; you know me, and you know that it is my custom to keep my word to the letter."

The boatswain's mate touched his hat, and went for'ard.

The next morning the ship was as nearly as possible on the equator. The weather was fine, and almost perfectly calm, though a long and heavy swell upon the water caused the frigate to roll considerably.

Soon after daybreak the mainyards were squared and the fore and aft yards braced up. The ship being now hove-to, a sail was stretched like a curtain across the deck, just in front of the foremast, greatly to the amazement of those who were not in the secret, who wondered what their shipmates were up to.

They very soon found out!

The moment four bells were struck, a young, smart-looking sailor, dressed, according to his own idea, to resemble a footman in gorgeous livery, came forth from behind, or rather from the front of the canvas curtain, and marching aft to the quarter-deck, where the officers had all assembled, turning his toes out, and simpering in a ridiculous manner to represent the ways of a mock-gentleman, bowed, and asked to see the captain.

"Yer honour," said he, when Captain Rodman stepped forward, "I come from my master's Great Neptune's Court to acquaint your honour how Neptune and his wife and court attendants be coming aboard to pay a visit to the Conqueror."

"I shall be proud to receive his majesty," replied the captain, bowing in return, "and shall feel my ship honoured by such a visit."

Hardly had the man returned to the forecastle, ere——

"Ship ahoy!" was bellowed forth, apparently from over the bows, in a loud gruff tone that resounded throughout the frigate.

"Hilloa!" replied the first lieutenant.

"Heave a rope for my car," said the voice. "I'm Neptoon—God o' the Sea—and I'm a comin' aboard to look arter my youngsters, as arn't been introdoosed to me yet, so's to receive their doo homage."

A rope was thrown, and presently the curtain was drawn aside, and seated on a gun-carriage (drawn by eight sailors, clad only in their trousers, with their bodies grotesquely painted, and their heads covered with wigs of oakum, ornamented with seaweed), appeared the god Neptune himself, who was represented by the chief boatswain's mate—the tallest and strongest man of the crew.

His godship was naked to the waist. His face was concealed by a hideous mask, and in his right hand he carried a pair of "grains" (a sort of small harpoon, with three prongs instead of one, used for striking dolphins, porpoises, &c.) to represent a trident. His enormous wig was made of oakum, well powdered with chalk, and his body was covered with paint. Thus attired, he sat crossed on the carriage, immovable and grave as a judge, while behind him, sitting astride the carriage, was his chief attendant and barber, with his razor—a piece of rusty iron hoop affixed to a wooden handle—over his shoulder. A small tub filled with a mixture of tar and "slush," or cook's fat, and other materials, which was used as a shaving box, stood before him, and in his left hand he carried a large tar-brush for a shaving-brush.

On a similar gun-carriage, following behind that on which her lord was seated, appeared Amphytrite, the wife of Neptune (a tall, stout sailor, dressed as nearly as was possible like a woman), wearing a frilled nightcap and a pair of huge spectacles. The lady's dress was profusely ornamented with seaweed, and in her lap she carried one of the ship's boys, attired in a long canvas gown, to represent her last baby, whom she constantly fed with pap ("burgoo," or thick porridge) out of a large tin pot, frequently rapping him with the spoon, when he squalled hideously. Half a dozen other men, fantastically attired, represented sea nymphs, mermaids, &c., all being highly rouged, as was their mistress, with red paint, and carrying looking-glasses, combs, brushes, and various other articles.

The cars were drawn aft to the quarter-deck, and the captain's steward then handed round a tray, on which were several glasses of stiff rum and water, Neptune raised his tumbler, his wife and attendants followed his example, and drank to the health of his royal brother, the King of England, and his Majesty's worthy representative, Captain Rodman.

"Now, yer honour," said Neptune, "havin' done my dooty to my brother King—George of England—which they tell me is a mighty fine country, as I means for to visit some o' these days—I must do my dooty to myself. I've heard say, yer honour, how there be a lot o' new subjecks of mine aboard this 'ere ship as wants washin' and shavin', and mayhap a trifle of physicking—d'ye see? And as neither you nor me has no time for to lose, both on us havin' our dooties to look arter, the sooner we sets about the job the better. My barber's here, all ready to go to work, with a fresh tub of lather, mixed this blessed mornin' for the wery purpose. So I'll just spell out the list—as Amphy here" (pointing to his wife) "writ out for me—and then my Tritons 'll seize hold on 'em, and the barber 'll give 'em a scrape, and so make 'em free o' my dominions hereafter and for ever."

So saying, Neptune read a list of names from a sheet of foolscap paper, commencing with that of the first lieutenant—who, though he had been many years at sea, had always served on northern stations, and had never crossed the line—and ending with ship-boys, and newly-enlisted marines.

The name of the first lieutenant being on the list, accounted reasonably enough for the fears of the boatswain's mate, that he would object to the performance, and induced him to apply for leave directly to the captain.

The lieutenant, however, and some others of the officers whose names were in the list, were readily permitted to escape the penalty by a payment of money, to be spent during the next leave on shore. The captain, of course, was exempt; besides, though he had never witnessed the scene, he had often crossed the line. Somehow or other, however, Neptune had heard that Captain Rodman had escaped free, and, taking advantage of the liberty and freedom of the moment, his godship looked up, and with a most comical expression on his painted visage —for he had removed his mask that he might speak more freely—he said (scratching his wig the while):

"Wishin' to pay all doo respec' to yer honour, I've larnt, from Amphy here, who keeps the books o' my coort, down below 'mong the marmaids, how yer honour ain't been reg'ler interdooced. And though yer honour's free, in vartoo of your high office, mayhap, on sich a interestin' occasion, yer honour, out o' your gracious generosity, wouldn't mind payin' the customary fee, which'll be wery welcome just now, for I can assure ye I find it dooced hard to collect my revenoo, and make both ends meet at the end o' the year?"

Captain Rodman laughingly tossed a couple of guineas into Neptune's horny palm, and received the hearty thanks of his godship, his wife, and his courtiers, and then the fun proceeded.

The names of the lieutenant of marines, and the purser's assistant, were read. Neither of these officers were much liked on board, and Neptune objected to accept a fee in place of their passing through the regular ceremony.

In vain they begged and implored. They were seized upon by the attendants and carried to the main deck, where, one after the other, they were seated upon a huge tub, over which a tarpaulin was tightly stretched, and, greatly to the delight of the marines, whom he drilled constantly, and whom, but for Captain Rodman's authority, he would often have punished for mere trifles, the poor marine lieutenant was made to sit down—his arms being held by the barber's assistants—while the barber lathered his face with the filthy, foul-smelling mixture in the "shaving-box," rubbing the rough brush over his mouth when he cried out, and then shaved off the lather with the iron-hoop razor. This done, the end of the tarpaulin was let go, and souse went the lieutenant over head and ears into the tub, which was nearly full of salt water.

"Puff-puff-puff-ugh-ugh—you shall pay for this!" he gasped forth, as he emerged from the water, a horrid sight to look upon, and spluttering for breath. He looked daggers at the grinning marines as he passed them by on his way to the ward-room to change his clothes, and wash the filth from his face. But though the men tried to look grave, they had not much dread of his threatened vengeance, for they knew that Captain Rodman would now allow anything like tyranny on board his frigate.

The purser's assistant had the pleasure of witnessing the barber's performance upon the lieutenant of marines, and of feeling, at the same time, that *his* turn would come next; and it did, with a vengeance!

The men had a notion that he extra-watered their grog, and cheated them, for his own profit, in the weight of the tobacco and other things they got from him, and he was almost choked with the shaving brush—the barber asking him if the mixture was strong and refreshing, and observing to him, as he soused into the tub, that he would find the water as mild as the six-water grog he mixed for the sailors.

Both these being officers, however, escaped comparatively easy. So did some of the sailors who had not previously crossed the line, and who were favourites with their shipmates; but woe to the unhappy wights who were disliked for their meanness or ill-nature.

These were choked with the lather, scraped with the razor till the blood ran

Lieutenant Peters dragged into the presence of Captain Rodman.

See page 16.

from the scratches they received, and pushed down and rolled over in the tub till they were well-nigh drowned; while their shipmates only laughed at their cries and threats of vengeance.

Those who took it good-humouredly got off best, and when at length the ceremonies were over, Neptune and his wife again saluted the captain, and drank a second time to his good health, and that of his officers, to a successful cruise to the frigate.

Then they were hauled for'ard, followed by their attendants, to the front of the curtain; and when that was hauled down, shortly afterwards, all had disappeared—had returned, as was pretended, to their palace at the bottom of the sea.

An extra allowance of grog was, according to the captain's promise, served out to all hands at noon, and as the weather continued fine, the rest of the day was kept as a holiday, no duty being required from the men beyond that which was absolutely necessary.

CHAPTER VI.

AFTER crossing the equator, the Conqueror speedily fell in with a fresh south-east wind, which carried her swiftly to the South American coast, running down which she, in a day or two, arrived off the harbour of Buenos Ayres.

It was well that Captain Rodman did not boldly enter the noble and spacious harbour of this great South American city, or the story of the cruise of the Conqueror had never been written.

Since the departure of the frigate from England, a fresh complication of difficulties had taken place in the city and provinces. Napoleon had, unknown to England, despatched emissaries for the purpose of rendering the great commercial interests of the country subservient to France. This had come to the knowledge of the admiral in command of the British squadron at the Cape of Good Hope, who, upon his own responsibility, had sailed with his squadron to Buenos Ayres, and had captured the French vessels in the harbour, and taken the city by surprise.

Not having a sufficient number of spare marines and sailors under his command to man and protect the forts, and considering that the English ships in the harbour were sufficiently capable of holding the place, he had left the forts unguarded, not being at all aware that a large body of French troops had, shortly before, marched inland from the city, in order to subdue the entire province. As soon, however, as it became known that the city was in possession of the English, the French general secretly marched his troops back, and under cover of the night entered the town and manned the forts, which completely command the harbour, and are mounted with tiers of heavy cannon.

In their turn the English were taken by surprise. Scarcely had daylight broke the next morning, ere a thundering cannonade was opened upon the vessels of the fleet from the heights above from every direction. To reply to it, or to remain in the harbour, and endeavour to force a landing and storm the forts, would have required a force at least three times as formidable as that under the admiral's command, and nothing was left for him but to make his escape with his ships—a feat which he only accomplished with great difficulty, and not without considerable damage having been done to some of his vessels. As he had no immediate expectations of reinforcements, and as it was useless to remain cruising off the coast to no purpose, the admiral returned to the Cape, happy, under all the circumstances, to have got away without being compelled to surrender any of the ships of the squadron to the enemy.

Captain Rodman was perfectly ignorant of this late occurrence when he sighted the coast, within six leagues of the harbour; and, but for a lucky chance, he would have entered the port, and have been compelled either to have surrendered his frigate to the French commandant, or she would have been sunk by the guns of the fort.

"How does the land bear, Mr. Peters?" he asked of the second lieutenant, as he came forth from his cabin after having been called and informed that the South American coast was in sight.

"Sou'-west by west, sir. The nearest point is about six leagues distance," was the reply.

"Ha! That is Cape Blanco. A very good landfall. But, Mr. Peters, we must not approach too near the coast until we open the mouth of the harbour. Luff up a point, sir, and steer due sou'-west, until further orders."

"Sail ho!" shouted a sailor, from aloft.

"Where away, my man?" inquired the captain.

"On the weather bow, sir, steering straight for the harbour."

"What does she look like?"

"I can but just see her topsails, from the crosstrees, sir; but from their general cut, I should say how she be a man-o'-war."

"Ha! ha! Is she a large vessel?"

"I can only make out two topsails, sir; but they looks uncommon narrer, and 'pears to be cut with a sheer. I take it as she's a brig, sir. But, steerin' our present course, we shall cut her off before she can reach the harbour."

"And that I intend to do, till I learn what she is, and whether she's friend or foe," said the captain.

"Call the first lieutenant, Mr. Peters," he went on. "Hoist our colours, and see the decks cleared for action—silently—no drum beat, nor anything of that sort, so that we may be prepared for any emergency."

These orders were promptly obeyed, and everything was prepared to welcome a friend, or fight a foe, long before the vessel's hull could be discovered from the decks of the frigate.

"She's a brig," said the captain, at length, after having examined the strange sail through his spy-glass. "We shall not need to fight, be she friend or foe, for she is not able to contend with a ship of this size. But to *me*, she looks like a French vessel, and she certainly *is* a ship of war. Ha! There goes her ensign! English, by Jove! Yet if that vessel *is* English, I was never more mistaken in the rig of a vessel in all my life. Hoist our flag, Mr. Peters."

Up went the British ensign, fluttering in the breeze.

As the vessels were steering, they might be supposed to meet each other just off the entrance of the harbour. But the stranger, who had hitherto been running swiftly, almost directly before the wind, now approached so unaccountably slowly, that she gave rise to some suspicion that—without shortening sail, which would have caused surprise—her progress had been checked, probably by towing a spar or a sail over her stern.

"I don't understand it," said Captain Rodman to his first lieutenant. "I have thought from the first that the vessel is French rigged, although she has hoisted the English colours; and now it is very evident that her speed is checked for some object or other, and *that* looks very suspicious. It appears to me that she wishes *us* to enter the harbour before she comes up with us, though for what reason I cannot understand, if she be indeed English. Hoist our private signals, sir, and inquire her name, and from what part she comes."

The private man-of-war signals were sent aloft; and then flags were hoisted, asking the questions demanded by the captain.

Flags were sent up on board the stranger in response; but neither the captain nor any of the officers could make head or tail of them.

"I thought as much, sir," said Lieutenant Peters. "She's hoisted false colours to deceive us. There's not a ship in the service, big or little, that couldn't answer the simple questions we've put. Besides, she has not replied correctly to our private signal."

"It's clear enough," said the first lieutenant. "She is lagging in order that we may enter the harbour, believing her to be English; and as soon as we drop our anchor, she'll alter her course, and make off."

The captain was of the same opinion; but in one respect both he and his officers were mistaken. The French brig—for such she was—wished the English frigate to enter the harbour, in order that she might escape being captured by her. But there was no fear of her making off, if once she had induced the frigate to enter the trap; for in such case the Conqueror would have found herself in the midst of a large squadron of French men-of-war which had lately arrived, one of which was an eighty-gun ship, carrying the flag of Admiral Liniers, and three or four of which were larger than the English frigate.

Captain Rodman of course was unaware of this fact, and it was lucky that he fell in with the French brig, or otherwise he would have been cleverly trapped.

He was not, however, to be deceived by the Frenchmen.

"We *will* enter the port," said he to his officers, "but not alone. In the first place we'll capture that brig, and then we'll carry her with us into port. Stand by to 'bout ship! Ready about there, for'ard! To your stations, my men!"

The orders were rapidly given. The frigate went round like a top, and in a couple of minutes she was standing out towards the French vessel in such a manner as to cross her bows within shot-range.

The Frenchmen, however, perceived that their *ruse* was discovered. The brig also was put about, and then, her yards having been squared, she ran off dead before the wind, followed by the frigate.

A long, stern chase ensued; but though the brig sailed fast, the frigate out-sailed her by two knots an hour. Before noon both vessels were far distant from the coast; but the Conqueror was nearly in range of the brig, and before darkness set in one of her bow-guns was fired, the shot *ricochetting* and skimming through the water far ahead of the chase.

The Frenchmen perceived that escape was hopeless. To show fight would have been sheer madness, for a single broadside from the frigate would have sufficed to sink the brig, whose captain now hove-to and lowered his flag (the French colours had been hoisted when the chase began) in token of surrender.

The French captain came on board the frigate, and delivered up his sword. He and his officers gave their *parole* not to attempt escape, and were allowed their liberty. The French sailors were confined between decks; a small prize-crew was put on board the brig, and the officer in charge was directed to follow the frigate, which was now many miles distant from the port which she was so near in the morning.

Captain Rodman spoke French with perfect fluency—as the readers of "Dashing Rodman" are aware. He had acquired the language through conversing with the governor of the fortress, and his wife, and his pretty young daughter, during his long imprisonment near Montauban, and spoke it so well that he might easily have passed for a Frenchman. As he paced the quarter-deck of the frigate in company with the French captain, the latter complimented him upon the excellence of his French, and seemed to be as contented as though his position were changed, and the English captain was *his* prisoner. The other officers laughed and joked, in broken English, with the British officers, and seemed quite at their ease; while the French seamen submitted to their fate with such a good grace, and talked and laughed, and sang so merrily, that at length Captain Rodman began to suspect that some mischief was afloat, though he could not conceive its nature.

Without attracting the notice of the French captain, he signalled to his first lieutenant to go below to his cabin, and presently followed him thither.

"I can't understand it, Mr. Bowling," he said, as soon as he and the lieutenant were alone; "but I am almost confident that there is some mischief brewing. These fellows appear as happy as if they had made a prize of the frigate! And, now I think of it, it's rather singular that the captain of the French brig did not make off when he *first* caught sight of us—which must have been long before we sighted him—rather than try to deceive us by hoisting false colours. In one case he was sure to get clear away, while, in the course he pursued, he must have known that he ran a great risk of being found out, as he was, and captured."

"It *is* strange, sir, when one comes to think it over," replied the lieutenant. "Frenchmen *do* certainly take misfortunes easier than we do. Still, these fellows are as merry as if they felt sure that *we* were caught in a snare. You read the French captain's commission, sir? That was all correct, I presume?"

"All correct, so far as *I* could perceive. The brig belonged to Admiral Liniers' squadron, from which, the captain said, he got separated some time since. The squadron sailed from Brest to cruise in the West India seas "——

"I ask pardon for interrupting you, sir," said the lieutenant; "but if Captain —what's his name?—Captain Riquet, got separated from the squadron, how came he to be in *this* part of the world? And why was he sailing into Buenos Ayres, instead of looking out for the lost squadron to which he belongs, among the West India islands? I wonder, also, where he was sailing *from*, when we fell in with him?"

"Very just observations, sir," said Captain Rodman. "There's some secret, you may depend upon it. I'll question Captain Riquet more closely, and if his answers do not satisfy me, I'll make a further search among the papers in the brig's cabin."

The two officers returned to the deck, where Captain Rodman rejoined the French captain, who appeared to be so much alarmed when he began to question him closely, that Captain Rodman at once determined—evidently to the great alarm or disappointment of *all* the French officers—to make a thorough search amongst the private papers of his prisoner.

"*Ah, mon Dieu,*" exclaimed Captain Riquet, when Captain Rodman demanded his keys. "*N'est-ce pas que je suis homme d'honneur?*" (Ah, my God! Am I not a man of honour?) "Why do you doubt my word, monsieur?" he continued in French, with many violent gestures and strange grimaces. "*Monsieur, votre conduite est honteuse—ignominieuse.*" (Sir, such conduct is shameful—disgraceful!)

All his protestations, however, united with those of his officers, were made to no purpose. Without replying to them, Captain Rodman, who went on board the brig with his second lieutenant—taking Captain Riquet also with him—made no reply, and after a long and vigorous search, his efforts were rewarded by the discovery of papers which informed him that the harbour of Buenos Ayres was full of French ships of war, and the forts garrisoned by French soldiers.

"Ah, ah, messieurs, whose conduct is disgraceful now?" said he, in French, to the discomfited French officers. "You have parted from your squadron—eh, messieurs? But it *was* but three days ago, when you left Buenos Ayres to cruise about off the coast, and bring back to your admiral information of any English ships of war that might be in the vicinity of the harbour, and to capture any unlucky merchant ship you might chance to overhaul. By George, messieurs, you played your part well, and very nearly succeeded in luring us into a trap! But if I don't double upon you, and make a cat's paw of *you*—to play your countrymen a trick that they little suspect—my name is not Tom Rodman!"

At the period to which this story relates, when England was, through the machinations of Napoleon Bonaparte, at one time or another, at war with almost all the nations of Europe, ships of war of the size of the Conqueror were provided with every conceivable description of disguise.

Captain Rodman consulted with his officers, and a most daring scheme was soon planned, which, if it should prove successful, would win him great credit, though it involved so much peril that, should it happen to fail—an idea which never entered the captain's head—he could not hope to escape severe censure, if he were not more severely punished, for his reckless daring.

Instead of sailing back with his prize to Buenos Ayres, the Conqueror was hove-to at a distance of fifty miles from the coast, and several days were occupied in completely altering the appearance of the frigate, and giving her a Frenchified look. Even the topmasts were struck, and lighter, but loftier, spars were sent up in their place; while the sails were set with a longer leach and a narrower spread.

The figure-head was removed, and a fresh one set up. The name was painted out of the frigate's stern, and the name of a French frigate, *Le Dedaigneux*—a vessel of exactly her size and armament—was painted in the space "The Conqueror" had occupied. The costume of the officers and seamen and marines was changed into the fashion of that worn in the French naval service, and every possible alteration was made to disguise the English appearance of the frigate, and make her look like a French vessel.

On board the brig a set of French flags and signals, with a book of descriptions for their proper use, was found, which greatly pleased Captain Rodman, who thought it, and the flags, might prove of the greatest service, and aid him materially to carry out his purpose.

All the while these alterations were being made, the French officers looked on with the utmost chagrin, though they were powerless to do aught besides, save to assure Captain Rodman that he would be unsuccessful, and that their day of triumph would soon arrive—an assurance which the captain and his officers, all of whom were young men, full of spirits and fun, only laughed at.

Among other things found in the cabin of the brig was a chart of the harbour of Buenos Ayres, with the depth of water in different spots, the position of the town, the forts, and the landing places, and that of the French ships of war then at anchor in the harbour.

This Captain Rodman studied attentively. So great was the terror with which the almost constant success of the British, in their naval combats, had, at this period, filled their foes, that, in spite of the number of vessels in the French squadron, all save one—a frigate of forty guns, which had been a late arrival—had anchored in the inner harbour, close under the forts, to avoid being cut out, and carried off by some daring Englishman; and Captain Rodman's chief anxiety was lest this vessel should have changed her anchorage, and also anchored beneath the forts.

The spot where she lay, as represented on the chart, was, he thought, out of the range of the guns of the forts, and if she still remained there, it would just suit his daring scheme.

When everything was prepared, the vessels made sail for the harbour, the French officers being now confined in the cock-pit, though they were allowed to walk about between decks as they pleased, and every comfort was provided them. They were, however, forbidden to come upon deck, lest they might somehow contrive to signal secretly to their countrymen on entering the harbour.

Among the officers of the frigate, the third lieutenant, the surgeon, and three of the midshipmen had been partly educated in France, during the period of the short peace. These officers, on their return to England when the war recommenced, had improved their knowledge of the language, and they all, as well as the captain, spoke French fluently.

Among the sailors, also, there were twenty-two French-Canadians from

Quebec, who, of course, spoke the language of their forefathers perfectly well, though they were British subjects, and Englishmen at heart.

These officers and men Captain Rodman thoroughly tutored, for he considered that they would serve his daring purpose admirably. The wind was from the westward; still, in a couple of days, the frigate and her prize, the French brig, beat up to the entrance of the port.

It was near nightfall, yet still sufficiently light to enable the crew of the frigate to see all the vessels in port, and to enable those on board the French vessels to see the frigate distinctly, though in another hour darkness would set in.

Captain Rodman considered that he could not have arrived at a more favourable time, and, to his great joy, he found that the French vessels still lay in the position indicated on the chart. A fine frigate of forty guns—*L'Impératrice*—lay a full mile apart from the other ships in the magnificent and spacious harbour, and, as Captain Rodman believed, certainly beyond the range of the guns of the forts, with probably one exception. But this was, after all, mere surmise on his part.

Through an excellent spy-glass that he possessed, he could discern the French officers on board the ships and in the forts, and the people on shore, all watching the movements of the frigate and brig—the former vessel having hoisted the French tricolour—with apparent curiosity, but without any signs of suspicion.

On entering the harbour, Captain Rodman carried his frigate a short distance inside the anchorage of the lonely French frigate; but let go his anchor in the outer harbour, at a safe distance from the fire of the other vessels of the French squadron.

He then clewed up his sails, without furling them, as though it were his purpose to await orders from the French admiral, or to take up a position, by-and-bye, in the inner harbour; and then boldly, and most audaciously, proceeded to salute the forts, and the admiral's ship, with the usual number of guns.

The salutes were responded to by the ship, and by the principal fort; and then a boat was seen to put off from the admiral's ship, and to pull towards the supposed *Dedaigneux*, to learn the latest news from Europe, that vessel being—as Captain Rodman had learnt from his prisoners—expected from France, and being of course supposed to have just arrived, by the Frenchmen. Almost at the same moment, a boat also put off from the shore. That from the ship arrived first. The officer hailed and was answered, in French, by Captain Rodman, who invited him to come on board. He complied; but as soon as his feet touched the gangway, he was disarmed, while his men were seized and made prisoners. The shore-boat, containing an officer from the fort, was soon alongside. He and his men were similarly served.

Meanwhile the brig, which had closely followed the frigate, was anchored a cable's length to leeward of the larger vessel.

Captain Rodman had another object in view besides the capture of a frigate. He expected that a letter from Lucy Sinclair was awaiting him at the post office; and what will not a sailor venture to obtain a letter from the maiden he loves? The town was in the possession of the French; but the young captain was not to be deprived of his letter, if it were at the post office, on *that* account. Almost immediately after the frigate entered the harbour, the little jolly-boat was lowered, and one of the midshipmen, who spoke French, with four of the Canadian sailors, were sent on shore, with orders to speak as little as possible, but to bring off, at all hazards, any letter or letters, in the post office, that might be addressed to Captain Rodman.

The jolly-boat was hardly midway to the shore, when another boat put off from another of the ships; then a third boat—all the French officers were so eager to hear tidings of the Great Napoleon, and to learn how he was thrashing the armies of those *coquins des Anglais.* (Those rascally English.)

The officers were disarmed, and the men seized and confined below, as their countrymen had been who had preceded them.

Captain Rodman himself politely escorted the officers to his own cabin, where the officers of the brig were confined, and where wine, and every refreshment and delicacy the frigate could afford, were spread out before them.

" *Entrez, messieurs,*" said the captain, with a polite bow; " *vous trouverez vos camarades ici. J'espere bien, messieurs, que vous vous enjouirez.*" (Enter, gentlemen. You will find comrades here. I hope that you will enjoy yourselves.)

" Steward " (to his own private servant), " bring champagne. Supply the gentlemen with everything they may require. Let them want for nothing that the frigate can afford."

And so saying he retired, leaving an armed sentry to guard the door, with orders to shoot any one who persisted in coming upon deck. But the unfortunate Frenchmen were so amazed, and taken-aback, as sailors say, that they submitted quietly, seeming as though they were perfectly bewildered.

The captain then returned to the deck, and at his directions the boats were quietly lowered, and filled with armed men—sailors and marines. An officer took his seat in each boat, save the pinnace, which was left to the command of the captain himself. The ship's guns were loaded and shotted, to be ready in case of necessity, though it was not thought that they would be needed. By the time these several orders were completed, Captain Rodman was anxiously looking for the return of his jolly-boat, and was also growing anxious lest the commanders of the vessels, who had sent their boats on board the frigate, should begin to wonder, or to feel alarmed, or suspicious, by reason of their not returning.

" The boat ought surely to be back soon," said he to the first lieutenant, who was, in fact, the only officer of rank left on board the frigate. " I am afraid the admiral will be sending another boat to inquire after the delay of the first one. Well, if he does, we must just seize it, and the officers and men, as before, though there are quite enough of the fellows on board now. . . . Hark! There is a gun from the admiral's ship to hasten the return of the boat! And see, they are hoisting lanterns on board all the vessels that have sent off boats! Confound it! What *can* be detaining our jolly-boat all this time? I hope the fellows have not come to any harm! . . . Ha! Here she comes at last. Boat ahoy!"

" Sir," replied the midshipman in command.

" Is all safe?"

" Ay, ay, sir."

" The letter! *Was* there a letter for me?"

" Yes, sir. A letter directed to Captain Rodman, of the Conqueror. To be left at Buenos Ayres till called for."

Captain Rodman's heart leaped in his bosom. He knew that from only *one* person could a letter arrived at Buenos Ayres for *him*.

" All right, my boy," he cried. " Hasten on board as quickly as possible. Now, sir " (to the first lieutenant), " we'll delay no longer. You have my instructions. See that they are followed to the letter. All will depend upon your promptitude. At the signal agreed upon—a lantern thrice dipped from the mizzengaff-end—you will instantly slip our cable. To wait to heave up the anchor is out of the question. King George, God bless him! can afford to lose an anchor and cable in order to gain a frigate, and I regard the French frigate, yonder, as already our prize. As soon as the cable is slipped, set sail upon the ship—they will do the same on board the brig—and follow the French frigate out of the harbour. You perfectly understand?"

"Perfectly, sir," replied the lieutenant, who would be left on board with no more men than were absolutely necessary to work the frigate. All the rest were in the boats alongside—the French boats having been also pressed into the service, and filled with Englishmen.

Captain Rodman now took his seat in the stern-sheets of the pinnace. The boat put off, followed by the rest, all being pulled with muffled oars.

Fortune proverbially favours the brave and daring. There was no moon; and, in the southern hemisphere, the stars are comparatively few and far between, clustered here and there in small constellations, which afford but little light, and leaving vast spaces in the heavens in perfect darkness.

Though the night was fair, the few stars that should have glittered were overclouded. Sea and sky were alike wrapped in inky blackness. It was just such a night as Captain Rodman would have chosen for his daring enterprise.

Suspecting no evil, the men on board *L'Impératrice* were—both officers and sailors—mostly below. Only a small night-watch was set, and the officer of this was lolling idly over the capstan, whistling "*Partant pour la Syrie*," and thinking of *la belle France*, so far away; while the men were dozing, or smoking on the forecastle. Even the gangway was left with a sentry. No one on board heard or saw the approach of the English boats. The pinnace was the first alongside the frigate, and Captain Rodman hailed the vessel in French.

"*Ha, camarade*," replied the young French officer. "You come from *Le Dedaigneux?* I am glad to see you. Come on board, and tell us the news from France."

"*Je viens, mon ami*" (I come, my friend), answered Captain Rodman, as he ran swiftly up the ladder.

The moment he reached the gangway, he seized the youthful officer by the throat.

"I mean you no harm, monsieur," said he, in French; "but be silent for your life. You are my prisoner. The frigate is my prize!"

Then calling to his own men, he said:

"Board from the boats, my lads. We *must* and will have the ship. Fight to the death if they resist; but mind—no needless bloodshed. Give quarter to all who surrender."

Up over each bow, over the quarters, over the stern, by the gangways, by the fore, main, and mizzen chains, the British seamen and marines came swarming, boarding the frigate from every direction. They raised a hearty shout. But that was no matter now; for, despite Captain Rodman's threat, the young French officer had given the alarm, and the Frenchmen came pouring upon deck from the cabins, and from every hatchway. They fought fiercely—savagely—with the utmost desperation; but they were bewildered, taken by surprise. Even now they could not conceive whom they were fighting, and the English, from the boats, numbered almost as many as the entire French crew.

Several men fell on both sides. Many more were desperately wounded. Captain Rodman received a severe cut on the left arm from an officer's sword. Lieutenant Peters, next in command, was shot in the leg. But, from the outset, the Frenchmen, brave as they were, thus taken by surprise, had but little chance of success. Surprised and bewildered, they knew not the number of their foes, nor whence they came, and imagined them to be more numerous than they really were.

After a few minutes of desperate conflict, they surrendered; and *L'Impératrice* became the prize of the supposed *Dedaigneux*—the real Conqueror.

Wounded as he was, Captain Rodman himself hoisted a lantern to the French frigate's mizzengaff-end, and dipped it thrice.

At the signal the order was given on board the Conqueror to slip the cable, and presently the loud rattle and rush of the massive chain was heard as it slipped swiftly through the hawse-hole. The sound must have been audible on board the ships in the inner harbour; but probably the Frenchmen thought that the supposed *Dedaigneux* (Disdainful) was letting go a second anchor, though such a precaution was quite unnecessary. At all events, they appeared to take no particular notice of the noise.

Meanwhile, several of the English sailors had climbed the rigging of *L'Impératrice*, and loosed her sails, at the same time as their shipmates on board the Conqueror were letting fall, hauling up, and sheeting-home *her* sails, which, as I have said, had been left unfurled. Both vessels were got before the wind, and in a few minutes the Conqueror, followed by her prizes, *L'Impératrice* and the gun-brig, was sailing out of the harbour before a fresh south-west breeze.

It soon became evident, however, that this daring and desperate adventure on the part of Captain Rodman and his officers and crew had not succeeded without attracting the notice of the officers of the French squadron. In the stillness of the night they had heard the report of fire-arms and the clash of steel; and coupling these sounds with the non-return of the boats they had sent off to board the new arrival, they became alarmed, and began to suspect that something was amiss, though they could not conceive what really *was* the matter. Two or three more boats, however, put off from the ships of the squadron, and one of them, ahead of the rest, came up with the Conqueror, hailed her, and demanded to be informed, in the name of the admiral, of the motive for her strange movements.

A gun fired from the frigate over the Frenchmen's heads—Captain Rodman did not wish to injure them if he could avoid doing so—was the answer they received. It was a polite hint to them to return, and they very wisely beat a retreat, and pulled back into the harbour.

In a quarter of an hour the Conqueror, with her prizes, had gained a good offing. The adventure had proved successful, and Captain Rodman had cut out an enemy's frigate in full view of the ships of the squadron to which she belonged, and from under the guns of half a dozen strong forts, with the loss of only six men, and with some twenty wounded!

The gallant captain had reason to be proud of his success. But how often does it happen that men's brightest hopes and proudest rejoicings are damped and dimmed by some secret sorrow?

Captain Rodman had not had a moment to spare in which to read the letter he had risked so much to obtain. He had placed it in his breast-pocket, where it remained, near his heart, until the action was over.

Now he found time to peruse it. Well he knew the handwriting of the superscription. Eagerly he broke the seal and opened the letter, and with a flush of pleasure he read over the first few lines. Then his countenance changed, and mingled feelings of sorrow and indignation succeeded to those of pleasure and satisfaction. His countenance darkened, and when at length he placed the letter on the table, he looked and felt as if he were overwhelmed with grief.

There was a paragraph in Lucy Sinclair's letter which, for the moment, rendered him forgetful of the deed he had accomplished—careless of the fame he had won—oblivious of aught besides the feelings of sorrow and indignation which filled his breast!

CHAPTER VII.

CAPTAIN RODMAN had retired to his cabin as soon as the Conqueror and her prizes, *L'Impératrice* (the Empress) and *L'Epervier* (the Sparrow-hawk), had gained a good offing. Day was already beginning to dawn, and very soon "eight bells" (four o'clock a.m.) were struck.

The watch was relieved. The sailors were on deck and at their several stations, the marines stood sentinels at the gangway, the front of the quarter-deck, and at the captain's cabin; the helm was relieved, and the quartermaster of the watch was at his post conning the frigate. Mr. Wilton, the third lieutenant, paced the quarter-deck impatiently, glancing every now and then angrily towards the companion-way that led to the ward-room, and then grumbling to himself as he consulted his watch.

"Half-past four, I declare!" he at length exclaimed. "Strike one bell* there, sentry. Upon my soul, it's *too* bad! Oh, here he comes at last;" and Lieutenant Peters, gaping and yawning, and smiling between whiles, as though he was the most punctual man in the world, made his appearance on deck.

"Chilly, rather, ain't it?" said he, addressing the third lieutenant. "Yaw-w-w" (with a tremendous gape), "I am confoundedly sleepy after last night's hard work, and my wound's a little stiff, though it's but a scratch. How far are we from land?"

"Upon my word, Mr. Peters, it's too bad of you to keep me on deck half an hour after your watch was called," growled the third lieutenant. "Every man of the watch, save yourself, has been five-and-twenty minutes on deck."

"Dear me," replied the second lieutenant, "is it *really* so late? 'Pon my word, I thought I turned out the moment I was called. I'm sorry"——

"Much good your sorrow will do me, after you've cheated me out of half an hour of my watch below!" grumbled the third lieutenant.

"Well—well, my dear fellow," said Peters, "what's done can't be undone. You should have roused me more thoroughly. I'll try and be more punctual another time."

"Pish! We'd need fire a gun close to your ears. I never knew a fellow sleep so soundly."

"How far are we from the land?" repeated the second lieutenant.

"About twenty miles, I should say," was the reply. "We made little way at first leaving the harbour; but this last hour she's been making twelve knots good."

"What are the orders?"

"To steer a west course till we get well out to sea. But the wind's veering round and freshening. I've been obliged to haul down the topmast studding-sails, and it's my belief that you'll have to brace up close to the wind before long, and to take in the topgallant sails."

"It *does* look breezy to windward," said Peters. "Where are the prizes?"

"There away, to leeward. It seems to be as much as they can do to keep up with us. Oh, by the way, you're not to alter the course, or shorten sail, without letting the captain know. Those were his last orders."

---

* The bells on board ship, denoting the progress of the watch, are struck every half-hour, from one to eight bells, four hours being the length of a watch.

"Very well. Good morning."

"Yes, you may well say good *morning*. It'll be broad daylight in half an hour, and I ought to have been snug in my cot long before this," and still grumbling to himself in consequence of the delay of the second lieutenant in relieving the watch, Mr. Wilton disappeared below.

Mr. Peters, who from his earliest days as a midshipman had a bad habit of coming late upon deck, and who, when a youngster, had had many a sly trick played him in consequence thereof, and had been frequently mastheaded in order that he might learn to keep awake, walked the deck for some time in silence, and apparently in deep thought.

Then, addressing himself to old Simpson, who was the quartermaster of his watch, he said:

"It looks gloomy to windward, Simpson, and the sea is getting up rapidly."

"Yes, sir," replied the quartermaster, "and it's as much as the ship 'll lie her course. We shall have the wind from the nor'ard and east'ard afore long, I'm thinkin'; and if I ain't mistaken, it'll blow pretty smart "——

"Keep her full, you booby" (to the helmsman). "Don't you see that the leach of the maintop sail is shaking?"

"She won't lie her course rap-full, sir," replied the helmsman. "She's broke off half a p'int just now."

Simpson glanced at the compass in the binnacle.

"We'll have to take another pull at the braces, sir, I reckon," said he to the lieutenant. "We'll have to brace sharp up afore long. The wind's veerin' round every minute."

Peters gave orders to brace for'ard the yards. This was done, and the frigate immediately felt the extra strain. The squalls caused her to lie over until the water washed her lee scuppers, and it was evident that she was carrying too much canvas.

The quartermaster glanced aloft, where the royal and topgallant masts were springing like reeds beneath a blast, and then looked at the lieutenant.

"I see, Simpson, that it is high time to furl the upper canvas," said Peters; "but my orders are not to shorten sail without acquainting the captain; and it seems a pity to disturb him if it can be avoided. How does she lie now?"

"She still lies her course, sir, due west; but though the yards is braced sharp up, I reckon how she won't lie her course much longer; and arxin' pardon for offerin' my opinion, sir, it's my belief how she not only wants her royals and topgallant sails taken off, but 'ud be all the better for a reef in the topsails into the bargain."

"I'll hold on as long as I can," said Peters, who continued to pace the deck, glancing anxiously from time to time at the gathering clouds to windward.

So long as the Conqueror carried a press of sail, the French vessels, her prizes, were compelled to do so, in order to keep up with her. But every moment Peters and the men of the watch looked for something to give way, and presently the *Impératrice* carried away her fore and main topgallant masts, and began to fall astern. It was high time to call the captain now, or to shorten sail without his knowledge. Peters looked at his watch. It was half-past six o'clock.

"Strike five bells," said he; and then he muttered to himself: "We surely must be far enough from the coast now—fifty miles at least, for we've been making more than twelve knots an hour since I came upon deck."

Captain Rodman had been twenty-four hours upon deck when, after leaving the harbour of Buenos Ayres, he went to his cabin, and for that reason Peters was unwilling to disturb him.

Now, however, he went below just as a heavy squall struck the frigate.

Expecting to find Captain Rodman sound asleep in his state-room, the lieutenant entered the outer cabin without knocking, and, to his great surprise, beheld the captain seated at the table fully dressed, and apparently in deep reverie over the contents of a letter which lay on the table before him.

He started at the noise Peters made, and looked up inquiringly.

"I beg pardon, sir," said the lieutenant. "Had I not believed you to be in your state-room, I would not have entered so unceremoniously. I have come to tell you that the wind is freshening, and veering round to the north-east with heavy squalls. The frigate will no longer lie her course close hauled, and it is necessary to shorten sail. The French brig has already carried away her topgallant masts, and ours are springing like whips.

"Ha!" exclaimed the captain. "How far are we from the coast?"

"I should say close upon fifty miles, sir," was the reply.

"Fifty miles! Impossible!"

"We quitted the harbour shortly after two o'clock, sir, and for the last four hours the frigate has been making twelve knots an hour."

"God bless me!" exclaimed the captain, passing his hand over his temples. "I've not slept, and yet I thought we had not left the harbour more than an hour. It seems incredible! . . . *Fifty miles*, do you say? We are far enough off, then, to render it improbable that any attempt will be made to recapture our prizes. You have seen nothing since daylight of any of the ships of the French squadron?"

"Nothing, sir. I suspect that none of them cared to leave the shelter of the harbour in order to give chase to us."

"You may bear away, then, to the southward. That will ease the frigate. Stay, I will go upon deck myself, and look around."

Captain Rodman followed the second lieutenant to the deck, and after casting a rapid glance aloft and around him, he ordered the quartermaster to steer a south-south-east course. This brought the wind which now blew fresh from the north-east, well on to the larboard quarter—in fact nearly aft. The frigate and her prizes—who followed her manœuvres—felt the relief immediately, and although, while close hauled, they could not safely carry their topgallant sails, they were now able to carry their royals with ease, and the larboard studding sails were again set—though until the *Impératrice* had sent up new topgallant masts, she lagged a little behind the other two frigates.

Captain Rodman's object in steering a course due west had been merely to get a good offing, in case the vessels of the French squadron should come forth from the harbour and make an attempt to recapture his prizes; for he was well aware that with so many officers and men absent from the frigate on board the two French vessels, he was not in a condition to meet a powerful foe, who would thus attack him at a disadvantage, while the danger was increased in consequence of the number of French prisoners on board the prizes, who, in case he were to be attacked, would make an attempt to set themselves free and assist their countrymen. Now, however, he resolved to bear away to the south-ward until he should fall in with the south-east trade wind, when he would bear up and run for St. Helena,* and get quit of his prizes as soon as possible.

---

* St. Helena, which is a very small island, lies right in the heart of the usually strong south-east trade wind, and is easily passed unseen, by reason of the mists (caused by the frequent rains) with which it is often surrounded. Vessels, therefore, bound to St. Helena, rarely attempt to beat into port, against the strong trade wind and heavy sea; but sail southward, often almost to the Cape of Good Hope, to catch the trade wind, and then bear up, and run before it for the island.

Captain Rodman, though, as I have said, he had not slept for more than twenty-four hours, remained upon deck, and tried, by superintending everything that was going forward, to forget his anxiety and trouble; but in vain. After shortening sail and setting sail, and bracing the yards and squaring them again and finding fault with this and with that, and putting his officers and men to all sorts of trouble, until they wondered what possessed him—for usually he seldom interfered with the duties of the ship except upon occasions of emergency—he would relapse into thoughtfulness, and then rouse himself and give all sorts of contrary orders over again.

That something had happened to distress and annoy him everybody saw though no one—save possibly Mr. Peters—had any idea what it was. I will however, make the captain's trouble known to my readers. I have already intimated that it was occasioned by a paragraph in Lucy Sinclair's letter. The paragraph ran as follows:

"And now, dearest Tom, that I have assured you that I think constantly of you by day, and dream of you at night, and that nothing can possibly change my feelings towards you, I must tell you something which I am sure will cause you as great pain, anxiety, and distress as it has already caused me. Still, dear Tom, it is but right that you should know all about the matter. You and I should hold no secrets from each other.

"About three weeks after you sailed from England, Captain Lord George Milford, an officer who formerly sailed as a fellow midshipman with papa, but who now commands the Acteon frigate came on a visit to the Grange. His attentions to me very soon became so marked that I found it necessary to avoid him, though he is a very handsome man, of thirty-five or thereabouts, and was always kind and polite in his behaviour.

"I suppose, dear Tom, that Lord Milford noticed my coolness, and spoke to papa about it, for a few days afterwards, while I was riding out with papa, he asked me why I shunned the society of our noble and gallant guest. It was an awkward question to reply to; but, though I hesitated and stammered a great deal, I at length gave papa to understand my motives. Imagine my surprise and consternation, dear Tom, when papa thus addressed me:

"'My dear Lucy, Lord Milford admires you very much. He is a handsome, intelligent, well educated, kindly-tempered man, and a thorough seaman. He is still comparatively young, and, on the decease of his father, the Earl of Camden, he will succeed to the title and estates, which yield a revenue of eighteen thousand a year. The Camden estates, lie, as you know, contiguous to mine. You, dear Lucy, are my sole heiress, and if you were to marry Lord Milford, you would eventually become countess—probably, indeed, in a short time, for the old earl cannot last much longer—and the two estates—which really appear as though they were intended to be united—would bring in an annual rental of nearly thirty thousand pounds! There is not a young lady in the county who would not rejoice to become their mistress, and you and Lord Milford would be the wealthiest couple in Cambridge-shire.'

"Papa became silent; but he looked as if he expected me to reply, and at length I said:

"'You forget, dear papa, that I am already affianced, with your permission, to Captain Rodman. How, then, can I offer any encouragement to Lord Milford, whom, in fact, I regard only as a friend?'

"'It is true, my love,' answered papa, 'that I offered no objections to your marriage with Captain Rodman, whom I both esteem and love. But I only accorded my consent to your marriage with him on his return from his present cruise, on condition that at that period you should both continue to be of the same mind. I did not *absolutely* promise that the marriage should take place; in fact, I regarded both you and Captain Rodman as perfectly at liberty to alter your minds, if either one or the other felt inclined so to do.' (This, dear Tom, is the fact, though we both looked upon papa's permission in the light of an express promise.) 'At that period,' continued papa, 'I had no idea that Lord Milford had any thought of paying his addresses to you; and, setting his lordship aside, I know of no young man whom I would sooner accept as my son-in-law than Tom Rodman. Still, dear Lucy, marriage is a serious matter to contemplate. Other things besides a mutual regard between the principal parties have to be considered. You will be comparatively rich under any circumstances. Rodman has nothing but his profession to look forward to, except the property his father may leave him; and though that may be considerable, it will be but trifling in comparison with *your* wealth. It is my opinion, too, that persons should wed their equals in wealth and social position, though remarking your attachment to Rodman, and having a real liking for him, I disregarded that equality in his case. However, nothing definite has been settled between you and Captain Rodman. Nothing, in fact, has passed between you beyond a mutual understanding that, if nothing occurred during Tom's absence to alter the state of affairs, you should be united in wedlock on his return to England. Now, my dear Lucy, this offer of Lord Milford's *does* place the matter in a very different light. I confess that I should wish to see you the Countess of Camden, and under any circumstances such an offer is not one to be lightly regarded.'

"Much more, dear **Tom**, papa advanced to the same purport, and, though I naturally felt bashful and diffident, I forced myself to reply to him.

"Among other things he said that Lord Milford, on the death of his father the earl, would retire from the service, and live the life of a country gentleman on his estates; while you, after your marriage, must necessarily continue to follow your profession.

"I spoke of your grief and disappointment in case I were to prove so fickle as to alter my mind, and break off what we both regarded as an engagement; but papa smiled at this, and said that sailors were not accustomed to take such matters seriously to heart, and that wandering about as they do, they are apt to seek a mistress of their affections in every port. He intimated, indeed, that you, dear Tom, might probably meet with some young lady whom you would prefer to me, in the society into which your present rank will lead you. I am afraid, dear Tom, that there is too much truth in what papa says regarding the fickleness of naval men. Still I do not, will not believe that *your* affections can change, any more than can my own.

"We conversed long and seriously upon the subject, and papa afterwards got mamma to talk to and reason with me. I, however, remained firm; and papa said he would never cause me to wed against my inclinations, much as he wished to see me a countess. I have never yet, dear Tom, opposed myself to papa's wishes, and the result of our conversation on the subject was that I assured him that so long as you remained true to me, I should regard myself as your affianced bride; that I would marry no other than you, but that I would never marry any one without his consent and blessing.

"Thus, dear Tom, do matters stand at present. Trust in me as I trust in you, and I hope and believe all will yet be well."

Lucy Sinclair also stated in her letter that the Acteon would shortly put to sea, and that her father had promised to say no more on the subject until Lord Milford's return from his forthcoming cruise.

"I know not exactly to what part of the world Lord Milford will sail," she wrote; "but he speaks very highly of you, Tom. He says he has often heard of you, and would like to become acquainted with you (of course he knows nothing of our engagement); but I should not be surprised if you and he meet each other abroad before you return to England."

It was this portion that I have recorded of Lucy Sinclair's long letter, which so greatly affected Captain Rodman as to make him, for the time being, forgetful of the daring and gallant deed he had just performed, and almost altogether heedless as to what became of him.

He was vexed with Lucy because she wrote that Captain Lord Milford was a handsome and agreeable man. He was jealous of her praises; and as he read the letter over and over again, he alternately doubted, trusted, felt angry with, and pitied her.

"Handsome!" he muttered to himself. "Yes, of course, a lord—the heir to an earldom, with eighteen thousand a year—is handsome and agreeable! I don't see what business such fellows have to command a ship! Remain true!" he went on. "Yes, until she's talked over to give her hand to my lord, when *I* shall be thrown aside without the slightest compunction! It's *too* bad of Captain Sinclair, by Jove! He *did* give his consent to our union, and I'll stick to it that he did! Lucy, if she had possessed any spirit, ought to have told him so, and have flatly refused to have anything to say to this sailor-lord! She's only tacking about till she can find an excuse for bearing up under his lordship's lee. *I* can see through her empty professions of trust and constancy clearly enough! But I'll be even with her. Sailors change their affections in every port, do they? Well, perhaps *I* shall act like the rest—though it's a confounded falsehood, and so Captain Sinclair knows it to be! And yet, after all, poor girl, she writes affectionately, and appears to be deeply grieved! What more *can* she say but that she will be true to me, as I, she believes, will be to her? I'm a brute for doubting her faith and constancy, and yet "——

And thus, as I have said, alternately doubting and trusting; now devoured by feelings of jealousy, and now overflowing with fondness and affection, Captain Rodman passed the hours, during which he was supposed to be asleep, until he was aroused from his gloomy reverie by the entrance into his cabin of Lieutenant Peters.

During the day he suffered from many relapses, and indulged in the most bitter feelings towards his supposed rival.

"I may come across him in the course of my cruise!" he muttered to himself "Yes, I *may;* and I hope I *shall*. I'll pick a quarrel with him, by George And then I'll call him out and shoot him as I would a mad dog! And yet I don't know what I could find to quarrel about, if, as Lucy writes, he knows nothing of our mutual engagement. Confound *him*, and everybody else!"

Sometimes he thought he would throw up his commission, leave the frigate and return home, and confront and upbraid both Lucy and Captain Sinclair, or he would persuade Lucy to elope with him. Then he thought he would seek out some desperate service from which there was no possibility of escape, and after running his frigate into the very midst of the enemy's fleet, or under the guns o some tremendous fort, would fight desperately to the very last, doing all the damage to the foe that he possibly could, until his ship was sunk or blown up when he would perish, forgetting all his woes, and be soon forgotten.

He harassed and tormented his officers and crew, as I have said, terribly until they began to think him crazy, and he thought and did all manner o foolish things, and all because the young lady whom he loved had written to inform him that she was admired and sought after by some one else!

Such, however, has been the effect of love and jealousy since the Creation, and so it will continue until the world's end. Solomon was the wisest of mankind and Samson the strongest, yet both did and said very foolish things when they concerned themselves with the fairer and gentler sex. And it was not to be expected that Captain Rodman should be wiser or stronger than they!

However, in course of time these keen feelings of doubt and jealousy lost their edge, and were kept under due control. Captain Rodman hoped that another letter from Lucy would relieve him from his anxiety.

This second letter he hoped to receive at Valparaiso, which was the next port at which he intended to call, and he became very eager to get there.

On the arrival of the Conqueror at St. Helena, her prizes were transformed into British ships of war, and after a brief stay at the island, Captain Rodman set sail for the South Pacific Ocean.

CHAPTER VIII.

LOVE matters are apt to be dull and prosy to record or to peruse, save to those whom they immediately concern. There is an amount of sameness peculiar to them, under any conditions, particularly at their commencement, and ere yet " the course of true love "—which, as Shakespeare wrote, " never does run smooth "—has begun to be disturbed or troubled by untoward circumstances.

To be sure, clouds appeared to be already rising in the distant horizon, and looming darkly over the love affairs of Captain Rodman and Miss Sinclair. But whether the obstacles which threatened to interpose in the way of their union were removed or overcome; whether Lucy Sinclair proved true or false; whether the lovers were eventually wedded, and made happy in their mutual affection; or whether the fond hopes of the young and gallant captain proved delusive, and were doomed to be blighted in the bud, I shall leave to be explained at a future period, when the subject will possess greater interest. Nor should I have yet alluded to it, nor have troubled my readers with the remarks which conclude the preceding chapter, were it not that I thought it desirable to inform them that Captain Rodman's ardent affection for Lucy Sinclair led, eventually, to one of the most intensely-exciting and interesting of the many spirit-stirring and daring and generous episodes that characterized his adventurous career.

The nature of this episode, however, I shall leave to be explained in its proper place, and setting love matters aside for the present, shall simply state that if Captain Rodman still cherished the feelings of doubt, mistrust, and jealousy to which Miss Sinclair's letter gave birth, he had sufficient pride and strength of mind to conceal them within his own bosom, and long before the Conqueror sailed from St. Helena, after having given over her prizes to the Government authorities, her officers and men had ceased to remark anything unusual in their captain's manner, the sailors were no longer harassed by reason of his ill-temper, and everything on board the frigate went on in the customary regular and orderly fashion.

At length the frigate arrived off Cape Horn. It is usual for vessels to keep well to the southward, and thus give the Cape a wide berth; but occasionally navigators keep close in shore in full view of the loftly rugged precipice and the singularly-shaped crooked peak on its summit, from which it acquires its appellation of " the Horn."

Captain Rodman kept near the coast, and passed the Horn within three leagues of the shore. Hitherto, the passage from St. Helena had been a remarkably fine one. The frigate had soon met with a fair wind, and had run before it with all sail set. It is seldom, however, that a ship can double either the Cape of Good Hope or Cape Horn without encountering a heavy gale, and now it seemed that the Conqueror was to meet with the usual stormy weather. The Cape was still in sight when the wind changed, and it came on to blow fresh from the south-west. It was soon necessary to reef topsails, then to furl the courses, and before darkness set in it blew a furious gale, and the frigate was hove-to under a close-reefed maintopsail and storm staysail.

In a good, stout, well-found ship, however, sailors care nothing for a gale of wind so long as they have plenty of sea-room. Indeed they rather like it, and certainly prefer it to a calm; for, when once the ship is " made snug," they have little or nothing to do except to keep the regular watches on deck, and, if helmsmen, to take their regular "trick" at the wheel.

"Well, Bob," said one of the sailors of the watch-below to a messmate, "this is the first v'y'ge as I've made round Cape Horn, and bless'd if I'd care to make another if it's allers such weather as this! Lord, how it do blow, surely! And summer time, too! Leastways, so I heard the officers say, though it's near Christmas! *That's* a thing as *I* can't understand anyhows!"

"Nor I neither, Jack," was the reply. "I heerd it explained once; but I warn't none the wiser arter'ards. I reckon how the sun's turned somehow or other wrong side up'ards, on this side o' the equator, and that's what brings it about. But I've been off Cape Horn at all seasons, and blow'd if *I* ever see much difference atwixt summer or winter."

"Stow yer talk there, boys," cried an old forecastleman. "It's Saturday night. There's an extra tot of grog in the can, and Joe Wilkins be agoin' to sing us a song as he's made up about sweethearts and wives."*

There was silence in the mess instantly, and, indeed, throughout the 'tween decks, for Joe Wilkins—a Cockney seaman, and a thorough good one—was acknowledged to be the best singer on board the frigate. Captain Rodman usually allowed his men an extra allowance of grog on Saturday nights, especially if the weather were cold or stormy; so, bringing forth the can and tin pannikins, the sailors settled down to enjoy themselves as well as they could; and while the ship rolled and pitched tremendously, and officers and men kept watch on deck, the watch-below listened in deep attention, while Joe Wilkins trolled forth his ditty:

> " 'Tis Saturday night, boys, and *our* watch below,
> So down to our hammocks we'll cheerily go;
> But before we turn in, boys, we'll each drink a toast
> To those in old England we honour the most,
> To the king; to our friends; and, the charm of our lives,
> The lasses we love boys—our sweethearts and wives!

> " The gale may blow strong, and the sea may run high,
> But no true-hearted sailor will whimper or sigh;
> Let happen what may, he's ne'er taken aback,
> For aye a stout heart in his bosom bears Jack:
> While he trusts to that Power that guards o'er his life,
> To take him safe home to his sweetheart or wife!

> " Let us sing and be merry, boys, still while we may,
> 'Tis enough that we're living and happy to-day;
> We live in the present, nor care we to know
> If the morrow shall bring us or pleasure or woe.
> We know we *must* go when our billet arrives,
> And behind us must leave, boys, our sweethearts and wives!

> " What matters? We're told, 'tis a comfort to know,
> That a Providence watches wherever we go;
> And whether we perish by wreck, steel, or lead,
> Or die, boys, like land-lubbers tucked up a-bed,
> That same Providence, boys, that guards over *our* lives,
> Will take care, when we're gone, of our sweethearts and wives!"

"A werry good song, and werry well sung; jolly companions every one!" roared out an old quartermaster, amidst the cheering and clapping of hands that resounded through the 'tween decks when Joe had ended his ditty.

---

* It is customary on board some ships to allow the sailors an extra allowance of grog on Saturday night, that they may enjoy themselves and drink to absent friends, and especially to sweethearts and wives; and where this extra allowance is not allowed, the sailors often save up a portion of their allowance that they may be enabled to drink to the time-honoured toast.

"And that 'ere song's yer own composin', Joe?" said one of the sailors.

"Yes, it be," was the reply. "Lor' love ye, boys, I've got half a dozen new ones. I made one about our captain t'other day. I composes 'em as I lays in my hammock, while you chaps is sleepin'."

"Then you're what they calls a pote, Joe?" said another.

"A pote! What the dickens be's a pote?"

"Why, a chap as makes up potry, to be sure. Look in the dixonary, mate, and you'll see."

"Bother the dixonary!" put in a boatswain's mate. "Let's have another song, Joe, my hearty."

"Sing us that 'ere song as you says you made about our captain, Joe," cried another.

"Ay, ay! The song about the captain, Joe!" roared forth a score of voices.

Joe Wilkins, who was proud of his voice, and of his own compositions—as is the case with many poets of much greater pretensions—and who was delighted with the praise he had received from his shipmates, was about to comply.

Silence was again called for, and the men sat around completely hushed, when suddenly a shout was heard upon deck. Then the boatswain's whistle sounded loud and shrill above the howling of the gale and the wild rush of the sea; and then a loud, gruff voice was heard, shouting:

"Tumble up! Tumble up, there, below! Tumble up, my hearties! Be smart, lads, and bear a hand upon deck, every man on ye!"

"What's up, boys? What's up now?" was the cry, as the watch-below sprang to their feet, and hastily put on their pea-jackets; those among them who had already turned in springing out of their hammocks, and hurriedly dressing themselves.

All knew that the ship had been made snug before they had come below, and was, as sailors say, "lying-to like a duck," scarcely taking a drop of water on board, although such a heavy sea was running. They knew also that all hands would not be summoned on deck except for some very serious matter, and though they had felt no shock, nor heard anything to cause them alarm, they gazed uneasily and with frightened glances at one another.

A general rush was made for the hatchways, each man striving to be the first to gain the deck, though when they got there nothing alarming was to be seen. The frigate was still lying-to with comparative ease, rising and falling gently with the waves.

Glancing, however, towards the quarter-deck, they saw that it was crowded with officers, wrapped in their boat-cloaks, and wearing their waterproofs and sou'-westers. Lanterns were being carried about, and a lantern was hoisted at the mizzengaff-end—the light from which caused the rain and spray drops on the officers' oilskin coats to glitter like diamonds.

Many of the officers had spy-glasses, which were pointed over the lee hammock-nettings, and one of the lieutenants and two or three midshipmen were fighting their way aloft, with their telescopes slung over their shoulders, though the wind blew so strong that they could hardly make headway, and were sometimes forced to cling to the shrouds with all their strength to save themselves from being blown into the sea.

"What is it? What's up, mates?" the men of the watch-below inquired of their shipmates—one of whom answered by pointing over the lee bow.

Then they saw the land, looming dark and gloomy, apparently a couple of miles distant; and wondered why the frigate was not wore round while there was plenty of sea room.

But another sailor, who had heard the eager questions, answered:

"What's up, shipmates? Look there! There's enough up, I reckon. There's a ship on shore on yonder point, and the sea is making a clean breach over her—the spray dashing completely over her mast-heads!"

Then they knew why the frigate was allowed to drift nearer and nearer to the dark, gloomy, rugged cliffs that towered aloft until their summits seemed to touch the black, lowering clouds that obscured the sky.

Captain Rodman was going to drift towards the coast, as near as it was possible to do so with safety to his own vessel, in the hope of being able to render some service to the crew of the doomed ship.

It was a desperate resolve, and the endeavour to save the crew, if it could possibly be attempted, must be made at the risk of life. Still, all were eager to make the attempt.

"Look, look!" cried several voices at once. "They see us now! They are making signals of distress!"

And as the men spoke, blue lights were seen burning on board the ship, and presently a rocket shot up high into the air, describing a fiery arc in the sky, and casting a lurid glare over the wild and dismal scene, that imparted to it a weird, unearthly aspect.

The rocket fell midway between the frigate and the shore, and then blue lights were burnt on board the latter vessel, to assure the crew of the doomed ship that their signals of distress were seen. And still the frigate was permitted to drift in-shore, until it would have been unsafe to approach nearer. Then she was wore round, and brought on the other tack, and the captain and officers consulted eagerly as to how it would be possible to render assistance to the shipwrecked crew amid the storm and darkness.

CHAPTER IX.

A MORE dismal scene than that upon which the seamen of the watch-below gazed when they were suddenly summoned upon deck from the snug, warm 'tween decks, just as they had settled themselves down to listen to Joe Wilkins's song about Captain Rodman, cannot be conceived. The sky was dark as pitch, save in one spot, where the half-moon shone palely out from between two parted clouds, away to leeward, just affording sufficient light to make, as it were, the darkness visible, and dimly to disclose the mad tumult of the elements. The sea was black as ink, save on the summits of the mountain waves, which, as they neared the rugged, gloomy cliffs, reared themselves higher and higher, until they broke upon the jagged rocks in snowy, glittering drift-like foam, scattering the spray in heavy showers. The wind howled fiercely, with a strange sound, at intervals, as though harsh human voices were mocking and jabbering in the air, while, to add to the terrors of the scene, vivid flashes of red forked lightning darted forth from the dark clouds from time to time, in zigzag lines of fiery brightness, and the thunder rolled as if heaven and earth were clashing together.

It was only when the lightning illumined the scene that the ship could be clearly discerned for an instant; but that instant was sufficient to show her hapless condition. She appeared to be lying broadside on, close to the cliffs; the seas poured continuously over her decks ere they broke in foam, hiding her for the moment from sight, and then she was seen again enveloped in a dense shower of spray. No one could have remained an instant upon her decks; but several dark forms could be seen clinging desperately to her shrouds, or sometimes swinging by their arms in mid air, when some towering wave broke over them, and washed them from their foothold. Then all would again be shrouded in pitchy darkness.

The frigate was now as near to the shore as she could approach with safety. It was necessary to wear her round—a difficult and somewhat hazardous manœuvre; for it is requisite in such cases that some head and after sail be spread, though sometimes this may be a dangerous risk. Moreover, a ship requires a great deal more room to wear than to tack—some ships spinning round like a top in tacking within their own length.

Fortunately, the Conqueror could be wore round with comparative facility without losing a great deal of ground, or Captain Rodman would not have dared to let her approach so near the cliffs. Her foretopmast-staysail was hoisted with no little difficulty, and a corner of the mizen-spanker hauled out, and under this canvas, and the close-reefed maintopsail, she was got round; and, the head and after sail being again stowed, was once more drifting slowly to seaward, under the reefed topsail only.

Now or never must help be afforded to the crew of the wrecked ship.

It was a question whether it were possible for a boat to live in such a sea, and whether, even if it could live, it were possible to lower a boat without swamping her alongside. Captain Rodman and his officers felt that in attempting to rescue the unfortunate crew they would be risking the lives of their own men, almost without a hope of success; and yet the captain could not bear the idea of leaving the poor creatures to their fate. The first cutter was lowered, and immediately swamped alongside.

"It is useless," said the captain; "we shall only lose our boats to no purpose, and we know not how soon we may need them."

Then blue lights blazed up again from the stern of the doomed ship, which was the only portion of her hull that was not constantly washed over by the heavy seas, and this fresh signal of distress caused him again to hesitate.

"We will try the pinnace," he said; and with the exercise of a great deal of care and caution the pinnace and the second cutter were safely lowered over the lee quarter, two men being in each boat to keep them from being crushed or swamped by the rolling of the ship.

"I can *order* no men thus to venture their lives," said the captain, as he looked over the quarter into the boats; "but if any man chooses to volunteer"——

"*I* will call for volunteers, sir," said the first lieutenant.

"No, sir," replied the captain. "As the first executive officer of the frigate, Mr. Bowling, I must forbid you to quit your post in such a gale as this. There are younger officers on board, sir. If any of them"—— He paused, and then went on: "When I was a lieutenant, or even when I was but a young middy, I would have been one of the first to volunteer on such an expedition as this. I would go *now*; but, as commander of this frigate, I must not leave her in her present position. And yet I don't know that such reckless daring is really praiseworthy."

Captain Rodman had spoken these words, as it were, to himself; but Lieutenant Peters, who was standing near him, had heard them.

"*I* will volunteer for the pinnace," he said. "Captain Rodman, the old Ajaxes will follow *me* to the death."

As I have said, a strong feeling of friendship existed between Captain Rodman and Lieutenant Peters. As the readers of "Tom Rodman's Schooldays" know, *that* friendship had its rise in a spirit of rivalry during the first week of Tom's going to school, and it had grown stronger and stronger, and become cemented until they felt towards each other as though they were brothers.

"I knew you would, Harry," said the captain, clasping the second lieutenant's hand. "I knew that when deeds of daring and humanity were required, Harry Peters would never be wanting. But—go if you will; but, for *my* sake, my dear fellow, be wary. Do not approach *too* near the shore. Save those poor fellows, or some of them, if it be possible. But, my dear Harry, if you perceive that it cannot be done without sacrificing our own people, do not permit any feeling of pride or false shame to prevent you from returning to the ship without attempting what you feel will be of no avail. We cannot do impossibilities."

"Never fear for *me*," replied Peters, with a smile. "Am I not always cautious? Remember the attack upon the barn at Coltsford, when I sallied forth to play the part of a scout" (alluding to a famous event in the days of their boyhood, which those who have read "Tom Rodman's Schooldays" will readily recall to mind). "Did I not *then* return to tell you that no more could be done? Help then came from a quarter little expected. Some opportunity that we cannot foresee may avail us *now*, and enable us to save those poor fellows."

Captain Rodman smiled at the recollection of the school affray thus called up.

"You will do your best, Harry—that I am assured of," he replied.

And Lieutenant Peters, stepping forward, said:

"Ajaxes, I go to the rescue in the pinnace. Who volunteers to go with me?"

The brief conversation I have recorded occupied but a few moments. The frigate was now, as I have said, drifting from the shore; but being hove-to, was, as every sailor will understand, drifting almost imperceptibly, and was appa-

The Fight on the Ledge.

See page 7.

rently as near the wreck as before she was wore round. The sailors, though eager to render assistance to the ship's crew—as, in such cases, sailors ever are—had still hesitated, seeing the hopelessness of the situation of the unfortunate men, and knowing the peril they themselves must encounter; but as soon as Lieutenant Peters spoke, the men who had served with him on board the Ajax frigate—"old Ajaxes" they were styled on board—who would have followed him into the very jaws of death, replied as one man:

"*We* will, sir! *We* will!"

"Nay, my lads," said Peters; "I need but eight or ten of you. You cannot *all* go."

"There is the cutter, sir. *She* must be manned too," was the reply.

But the ready response of the Ajaxes had aroused a spirit of emulation amongst others of the crew, who, though they had so lately hesitated, were now eager to risk their lives to save the lives of the wrecked seamen.

"The Ajaxes go in the pinnace," they cried; "let *others* man the cutter."

"Bravely spoken, men," cried Mr. Benson, a young master's mate, who was about to enter the cutter, when Lieutenant Wilton interposed.

"That is *my* place, Benson," said he, laying his hand on the young officer's shoulder. Three or four of the elder midshipmen had also come forward to claim the honour of commanding the cutter. But now Captain Rodman again interposed.

"Let Benson go, Mr. Wilton," he said. "I appreciate your courage and devotion, sir; but it is well to stimulate a spirit of heroism among these youngsters; and it is your place, as third lieutenant of the frigate, to remain on board."

Young Benson, therefore, was permitted to take his place in the stern sheets of the cutter, and one of the elder midshipmen also went in each boat—those who were selected for this post of danger being the envy of their fellows; for the spirit of ocean-chivalry was now fully awakened, and all were alike eager to show their contempt of hardship and danger.

So the two daring boats' crews went forth into the storm and darkness, where every mountain wave that rolled towards them threatened to engulph the boats, which were lost to sight as they sank into the trough of the sea, and which indeed—so intense was the darkness of the night—were visible, even when tossed high on the summit of the foaming billows, only when the vivid flashes of lightning darted forth from the dense black clouds, and cast, for the moment, a fitful, lurid glare over the dismal scene.

The wind howled savagely, and the sea roared around them; the thunder rolled in terrible peals above their heads; and they were half-blinded by the spray, and the fierce, drifting sleet which accompanied every squall, and which pricked their faces like needles as it was driven furiously by the gale across the stormy waters. Still the rowers desperately plied their oars, while the officers peered intently through the gloom to catch a glimpse of the doomed ship whose crew they sought to succour and save.

It may appear strange why boats were sent forth to render aid, and why it was not sought to throw lines to the wreck from on board the frigate. Such an endeavour *would* have been made had it been daylight, and had not the tempest blown so fierce and strong. But, as it was, the frigate dared not approach sufficiently near the shore. Had she done so, she would herself have speedily been wrecked. It would have been madness for Captain Rodman to approach more near than he had done.

The boats were therefore provided with life-lines, and with the means of shooting them on board the wrecked ship; and to these life-lines life-buoys and cork belts were attached, so that when they were thrown on board, the wrecked seamen might fasten the buoys and belts around them, and then, throwing themselves into the sea, might be drawn by means of the lines on board the boats.

Every officer and man of the boats' crews also wore his cork jacket; and a number of spare life-belts were put on board the boats, together with brandy and such restoratives as it was thought the wrecked men, if they could be rescued, would probably need.

As the boats, after severe toil on the part of the rowers, and many narrow escapes from being swamped by the waves, drew near the cliffs, and the wrecked ship became more plainly visible, the prospect of saving the crew appeared hopeless indeed! Her decks were swept clean, her bulwarks gone, the maintopmast alone was standing, and each tremendous sea that dashed against the cliff hid her hull entirely from view as it passed over her. It was evident that many of her crew had perished. Still the maintopmast shrouds were full of despairing sailors, who seemed already to have almost lost consciousness, but who clung to the rigging with the desperate grasp of dying men. The ship, a vessel of six hundred tons burden—the Ranger, of Liverpool—lay quite close to the cliff; for on this coast the water is generally deep close in shore. But the side of the cliff was so perpendicular—in fact, in some places projecting—that it afforded no chance of escape. A cat could not have clambered up it.

The boats got near enough to enable the voices of the men to be heard during the lulls of the tempest, and sufficiently near to shoot a line on board the wreck. Still the darkness was so extreme that the hapless seamen in the rigging could only be distinctly seen when the fiery lightning flashed.

It required the utmost skill and strength of the rowers to enable them to back-water with their oars, and keep the boats from broaching-to, or from being swept alongside the wreck by the tremendous seas that washed over her. They were as near as they dared to approach.

"Shoot a line on board," said Peters to the men in the boats' bows. Then, taking advantage of a short lull, he shouted at the top of his voice:

"Ship ahoy! Look out, you on board—you in the topmast rigging. Look out to catch the line, and haul the rope on board!"

To this cry no answer was returned. The first line that was shot into the maintop was unheeded, and was drawn back again.

"Rouse yourselves—for your lives, men!—for the sake of your own lives! Now, look out for the line again!" shouted the lieutenant, when another brief lull in the storm permitted his voice to be heard. "We dare not remain much longer," he added. "The strength of the men is failing them. Look out, or we must leave you to your fate, and return to the frigate."

This time some of the poor men seemed to become conscious of the fact that an attempt was being made to rescue them. Three men caught hold of the line, but their limbs were so numbed that they could hardly clutch it in their fingers. Two of them fell from the shrouds into the sea. One of them was swept away instantly; the other, luckily, was swept towards the boats by a receding sea, a life-buoy was thrown to him, and, by dint of great exertion, he swam towards it, and caught it just as the returning wave caught him, and would have swept him, with irresistible force, against the cliff. The men in the boats tugged at the line attached to the buoy, and the poor wretch was dragged into the cutter, though he was by this time senseless, and almost cut in two by the line round his body. The third man tugged at the line, and drew the stronger rope, and the life-belts attached to it, into the rigging. Some of his shipmates now came to his assistance, and other ropes and buoys were drawn on board, and two or three men fastened the belts to their bodies, threw themselves boldly into the sea, and were, with great difficulty, drawn to the boats and taken on board.

Others, however, slipped from the belts, and were swept away and drowned, and still others had not the courage to cast themselves into the raging waters, even when they had fastened the life-belts round them. They hesitated, remained clinging to the rigging, and paid no heed to the repeated calls from the men-of-warsmen.

"Look out! Look out, there!" shouted one of the midshipmen in the pinnace.

"*To your oars, men!*" cried Peters, after casting a glance across the raging waters. "*Double bank them. Back water, hard—ha-ard!*"

A mighty wave, which to those in the boats appeared to tower aloft to a greater height than the masts of the frigate, was rolling towards them, gathering force and greater volume as it rolled on. With tightly-clenched teeth, and with every muscle strained to the utmost, the sailors—two to each oar—held water, and managed, with their herculean strength, to prevent the boats from broaching-to. But they were swept swiftly aloft, as though they would reach the skies; then they sank down deep into the trough of the sea—a wall of dark water enclosing them on every hand, and then again were they swept aloft on the foaming crest of the billow, so rapidly that they almost lost their breath.

While resting for a moment on the summit of this mountain wave, the dark clouds opened above their heads; fierce flashes of red-forked lightning darted forth in every direction around them, illuminating sea and sky with an awful lurid glare, and causing the faces of the sailors to appear pale and livid as those of corpses. At the same instant the thunder pealed with a deafening sound, louder than the roar of a hundred parks of artillery, rolling, as it seemed, to and fro, and reverberating amongst the rocks and cliffs on shore, until its rumble was lost in the far distance. Then intense darkness succeeded to the dazzling, unearthly glare; and amidst the darkness the boats rushed swiftly down the side of the mountain billow into the deep trough beneath, as if they were being borne headlong to destruction. The men were obliged to lift their oars; all control over the boats was temporarily lost; the swiftness of their descent, which fairly took away the breath of the sailors, alone saved them from broaching broadside on, and being engulphed in the tumultuous rush of waters. Then there came a brief lull in the storm after this tremendous burst of fury. The sailors seized their oars, and drew a long breath of relief as they strove, amid the darkness, to gaze into each other's faces. Then again the lightning glared, the thunder rolled, and the wind howled around them, as though it had gained strength after the brief lull. But the tempest was not so fierce, nor was the lightning so vivid as before, though it was sufficient to illumine the dark expanse of ocean around them, and to show that the seas broke over a vacant spot where the ship had lately lain! The dark, frowning, perpendicular surface of the cliff was visible, with the glittering spray dashing furiously against it, and rising nearly to its summit; but of the wreck not a vestige was now to be seen!

Those last tremendous waves had dashed her to atoms, and scattered her spars and timbers wide adrift, together with the living freight that had still remained on board her. No signs of one or the other were ever seen again!

"That was fearful—awful!" exclaimed Lieutenant Peters, breaking the silence the men had maintained. "All is over; it is useless to remain any longer. Back to the frigate, my lads, while this lull lasts. Thank heaven that we are safe so long! The ship has gone. A minute ago I thought it was all over with *us* too."

The sailors drew a long breath of relief, and once more bent to their oars, They could only guess in what direction the frigate lay, the darkness was still so great; and even when the boats rose to the summit of a wave, they could see her but for a moment, when the lightning illumined the dismal scene.

"There—there she is—there!" cried a sharp-eyed middy, as, for an instant, a lightning flash disclosed her dark hull. "See, they are burning blue lights to attract our notice."

"Pull, men—pull!" cried Peters. "I see her now, even through the darkness! But, for your lives, boys, watch the seas, and keep the boat's bow no to them."

The frigate had again wore round, and was drifting slowly towards the boats. It was a fearful tug to pull against the heavy cross sea; but in ten minutes the boats were within hail, and the gale had lulled sufficiently to enable the human voice to be heard.

"They see us on board! See, they are getting ropes ready to throw to us! Pull, my lads—pull strong. Another minute and we shall be safe and snug on board once more!" shouted Lieutenant Peters.

The pinnace was so near that a rope, with a life-buoy attached, had already been thrown to her. Lieutenant Peters tried to catch hold of the buoy as it floated near the stern of the boat, and, to aid his effort, the bow-oarsman caused the pinnace to swerve slightly round. At this instant a cross sea lifted her, and Peters lost his balance, and was thrown overboard into the raging waters.

He was seen from the ship, and a cry of terror broke forth from the men on board, while those in the boats tried in vain to pull towards him.

Captain Rodman saw the deadly peril of the friend of his boyhood, who was to him as a dearly-loved brother. The many fond ties of friendship which bound them together flashed to his memory, and regardless of his own peril, he flung himself into the sea, and swam to save the young lieutenant.

It was a rash action, for it only increased the alarm and confusion on board, and added to the difficulty of the men in the boats. In such a sea it was both difficult and dangerous to alter the course of the boats, and for some moments it was thought that both officers must be lost. Still, had not Captain Rodman acted as he did, Lieutenant Peters would certainly have perished—thus a rash action is sometimes well rewarded.

Peters swam well, but, probably through the coldness of the sea, he was suddenly seized with cramp. Springing out of the water, he threw up his hands, fell backward, and disappeared. Captain Rodman was close to him at this moment. A heavy sea rolled by, and when it passed on, neither the captain nor the lieutenant were to be seen.

Again a fearful cry arose.

"They are both—both lost!" shouted a score of voices.

Then the captain was seen to rise far astern, holding the collar of Peters' jacket between his teeth, and thus, though with difficulty, keeping his head above water. It was long before the boats could reach them, and both boats were more than once nearly swamped in the attempt. At length they were taken on board the pinnace, and a few minutes afterwards the boats, by dint of great exertion, got alongside the frigate, and they were lifted on board the ship in a state of utter exhaustion.

It was well that the tempest in some measure subsided, after the fierce tumult of the elements, amidst which the wreck disappeared, or both the captain and lieutenant must have perished; nor is it probable that the boats would have regained the frigate.

The two officers, however, soon recovered consciousness, and then the captain learnt from Peters that of the whole ship's company of the Ranger—comprising thirty hands, all told—four men only were saved! Still, but for the daring courage and generous humanity of the officers and crew of the Conqueror, these four men must also have perished.

"It is worth all the risk we ran," said Captain Rodman, "to have saved four human lives."

Afterwards he learned from the rescued seamen that the Ranger was bound from Liverpool to Peru, and that she had missed her reckoning, ran too near the coast, and been driven on shore by the gale.

The men who were rescued from her gladly entered, as able seamen, on board the man-of-war.

CHAPTER X.

THE gale broke after it had culminated in the fearful tempest I have endeavoured to describe; but only to be followed by others, though of lesser strength. For five weeks the Conqueror was thus allowed to drift to and fro at the will of the winds and waves; for as she was bound to no particular port, and her captain was left free to be guided by his own judgment, he hove the frigate to during the gales, satisfied that with her sails furled and all made snug on board, no weather could do her harm; and he thus, perhaps, saved her from the fate which befell so many ships that, in their endeavour to make their destined port, beat against the fearful tempests that prevailed off Cape Horn that terrible summer, until they were driven on shore, and all on board perished.

The crew of the Conqueror grew weary of the continuous stormy weather, otherwise they had an easy time of it. Confident in the strength of the gallant frigate, and the skill of her captain and officers, they cast aside all fears, kept watch and watch—having little or no work to do, and, during their watch below, amused and enjoyed themselves as comfortably as though they had been on shore —though those who now visited Cape Horn for the first time wondered, if this were summer, what the weather would be like in winter.*

When at length fine weather came, the frigate had drifted far into the Pacific Ocean. A brisk breeze then sprang up from the southward, and she ran before it, every day getting into warmer weather, though no land was visible, until she had entered the tropic of Capricorn.

Then one morning the glad cry of "Land ahead!" was shouted by the sailor from aloft.

The land was, in fact, visible to all on board. A mist had prevailed, which had suddenly lifted, and disclosed a small, low, and seemingly fertile island, not more than two leagues distant.

As the frigate bore down towards it, it showed a rich luxuriance of vegetation, being in some places covered with forest trees, and in others displaying level tracts of apparently fine meadow land.

At this period much less was known of the Pacific Ocean than is known at present. Captain Cook, some years before, had astonished the civilized world by his discoveries; but since his death the nations of Europe had been too earnestly engaged in warfare to pay much attention to aught besides.

Pat Hennessy, the brave Irish sailor, had been appointed by Captain Rodman coxswain of his barge. In fact, honest Pat was a great favourite of the captain's, and he happened to be at the helm when the land appeared in sight.

* In some seasons the weather in the vicinity of this Cape is more tempestuous than it is in others. At the period to which I allude in this story, no less than seventeen vessels were wrecked during the summer months on the coasts of Terra del Fuego and the islands to the southward. The truth is that the summer in this dreary part of the ocean is more stormy and disagreeable than the winter. So Captain Fitzroy and other navigators, who have had experience of the weather in both seasons, have described it, and so I (the present writer) certainly found it to be. I once sailed round Cape Horn, close in shore, in December—the midsummer month—and met with almost continuous gales, accompanied by storms of snow and sleet. The thermometer ranged, often in a few hours, from sixty down to thirty degrees Fahrenheit. But on returning eighteen months afterwards, in July—midwinter—the weather, though cold, yet seldom *much* below the freezing point, was generally fine and clear, and we met with but one smart gale. Very intense cold is rarely experienced near Cape Horn, which lies only in 56 degrees south latitude—the latitude (only south instead of north) of the north of England

"Keep her full, and steer steady for yonder point, Pat," said Captain Rodman, as he closed the telescope through which he had been steadily peering.

"Arrah, thin, won't I do that same, surr," answered Pat. "Sure it's a pleasure to see the green fields and the trees whin a body's not seen anything but salt wather for so long. Is there people on that island, surr, may I make bould to ask?"

"None that I can perceive; yet it looks singularly fertile," was the reply. "One might imagine the land to be cultivated. But many of the Pacific islands are very beautiful, and some of the most beautiful are uninhabited."

Captain Rodman took two or three turns on the quarter-deck, and then, again addressing Pat, said: "Are you in the mind, Pat, for a trip on shore?"

"Sure, surr, I'd like it exthramely above all things," was the reply.

"Well, then, I'll tell you what. The wind's dying away; I'm afraid it will soon fall calm. I'll back the mainyards when we get a bit further in, and you shall take the gig on shore with four hands. We want some sand, the first lieutenant tells me, and there appears to be a fine sandy beach. Bring off a few bucketfuls with you, and take a look around you. See if there are any trace of inhabitants; only, if there be, be cautious, and don't go too near them till you know how they feel disposed. I shall expect you to bring me a faithful report, and if your report be favourable, I shall probably go on shore myself."

Pat was delighted with anything that savoured of adventure. He jumped at the captain's offer; and though all hands were just piped to breakfast, he, and the four men who formed the boat's crew, would not wait, but took their breakfast along with them, and the light gig was soon dancing merrily over the sparkling waters on its way to the beach of which the captain had spoken, while the frigate, with her mainyards backed, lay to, about a mile from the land.

The boat soon grounded on the shelving beach. One of the crew remained on board to mind it, the other three leaped on shore with the buckets, which they proceeded to fill with sand, while Pat Hennessy, in order to furnish his report to the captain on his return, walked away into the interior.

Captain Rodman, from time to time, watched them through his spy-glass. The buckets were filled, and the last one was being put on board the boat, when Pat Hennessy suddenly made his appearance, running at his utmost speed. He apparently spoke a few words to the other sailors, who started and looked behind them, as if in alarm, then hastened into the boat, followed by Pat, who almost tumbled on board in his hurry. The boat was put off, and the men pulled with all their might for the frigate.

Suspecting that an attack had been threatened by the natives, Captain Rodman said to Peters, who stood near him:

"The island must be inhabited after all, and the natives must be a savage lot to terrify a bold fellow like Hennessy in such a manner."

He continued to peer through his spy-glass, expecting some of the savages to make their appearance on the beach, and presently he saw what he supposed to be human beings, a long distance off, beneath a cliff at the extreme end of the island. They seemed to be busy over what he fancied was a canoe, which they quickly launched, and a party of them entering the canoe, paddled or pulled off towards the frigate, though they were so far distant that nothing more than the outlines of their forms could be discerned through the glass.

"At all events," continued the captain, "they have no fear of *us*. It is strange that the men should put off in such haste, for I have always found that *savages* are frightened themselves at the visit of white men. Those who willingly trust themselves near or on board a ship, are generally a gentle, kindly race!"

The gig was soon within hail.

"Boat ahoy!" cried the captain. "Coxswain, what is the reason of your returning in such haste?"

"Och, yer honour," answered Hennessy. "The drollest thing in the world, intirely! Sure that same bit ov an island be's bewitched! The white naygurs, surr, came afther us, and sure we run—for we didn't know but we'd be bewitched ourselves, av we stayed!"

"You foolish fellow! What do you mean by white naygurs? Have you brought off the sand?" said the captain.

"Yes, your honour," was the reply, "an' mighty fine sand it be. Av we'd stayed, we'd have emptied the buckets aboard, and filled 'em ag'in."

By this time the boat was alongside. The buckets were hoisted up, and Pat and the other sailors came on board.

"Now explain what you mean by white naygurs?" said Captain Rodman.

"Look there" (pointing to the distant canoe). "White or black, they are coming off to the frigate. Did they threaten or offer to attack you?"

"Sure, they spoke to us *in English*," said Pat, "though I was too frightened to heed what they said."

"You stupid fellow! Doubtless they are English seamen, who have been wrecked on the island!"

"Niver a bit ov it, beggin' yer honour's pardon for conthradictin'. Sure they hadn't the looks of English saymin; and their clothes, bedad! Sure the duds they wore was the dhrollest things in the wurrld!—just made of the stuff the naygurs weave, cut and sewed into reg'lar frocks an' trousers, all the same as rale white men 'ud be afther wearin'! 'Tis bewitched the place is for sartin, yer honour, an' the other min 'll tell ye the same."

"You might have waited to learn what they wanted, at least."

"Sure, surr, 'twasn't raisinable that we'd wait to convarse with naygurs that wor white, and talked English!"

"Well, well," said the captain, perceiving that it was useless to attempt to reason Pat out of his prejudices, "the canoe is drawing near, and we shall soon learn from themselves what they want."

"They *do* really look like white men, sir," put in a midshipman, who, while the captain was speaking, had been watching the canoe through his telescope.

Captain Rodman placed his glass to his eye.

"They are—they must be wrecked seamen," he said. "Though they appear to be clad in native cloth, their garments are shaped like those worn by sailors."

"Ship ahoy!" the head man presently shouted, in pure English. "What ship's that?"

"His Majesty's frigate Conqueror," replied the captain. "Who and what are you?"

"We are natives of the island, sir," was the reply. "Will you permit us to come on board the frigate? We have brought you off some vegetables and fruit."

The officers and sailors looked at one another in amazement.

"Begorra, didn't I tell his honour how it was?" said Hennessy. "Sure, there's witchcraft there, b'ys!"

A sudden idea seemed to strike the captain.

"Come on board," he cried. "We will throw you a rope."

Then he called to his servant to bring his chart upon deck.

"It *will* be about the spot," he said, after examining his chart—"latitude 22 degrees south, longitude 130 degrees west." Then, addressing the officers who stood near him, he went on: "That land must be Pitcairn's Island, and these men in the canoe are the descendants of the mutineers of the Bounty."

Most of my readers will probably have read or heard of the strange story of the mutiny on board the Bounty, a small ship of war sent out by Government under the command of Captain Bligh, in the latter portion of the last century, with the object of bringing from the islands of the Pacific specimens of the bread fruit tree, which grows there in great abundance, and trying the effect of transplanting the tree in the West India Islands. The greater portion of the crew mutinied under the command of Edward Christian—a young midshipman of good family—and placing Captain Bligh, and those who refused to join them, adrift in a boat, made off with the ship to Otaheite. Severity on the part of Captain Bligh, together with the attachment the mutineers had formed to certain of the Otaheitan females, is supposed to have led to the outbreak; but on the arrival of the mutineers at the island of Otaheite, they quarrelled among themselves, and with the men of the island, who were jealous of the favour shown to the white men by the women. Bloodshed and murder ensued. Most of the white men perished; but the midshipman, Christian, a man named Adams, and some others, escaped in canoes, taking some of the females with them, and after drifting about the ocean for some time, landed on Pitcairn's Island—until then uninhabited—where they founded a colony. The native women bore them children; but the mutineers still continued to quarrel amongst themselves, until at length all but Adams perished. Thus left to himself with the native women and children, Adams sincerely repented of the part he had played, and resolved to lead a new life. By means of an old Bible and some other remnants of old books, he taught the children to read, and educated them to the best of his ability as Christians, besides teaching them all he knew respecting his native land, and other civilized countries. The children, under his constant care, grew up a fine, hardy, strictly moral, and religious race. When they grew to manhood, he acted the part of a priest, and wedded the young men and women to one another. Years passed away, and at length, when Adams had grown to be an old man, and many children, almost as white as Englishmen, and possessing English features, had been born to the wedded couple, a man-of-war, by chance, touched at the island, and the captain and crew were greatly amazed on being boarded by young men who spoke English, and who, when they came alongside the ship, cried out, "Won't you throw us a rope?" The captain landed, saw old Adams, and was greatly pleased with the simple, kindly manners of these descendants of the mutineers. Adams would have surrendered himself to take his trial in England for his past misdeeds; but the young men and women clung around him, and besought him not to forsake them, and the captain of the ship of war thought he had well earned his pardon, and left him, after supplying the interesting colony with many useful articles which he could spare from the ship. On the return of the ship to England, the news she brought caused much wonder and excitement, and it was thought desirable to send out missionaries and teachers to the island, to fill Adams's place when he should be should be taken from them. But, as I have said, Europe then, and for many years afterwards, was engaged in deadly warfare, and a long time passed away before much was done to help these simple islanders, who, in course of time, became so numerous that it was found necessary to remove them to a larger and far-distant island, where they exist at this present period—still an innocent, simple, kindly race of people.

Only some four or five ships had touched at the island when the Conqueror visited it, by chance. Many people in England had never heard of its existence;

but Captain Rodman, as I have shown, suddenly recollected having heard som
thing of it, and, after looking at his chart, found that the frigate was near tl
spot where the island was said to be situated. He had until now been ha
inclined to regard the story as a myth, and he was delighted to find that it w
indeed a reality.

He heartily welcomed the islanders—the chief of whom was Thursday Octob
Christian, the son of the mutineer midshipman—on board his vessel, and dete
mined to anchor his ship, and remain a few days at the island. Young Christia
who had been christened Thursday October by old Adams, because he was tl
first-born child, and was born on a Thursday, in the month of October, w
greatly pleased at the captain's decision. He offered to pilot the frigate to
safe anchorage; and soon she was snug at anchor, with her sails furled. O
Adams presently afterwards came on board to pay his respects to the captain, a
to invite him and his officers to visit the shore.

"Well, I'll be blowed if this 'ere ain't a rum go, for to find a little Englar
out here in this 'ere wide out-o'-the-way ocean!" exclaimed one of the sailors,
the mess to which he belonged were seated in the 'tween decks that same evenin

"And Pat Hennessy for to go to say how the island were bewitched!" sa
another.

"Be jabers!" cried Pat, if you had been ashore, lookin' out, as naturally
would be doin', in proper raisin, for a lot o' black naygurs, and was suddently
see a lot ov outlandish-lookin' crayters, whiter nor yerselves, and spakin' goo
English—faix, ye'd be afther fancyin' as there wor witchcraft in it, I'm thinkir
Bedad! I'm not half satisfied yet that it's all as it should be, b'ys."

"Never mind. We shall all get leave to go ashore, and see for ourselves in
day or two," cried a boatswain's mate. "Now that we're all snug, let's have
song. Joe Wilkins, my hearty, you never yet sung us that 'ere song as you mac
up about our captain, wot you was a-goin' to pipe, when we wor roused up to gi
help to the ship as went ashore off Hoste Island, near Cape Horn. Come, o
chap, give it us now. You'll never have a better oppertoonity."

"Silence, my jolly tars, for Joe Wilkins' last new song!" cried sever
voices, while the boatswain's mate handed Joe a tot of grog to clear his windpip

Joe drank off the grog, with a smack of his lips, and then humming ar
ha'ing to clear his throat, commenced in a loud clear voice, to sing the song th
was called for.

> Tom Rodman, when a schoolboy gay,
>   Had heard the oft-told story,
> How Britain's navy was her stay—
>   The nation's pride and glory.
> His youthful spirit sighed for fame,
>   A sailor bold he'd be;
> And so, to win a glorious name,
>   Tom Rodman went to sea.
>
>> Then cheer, boys, cheer! we have no fear,
>>   If seas run high or low;
>> We'll drink and sing, long live the king,
>>   While stormy winds do blow.
>
> On board the Monarch, staunch and true,
>   A middy Tom was rated;
> A gallant youth, with hardy crew,
>   And captain bold—well mated.
> To knot, to reef, to hand, to steer,
>   He learnt with ready speed;
> And noted was his youth's career,
>   For many a gallant deed.
>
>> Then cheer, boys, cheer, &c. .

And when borne down beneath the gale,
   In Biscay's stormy Bay,
Her topmasts gone, and rent each sail,
   A log the frigate lay.
'Twas Tom, when none dared leave the deck,
   So fierce the tempest blew,
Who bravely cut away the wreck,
   And saved the ship and crew!

      Then cheer, boys, cheer, &c.

Years passed away, and time rolled on,
   So quick, 'twas scarcely noted :
And gallant Tom, to manhood grown,
   Was, for his worth, promoted.
And then again he went to sea,
   On board the famed Leander,
Appointed in that ship to be
   Lieutenant and commander.

      Then cheer, boys, cheer, &c.

To serve his friends, to fight his foes,
   Tom Rodman aye is ready ;
For honour in his bosom glows,
   With flame both bright and steady.
Like glorious Nelson, e'er he'll try
   To tread the path of duty—
Like him, prepared to fight or die
   For England, home, and beauty!

      Then cheer, boys, cheer, &c.

Now captain of a frigate trim—
   Rightly the Conqueror named—
For long that frigate, sailed by him,
   Shall be for victory famed.
Tom Rodman will be staunch and true,
   E'en to his latest breath :
And we, brave boys, his trusty crew,
   Will follow him to death!

      Then cheer, boys, cheer! we laugh at fear ;
      Let seas run high or low,
      We'll drink and sing, long live the king,
      While stormy winds do blow.

"While seas run high, and stormy winds—do blow—do blow—d-o-o blow. We'll drink and sing, long live the king, while storm-y winds d-o blow !" roared forth the whole watch, at the conclusion of Joe's song.

Joe Wilkins belonged to No. 7 mess, and though the whole watch-below had listened to his song, the men of his own and the adjoining mess had alone joined in the chorus; but the refrain, "While stormy winds do blow, do blow, d-o blow," was finally caught up by the entire watch-below, and roared forth by two hundred stentorian voices, until the timbers and rafters above their heads echoed and re-echoed the sound from one end of the 'tween-decks to the other.

"A good song that 'ere. 'Cos why, Joe? 'Cos it's true, shipmate—'cept in *one* little sarcumstance," said old Simpson the quartermaster, when the noise and stir had subsided.

"What *is* that 'ere sarcumstance, Simpson?" asked one of the sailors.

"Why, mate," replied the quartermaster, "I've know'd Captain Rodman ever since he was a young reefer, when he used to come aboard the Ajax 'long with Mr. Peters, as is now our second leeftenant, and there was no end o' sky-larking 'mong the young genelmen in the cockpit; and if *my* reckonin' be correct, Captain Rodman warn't rated as a commander till he went to Afriky, in the Alert gun-brig."

D

"You're right there, quartermaster," said Joe. "But d'ye see, mate, that's what they calls a poet's license. I heard the chaplain say one day how poets—reg'lar-built, 'long-shore poets I means, of course—takes out licenses. I don't know ersackly the meanin' on't; but summat like publicans' licenses, I suppose. Anyhow, it gives them the privilege of twistin' and turnin' the king's English anyways as suits 'em when they wants words to chime together like. Now, I couldn't make commander and Alert chime together nohows. Charles Dibdin, as is the greatest poet that ever lived, couldn't do *that*; so I took the liberty of rhimin' commander with Leander—a word as seemed made for the werry purpose."

"Werry good, shipmate," said Simpson; "but I reckon how you're wrong in sayin' as Charles Dibdin couldn't ha' made commander and Alert chime together —that is, if so he'd set his mind on doin' so, d'ye see? I reckon there ain't *nothin'* in the way o' song-writin' that Charles Dibdin *can't* do. And as to po'try —why, that 'ere song o' hisn, 'Here a sheer hulk lies poor Tom Bowline,' is what *I* calls a reg'lar pictur' of human natur' wrote out in words!"

"True, mate; and I takes Dibdin for my moral (model). I follers arter him."

"A long ways arter him, I reckon, Joe," sang out a young sailor from the adjoining mess.

"Now you just clap a stopper on your slack jaw, Dick Bunting," said Joe. "Don't you be a-payin' it out so fast. Wait till *you* can make up a song yerself afore you goes pokin' yer fun at other folk. But, as I was a-sayin', I takes Dibdin as my moral; but say what you like, quartermaster—though I'll allow as he can do most anythink, and can write fust-rate songs as easy as you or me could strop a jewel-block—I'd take my Andrew David (affidavit) afore the First Lord o' the Admi*rality*, and that's sayin' a good deal, as neither he nor nobody else could make commander rhime wi' Alert, nohows he could fix it."

Old Simpson shook his head. He was not to be persuaded out of his firm belief in the ability of Dibdin to make any words he chose rhyme together, "if he sot his mind on doin' so."

Some took sides with him, while others said, with Joe Wilkins, that commander and Alert could never be made to rhyme together as long as the world should stand.

An earnest discussion arose upon the subject, which was kept up long after the men had turned into their hammocks, until one after another dozed off, and at length the sounds of snoring which prevailed throughout the 'tween-decks proclaimed the fact that the whole of the watch-below were sound asleep.

The men went ashore in turns on Pitcairn's Island, and were much amused with the simple habits and manners of the natives; and after Captain Rodman had supplied old Adams with some books and a quantity of stores from the frigate, the Conqueror again put to sea.

One day, whilst at Isly, Captain Rodman was informed by the master of a whale ship that an English naval officer who had taken service with the Peruvians, had been made prisoner, and was condemned to be shot. The officer, he added, was then confined in the castle at Arica—a Peruvian port—then occupied by the Chilians.

"He has brought his fate upon himself," said Captain Rodman. "England has no right to interfere; neither have the officers of the navy, who represent their country in this part of the world. Officers who quit the British service to take service under a foreign Government, forfeit, justly, all claim upon their country. It is a hard case; but I am sure the admiral on this station will not interfere, and I don't see how anything can be done in his behalf. Do you know the name of this officer?"

"Yes, sir. The name is Fleming. He was formerly a lieutenant in the British navy, and, as I have been told, he is still quite a young man, though brave as a lion."

Captain Rodman started at the name of Fleming. It was the name, as those who are familiar with the captain's earlier history will recall to mind, of one of his former fellow-midshipmen, who had been a great friend and favourite, and whom he had often protected from the tyranny of his senior brother middies. He had heard that Fleming—for the sake of the higher pay, which enabled him better to support his mother and sister, who were entirely dependent upon him—had entered the Peruvian service, though it had temporarily slipped his memory.

He said no more to the whaler captain, who returned to his ship. But he was no sooner gone than Captain Rodman consulted with his first lieutenant, and with Peters, and told them what he had heard.

"I said I had no right to interfere," he added ; "nor have I. But I must—I *will* save poor Fleming—'Little Fleming,' as we used to call him, poor fellow—if it be possible. Ay, though I have to run my ship under the guns of the fort, and make an assault upon the castle ! I shall be blamed, probably—perhaps reprimanded severely. The admiral would likely forbid my interference if he were aware of my intention. But he shall know nothing of it until it is over. Let what will come of it, I will not leave poor Fleming to suffer without making an effort to save him. See all clear for action, gentlemen. We'll get the frigate under weigh immediately. Arica lies but fifty or sixty miles to the southward, and with the present breeze we shall reach the port before noon of this present day."

In less than an hour the Conqueror sailed out of the harbour, and everything was made ready for battle. The frigate was bound on a desperate adventure, if, as was most probable, the Chilian authorities should refuse to hearken to Captain Rodman's imperious demands.

CHAPTER XI.

THE port of Arica lies in about eighteen degrees south latitude, at the base of a range of lofty mountains, amidst which are situated some of the richest silver mines in South America.

It is this great mineral wealth that renders the place of importance; for the coast for several miles inland, being barren and sandy, and almost destitute of vegetation, would otherwise be regarded as almost uninhabitable. As it is, a town of considerable size has arisen in the midst of this sandy desert, whose population is prosperous and thriving, though the cost of living is great, provisions having to be brought in from a considerable distance.

The port and harbour of Arica are protected by a fort and a castle, each possessing a heavy battery which command the greater portion of the harbour.

The castle is maintained as a place of confinement for political offenders and prisoners of war; though, by reason of the sanguinary laws which exist in all these South American Republics, prisoners brought to the castle seldom remain long in durance, being generally executed a few days—sometimes a few hours—after their capture.

The port—as I have said—though it properly belongs to Peru, was, at the period of which I write, in the occupation of the Chilians, who maintained a strong garrison in the castle.

At this port the Conqueror arrived after a short passage from Isly; and as soon as the frigate had entered the outer harbour, which is beyond the range of the batteries, she saluted the fort, her salute being answered by a similar number of guns. The custom-house boat then put off to the frigate to make the usual inquiries, and to receive assurance of the health of the crew; and when the boat was leaving, Captain Rodman sent a message, by the officer, to the commandant, stating his intention immediately to pay that officer a visit.

The captain's barge was then lowered and manned, and in a few minutes Captain Rodman appeared on the frigate's quarter-deck in full uniform.

"Have everything prepared for action," he said to his officers. "But do things quietly. Make no threatening display. It may be that the commandant will show himself willing to accede to my request; and, in that case, I would not have it known or suspected that we assumed a threatening attitude. I had rather that they should imagine on shore that we have merely called in to pay a passing visit; for, though I am determined to effect the release of Lieutenant Fleming, if it be possible, and even go to the length of making war upon my own responsibility, I really have no authority to do so, and my conduct may draw down severe reproof from the Admiralty. *That* I would gladly avoid if I can effect my object quietly."

"Not much fear, sir, I reckon, if we compel these bloodthirsty creole Spaniards to give up an English prisoner," put in the master. "The Government folk may object, and some of those fellows who have always some grievance to complain of in Parliament, because otherwise, as nobody cares for 'em, they'd have no chance of making their voices heard—some of these chaps, I say, may ask by what authority the captain of one of his Majesty's ships of war ventured to interfere with the rights of others, and to risk a war with a feeble Power in order to rescue an Englishman, who, by his own action, has placed himself beyond the protection of his Government. But nobody heeds what these grumblers say, sir, and John Bull *does* like to boast that his might is his right. Rescue this gentleman, sir, and we'll have the whole people with us."

"No doubt you are right, master," replied Captain Rodman; "and should the commandant accede at once to my demand, I shall be commended for my conduct, although I shall stretch my authority to its utmost. But though the whole of the Spanish-American Republics united would be regarded as contemptible foes by England, it is a question, I doubt, whether the guns of those two strong batteries will not be too heavy for us, if we *should* be compelled to resort to strong measures. However, the young officer condemned to be shot as a prisoner of war was a brother midshipman, and a staunch friend and favourite of mine, and I am resolved to proceed to any length to save him."

The officers generally agreed with the captain. Englishmen thought much of themselves at that period—they think something of themselves still; and the young officers said that it wasn't to be admitted for a moment that a petty Republic like that of Chili was to sacrifice Englishmen in a spirit of revenge, or was to refuse to accede to the demands of the captain of a British ship of war, who was the representative of his sovereign in the ports of a foreign people. As to the sailors, though they neither knew nor cared what the dispute was about, they were ready for anything in the way of a " scrimmage."

In a few minutes Captain Rodman was on his way to the shore in his eight-oared barge. A Chilian guard of honour was sent down to the landing-place to receive him, and, accompanied by his second lieutenant and a midshipman as his aide-de-camp, both being, like himself, in full uniform, he was escorted by the guard to the castle, where he was received by the commandant (a Chilian general officer) in person. The commandant expressed the delight he felt at being honoured by a visit from the English captain, and in the hyperbole peculiar to Spanish phraseology, wished that he (the captain) might live a thousand years, and declared that the castle and town, and all they contained, were at his service.

Spanish is by no means a difficult language to acquire, especially to those who have a knowledge of French or Latin; and Captain Rodman, who spoke French fluently, had, during his visit to South America, when a midshipman, acquired a sufficient knowledge of Spanish to enable him to understand and carry on a conversation intelligibly.

"I have no intention to test the friendship and goodwill of your excellency to such an extent," he smilingly replied. I certainly *have* a favour to ask, but it is a very trifling one."

"Consider it as already granted, senor capitano," said the commandant.

"But your excellency must first hear what it is," answered Captain Rodman. "It is merely that you shall release a countryman of mine, formerly my brother officer, now a prisoner of war, in this castle, and deliver him over to me on consideration of his promise not again to bear arms against the Chilian Government."

The countenance of the commandant had darkened as he listened to the request of the English captain.

"Are you aware, senor capitano," said he, " that this officer is under sentence of death, and that—but for an exhibition of unusual clemency—his life would already have been justly forfeited?"

"It is for that reason I make this request," replied Captain Rodman, " although I cannot admit that a prisoner of war is deserving of death. The practice of condemning such prisoners to death is inhuman, and opposed to English usages."

"It is not for England nor for English officers to dictate to the Governments of other countries," commenced the commandant, in a haughty tone of voice. But checking himself, as if endeavouring to control his temper, he added, in a politer tone: "Remember, senor capitano, that Great Britain is powerful, and can therefore afford to be generous. This Republic is weak, and we are forced to severity. More especially when we make prisoners those of other nations, who have no cause of quarrel with us, yet who, for the sake of reward, place their skill and courage at the command of our foes. I will not deny—nay, I will freely acknowledge—that the young officer whose life and liberty you ask is brave, and skilled in his profession. He has caused us the loss of three of our best vessels of war already. It is his spirit and courage that have animated our opponents, who otherwise would have been defeated long ere now. It is he, and such as he, who prolong the war, and when we do get such a promoter of discord in our power, it is but just that we should make an example of him. Nay, more, senor capitano, the duty we owe to our country *demands* his death."

"Yet," said Captain Rodman, "you Chilians also have both English and French officers in both your naval and military services?"

The commandant shrugged his shoulders. "We must do as others do, senor," he replied. "One evil causes others."

Much more was said on both sides. Captain Rodman resolved to do his utmost to save his friend; yet, anxious to avoid threats which might lead to hostilities, for which, especially if the result should prove disastrous, he would be severely blamed, and would lay himself open to a trial by court-martial, and probably to severe punishment—he pleaded that the condemned officer was a personal friend, and asked for his pardon and release, as a special favour to himself.

"Any other favour that you can ask, senor capitano," replied the commandant.

"Yes," said Captain Rodman, with a sneer; "any *other* favour but that which I do ask. The castle and town, and all that they contain! Anything but the life of my friend, whom you would sacrifice, out of your Spanish-Creole spite and vengeance, because he is braver than you and your cowardly countrymen!"

"Senor capitano," cried the commandant, in a savage tone, and with a stamp of his foot, "the Chilians are brave. They are not cowards. And *I*, senor, *I* am of pure Spanish descent. I am no Creole. My father was an hidalgo of Spain!"

"So much the more to his son's shame and discredit," replied Captain Rodman.

After this, as may be imagined, the Englishman and the Chilian alike forget their politeness, and interchanged taunts and threats, until at length Captain Rodman said: "Then your excellency refuses my request?"

"My duty to my country compels me to do so," was the reply.

"Then I no longer make a request, but a *demand*. Release my countryman and friend, senor, or take the consequences"——

"And they, senor?"

"You shall soon learn what they are, senor. Dare to injure my friend in any way whatever, and I will lay your town in ruins."

The commandant pointed to the guns on the batteries.

Captain Rodman smiled disdainfully.

"We shall see whether you dare to use them!" he said. "Addio, senor."

"Addio, senor!" replied the commandant; and with an outward semblance of politeness, and with deep feelings of pride and anger at heart, the English and the Spanish officer separated.

The interview had been a private one. The second lieutenant and the midshipman had remained in the ante-room; but Peters saw at a glance, when Captain Rodman rejoined him, that the captain had failed in his object.

Together they returned to the boat in silence. Peters waited for the captain to speak. Intimate and friendly as they were, there were times when Peters dared not address his captain until he was spoken to, and the frown on Captain Rodman's brow told that this was one of those times. It was not until they had taken their seats in the stern-sheets of the barge, and the captain had ordered the men to shove off, that, addressing himself to the lieutenant, he said, calmly:

"The commandant has refused to accede to my request."

"So I supposed, sir," replied Peters. "And now"——

"And *now*, sir," interrupted the captain, "we shall see whether he will dare to refuse my *demand*, supported as it will be by the guns of the frigate."

This was all that was said during the passage from the shore to the ship; but the sailors—as well as the lieutenant and midshipman—had heard the captain's words, and they all knew full well that the implied threat would be carried out at all hazards.

When the ship was reached, it was seen that during the absence of the captain everything had been quietly prepared for action. The hammock-nettings alone had not yet been triced up; but this could be done in a minute.

Captain Rodman, without speaking a word, descended to his cabin.

"By George! The captain's in a terrible temper," said the first lieutenant to Peters. "The journey has been a failure—eh?"

"Yes," replied Peters. "We're in for it. The commandant has refused his request, and he is determined upon saving poor Fleming at any cost."

Before anything further was said, Captain Rodman reappeared upon deck.

"Mr. Bowling," said he, to the first lieutenant, "send the men aft."

"Ay, ay, sir," replied the lieutenant; and presently the boatswain's whistle was sounded.

"All hands aft!" succeeded to the call.

In a few minutes the men stood ranged in files, in front of the quarter-deck.

"My lads," said Captain Rodman, "an Englishman, a true-hearted sailor, a friend of mine, and one whom some among you have known in days gone by, lies under sentence of death in yonder castle—his only crime being that he has shown so much skill and courage in battle, that these Creole-Spaniards envy and hate him, and are determined to sacrifice him. To-morrow morning, at sunrise, he will be shot to death, like a dog, in the courtyard of the castle, unless we can deliver him. I have asked for his pardon. I have condescended so far as to plead in his behalf my own boyish friendship for him, to no purpose. At length I *demanded* his release, in the name of my king and countrymen, alike in vain. The commandant refuses to listen to me, and when I spoke more warmly, he sneeringly pointed to the guns on the batteries.

"My lads, I think the guns of this frigate are as much to be trusted as are those of the castle and fort. I *know* the men are more to be trusted than all the soldiers in the Chilian army. I am determined, if it be possible, to rescue my gallant young friend, Lieutenant Fleming, from these bloodthirsty scoundrels. I intend to carry the frigate past the guns on the batteries. If the commandant dare to fire upon us, I shall return the fire with interest, and then shall land, and carry the fort and castle by storm. This I *can* do, my lads, if you stand firm and true"——

"We will—we will—to the last man, sir!" shouted the sailors.

"One word more, my brave fellows," continued Captain Rodman. "I don't think they dare proceed so far as to fire upon the frigate. If they do, I am confident that they will meet their match. In such case, however, I shall return but one broadside. Then I shall man the boats, which will be lowered in readiness, and lead you in an assault upon the castle. I forbid you to interfere with the townspeople unless they unite with the soldiers against us. In that case, strike at all who oppose us; but spare the women and children, and give instant quarter to all who surrender. Follow me and your officers to the castle, and we will bear Lieutenant Fleming off in triumph."

The sailors gave three hearty cheers, and amidst cries of "Hurrah for Lieutenant Fleming!" they proceeded to get a spring upon the cable; so that, without the necessity of upheaving the anchor, the frigate was enabled to drift down the harbour towards the batteries.

Several of the sailors *had* known young Harry Fleming as a midshipman, and these were ready to risk anything to rescue him.

They imparted spirit and confidence to their shipmates; and as the gallant vessel neared the fort, all were eager for the affray.

The falls were laid down, so that the boats could be lowered at a moment's warning. Firearms and cutlasses were placed in the boats, and separate parties of marines were drafted to each. Then, when the frigate was within speaking distance of the fort battery, Captain Rodman seized his trumpet, and shouting through it to the officer on guard, demanded an audience of the commandant, who presently made his appearance, evidently much excited; and, to the imperative demand of Captain Rodman for the release of Lieutenant Fleming, returned a prompt and passionate refusal.

Captain Rodman ordered his boats to be lowered, and the guns of the frigate to be thrust out and pointed upwards.

"If you, senor capitano, persist in your present aggressive measures, I shall fire upon your frigate," exclaimed the commandant.

"Fire at your peril!" was the reply; and the sailors gave a hearty cheer.

It was a moment of extreme excitement and great peril. Captain Rodman had run his ship so close to the shore that she lay directly under the batteries; consequently most of the shot, had the Chilians fired, as they threatened, would have passed over her. Still, a sufficient number of guns might have been brought to bear upon her, as would in all probability have sufficed to sink her, while the frigate's broadside would have swept the parapet, but could have had little effect upon the batteries themselves.

Of this Captain Rodman and his officers and crew were perfectly aware. The ship was so close in that the wild passionate ravings of the Chilian officers and soldiers could be distinctly heard. Many of the younger officers were heard to urge the commandant to take no heed of threats nor consequences, but to blow the audacious Englishman to atoms. Yet so great was the dread in which, at this period, the British navy was held, and so great the terror with which the British Government was regarded—so confident the belief that England would take terrible vengeance upon any Government or people who would dare to offer insult or injury to British officers or subjects, even though such insult or injury were brought upon them by their own rash or reckless conduct, that Captain Rodman firmly trusted to these feelings to enable him to carry his point, perilous as was his present position. The younger officers, he thought, might be urged by pride and passion to proceed to take desperate measures; but however much the commandant and his chief advisers might threaten, he (Captain Rodman) believed that fear of consequences would overcome their passions, however violent.

Still, as I have said, it was a moment of fearful peril. The slightest overt action on the part of any over-zealous young officer, or even of any soldier, might lead to results that could not be contemplated without feelings of dread and horror!

The frigate was under her topsails only. All the lighter sail had been furled, and the courses were hauled up; but under her topsails, with a light breeze abeam, she was slowly gliding past the batteries, and would, in a few minutes, be perfectly safe from any damage from their guns. The boats, five in number, were alongside, filled with seamen and marines—an officer sitting in the stern-sheets of each boat.

Hardly an audible word was spoken on board the vessel. Orders were quietly given. The people on shore could see that men were stationed at every gun, and every order was promptly obeyed; but Captain Rodman, whatever might have been his feelings, betrayed no signs of alarm, nor of unusual excitement; and neither he nor his officers appeared to take the slightest heed of the threats that were hurled at them from the Chilians. They acted as though they did not hear them.

This contemptuous conduct served still further to exasperate the commandant, and those who stood around him.

"Bring your ship to, or I fire!" he shouted through his clenched teeth, using as the same time violent gesticulations. In fact the Chilian officers, had they been seen without being heard, would have appeared like so many huge apes in uniform, savagely grimacing.

No notice was taken on board the frigate of this last threat; and at an order from the commandant, the soldiers were seen to cluster round the guns, while the gunners seized their lighted linstocks.

Captain Rodman simply waved his hand, and the captains of the guns stood ready, at a moment's warning, to fire a broadside. Now was the dread moment Another minute of inaction on the part of the soldiers, and the great peril would be past.

The commandant and Captain Rodman stood steadily regarding each other, as though each was watching for the other to give some decisive order. The commandant had ceased his gesticulations, and now stood firm, with folded arms —his eyes steadily fixed upon the ship, while the officers, both on shore and aboard ship, stood intently regarding their chiefs.

The frigate slowly glided along, and was soon inside the batteries. One dread peril was averted!

Fierce mutterings were heard to proceed from the groups of Chilian officers; but the commandant stepped forth from among the older officers, and waved his hand as a signal for a parley.

Captain Rodman waved his trumpet in response, as he stood on the hammock-nettings of the frigate, just abaft the gangway.

"Senor capitano," said the commandant, with assumed calmness, "you act without authority."

"I act on my own responsibility, in case of emergency," replied the captain.

"Still, senor, without authority from your superiors," continued the commandant. "Hearken, senor. I have permitted you to come thus far, and to set at defiance the lawful authority which I claim, rather than involve myself in a quarrel with your country. Wait, and procure authority to act from the British admiral on this station, and your demand shall be taken into consideration."

"Where is the admiral now to be found?" answered Captain Rodman. "His ship is cruising in the Pacific! Can you, or any one tell me, where is he at this moment? I demand the release of Lieutenant Fleming, in the *first* place. Then you can make your appeal to the admiral, and if he hold me to blame, I am prepared to abide the consequences."

"The life of the prisoner shall be safe until the result of an appeal to the admiral shall be known," said the commandant.

Captain Rodman shook his head.

"I cannot trust to your promise," he replied. "Your word may be over-ruled."

"No, senor. On the honour of a Chilian officer."

"That pledge has, ere now, been tested, senor commandant, and found false. Remember the case of General Salavéra."*

The commandant ground his teeth with rage.

"I give you my word of honour, senor capitano," he said, with difficulty smothering his passion. "The prisoner's life shall be, for the present, safe. But I dare not set him free on my own responsibility."

"*I* dare and *will* act upon *my* own responsibility," replied Captain Rodman. "I will take no man's word."

The boats were now cast adrift, with the exception of the captain's barge, into which Captain Rodman now descended, and putting off from the ship's side, he led the way towards the landing-place. The first lieutenant was the only officer left on board the frigate, which was now safe from attack.

"They may hasten the execution out of revenge, sir," said Lieutenant Peters, as the barge pulled past the pinnace.

"If they do, Fleming shall be fearfully avenged," was the captain's stern reply. "But I have little fear of that. Pull after the barge, sir. If they oppose our landing, we must fight for it. I have gone so far that I care for *nothing* now. It is my intention to storm the castle."

---

* General Salavéra, a Spanish officer in the Peruvian service, was taken prisoner, and, as usual, condemned to die. On the strong remonstrance of the Peruvian Government, a reprieve was granted until his case should be further considered. A council was held, and it was decided that the general should be set free on certain conditions. Then it was made known that he had been shot dead, at the time appointed for the execution. The governor of the fortress was blamed, but not punished for his precipitation. The Peruvians were, at this period, equally false to their pledged word.

CHAPTER XII.

THERE was no doubt, now that the frigate had passed beneath the batteries, and lay snugly anchored in the inner harbour, beyond the range of the guns, of the success of the expedition. The sailors and marines who manned the boats were sufficiently numerous to be more than a match for the Chilian troops that could be brought to oppose their landing; and the townspeople, being naturally cowardly, and by no means well-affected towards the Government or military, would not interfere on one side or the other. Still, Captain Rodman wished, if possible, to avoid bloodshed, especially in a cause in which it was doubtful whether he would meet with the support of the admiral of the station and his superior officers, many of whom were envious and jealous of his well-earned fame, though he was confident, if he succeeded in carrying out his purpose, of meeting with the support of his countrymen at home.

He therefore issued orders to the officers in each boat to exercise a control over the men.

"I am determined to land, and march to the castle," he said; "but though no doubt they will oppose our landing, use no violence if it can be avoided. If the authorities are determined to oppose us, and order an attack upon our men, *then* I leave you to your own judgment, only stating that it is my command that you push forward at all hazards. We can take and hold the town and castle if we will, but I do not wish to resort to such extreme measures. Now you know how to act, and knowing you as I do, I place implicit confidence in you, one and all. I hope I shall have no reason to regret my trust."

The officers and soldiers of the garrison were goaded almost to madness by the cool contempt manifested towards them by Captain Rodman, and by the thought that, through their fear of precipitating a collision, they had let slip the only chance they had of successfully opposing the demands of the English captain, by permitting the frigate to pass the batteries, and leaving the town open to the assault of the seamen.

Actuated by the revengeful feelings which seem to be inbred amongst the Spanish Creoles, the soldiers were ready to resist to the uttermost the landing of the English sailors, though such resistance should cost them their lives; for the descendants of the Spanish people in South America inherit, to a great extent, the mere animal courage of their Spanish ancestors.

They yelled and hooted, and danced with passion on the quay, brandishing their weapons, and swearing that the Englishmen, if they landed, should wade through blood. The townspeople shut up their shops and hid themselves, anticipating a furious conflict in the streets, while many of them called upon the authorities to deliver up the prisoner to the British, and thus prevent the dreadful affray that was threatened. *Carrajos!* and *Carambas!* hissed forth from between the teeth, were heard in every direction, and a serious and savage conflict appeared to be inevitable.

Still, now as heretofore, the calm, quiet firmness of the British officers, seamen, and marines, had an overpowering effect upon the Chilian commandant and his officers. Had the sailors shown signs of passion, a fierce conflict could not have been prevented. The slightest display of anger would have led to an outbreak; and the passions of the Creole soldiers once fully aroused, every effort of their officers to control them would have been unavailing.

The boats were at the landing-place—a long jetty which ran out a furlong from the beach. Captain Rodman rose, and giving some brief commands to his officers, stepped from the stern sheets of the barge on to the jetty. He and his officers wore their swords, and were provided with pistols; but the swords were sheathed, and the pistols concealed. The sailors were armed also with cutlasses and pistols; but no offensive display of the weapons was made, and the marines, with their loaded muskets, to which bayonets were fixed, sat with the muskets lying across their knees, to all outward appearance as unconcerned as though they were merely going to a parade on shore.

The commandant held a brief council with the superior officers, and was advancing to meet Captain Rodman, when a party of soldiers, excited to frenzy, rushed forward without orders, swearing savage Spanish oaths, and vowing that they would drive the accursed Englishmen into the sea to which they belonged.

So rapid were their movements, that a calm looker-on would have thought that nothing could prevent them from carrying out their fell purpose.

Captain Rodman, two or three of his officers, and some dozen or so of seamen only had yet landed, and these appeared a contemptible force opposed to their ferocious assailants. Had the Englishmen then wavered, there is no telling what the result would have been. The attacking party would have been supported by their comrades, and though the sailors and marines would most probably have eventually overpowered them by their superior muscular strength and greater coolness, the beach and jetty would have been deluged with blood.

Neither Captain Rodman nor his officers, however, even drew their swords. The gallant young captain merely turned about, and gave some brief orders to his men.

In an instant thirty sailors and as many marines sprang to their feet as if by magic, or rather as if moved by machinery.

"Keep back at your peril, every man of you!" cried the captain, in Spanish.

The greater portion of the Chilian party, startled by the sudden aggressive movement of the Englishmen, checked themselves in their wild career.

Six or seven, however, rushed on with drawn swords, and before they had advanced half a dozen yards, were swept down to a man by the skilfully-directed fire of the marines, who instantly afterwards sprang on shore, followed by the sailors, and both sailors and marines prepared to charge.

"Avast there! Keep back, my lads!" cried Captain Rodman; "but be prepared for action."

Then, raising his voice, he said in Spanish, addressing the Chilian officers:

"You have brought this upon yourselves by opposing my landing. I wish to avoid bloodshed if possible. Let me speak once again with the commandant."

A sharp report was heard, and a musket ball whizzed past him, close to his ear.

The main body of the Chilian troops had drawn back, and now stood in groups eagerly conversing, while they cast around them startled looks of amazement, as if overawed by the coolness of the English captain, and wondering what would come next.

The commandant, accompanied by a sergeant, who bore a flag of truce, stepped forward.

"Stay, senor commandant," said the captain. "Before I can enter into any terms with you, I call upon you to deliver up the assassin who fired at me, without orders from any officer."

The Lieutenant of Marines introduced to Father Neptune.

See page 86.

There was some demur and hesitation. The commandant wished to explain, and the soldiers seemed desirous to shield their comrade; but Captain Rodman stood firm, and waved the commandant back.

Some discussion followed; but presently the soldier who had fired the shot was led forward by a sergeant and a file of his comrades as meekly as though they were obeying the command of one of their own superior officers.

A couple of marines, by Captain Rodman's orders, seized the offender, and conveyed him to the pinnace.

Then Captain Rodman and his lieutenants met the commandant and his staff midway on the jetty.

"Your excellency can see the force I have at my command," said the captain. "My men equal your troops in number, and the guns of the frigate can be brought to bear upon the town. Your batteries are impotent to do us harm. At a word from me your town can be laid in ruins, for the townspeople will stand neutral. Deliver up your prisoner, and I will return to my ship and quit the port. Refuse, and I will take by force what you will not peaceably surrender."

The commandant and his officers appeared to be completely cowed. They could have understood a fierce display of passion, similar to that manifested by themselves; but the calm sternness of the English officers awed them.

"Senor capitano," said the commandant, after a brief conversation with his officers, "the town is at your mercy. I cannot oppose you; but I dare not deliver up the prisoner without permission, under the seal of the commander-in-chief. He is at Arequipa, thirty miles distant. A messenger shall be despatched to him instantly, who will state how affairs stand. I have no doubt permission to deliver the prisoner into your hands will be immediately accorded, and by daybreak to-morrow he will be free. Meanwhile, his life is safe, for we are in your power and cannot contend against you. I should also inform you, senor capitano, that the mother, wife, and sister of the prisoner are within a few miles of the town, and will arrive this evening. You will judge for yourself how best to act. The ladies will be admitted to the prisoner immediately upon their arrival. Perhaps it were better that they should know nothing of the measures now being taken for the prisoner's release until the order shall arrive from the commander-in-chief."

Captain Rodman had no desire to push matters to extremities. He knew that by holding the castle—which he intended to do—no force that the Chilians could immediately oppose to him could avail them anything, and until the order for the prisoner's release, properly signed, was delivered to him, he thought it was perhaps as well that Lieutenant Fleming and his female relatives should remain in ignorance of the nature of the efforts being made for his release. Still, he insisted that the lieutenant and his relatives should be informed, immediately on the arrival of the latter, that the prisoner's sentence was stayed, and that his speedy release was certain; and to make assurance doubly sure, he insisted that a hostage, in the person of an officer of the commandant's staff, should be given up to him and conveyed on board the frigate, there to remain until the appearance of the English lieutenant, when he should be forthwith released.

This he stated to the commandant, and moreover, expressed his determination to hold possession of the castle until the arrangements agreed upon were satisfactorily concluded.

These were harsh terms. But after some hesitation the commandant was compelled to submit to them. A Chilian colonel was delivered up as a hostage for the safety of the prisoner, and the colonel having been sent on board the frigate in charge of the third lieutenant, who had orders to treat him with every consideration, Captain Rodman and Lieutenant Peters, the lieutenant of marines, and between sixty and seventy sailors and marines, forthwith took possession of the castle—the marines keeping sentry over the batteries in lieu of the Chilian soldiers, who were disarmed; and though allowed their liberty within the precincts of the castle, were actually, for the time being, prisoners to the English.

Lieutenant Fleming was informed that he would be set free on the morrow; but he was not told what were the means by which his deliverance was effected, until the arrival of his pardon.

The messenger despatched to Arequipa made a quick journey, and whatever communication was made to the commander-in-chief of the Chilian forces, it had a prompt effect. The pardon of Lieutenant Fleming, of the British navy, late captain in the naval service of Peru, was delivered into the hands of Captain Rodman before daybreak the next morning—the only condition attached to his release being that he was required to give his word of honour not again to bear arms against the Chilian Republic.

Before midnight, the sister, wife, and mother of the prisoner arrived at Arica, expecting to be admitted to the lieutenant only to take their last farewell of him. They, however, were informed, instantly on their arrival, that the condemned prisoner was already pardoned, and would be released in the morning, though by what means the pardon was obtained they knew not.

At gunfire in the morning—the hour at which the execution was to have taken place—Captain Rodman and Lieutenant Peters entered the cell in which the prisoner was confined, the captain carrying the sealed and signed pardon in his hand.

The ladies had passed the night with the prisoner, hoping—as did the lieutenant himself, that the news they had heard relating to his pardon and release was true; but doubting—so feeble was their faith in Chilian truth and honour—whether they were not deceived for some purpose unknown to them.

As may be imagined, they had passed a miserable night. The young and beautiful wife of the lieutenant had fainted several times, and now lay, half unconscious, in her husband's arms. The sister, also a young and pretty woman, had suffered from hysterics, from which she had only found relief in tears. She was still weeping bitterly, and clinging to her brother, refusing to be comforted, when the cell door was thrown open. The poor mother, pale as a ghost, was striving to afford to the others the comfort that was denied to herself. It was a mournful group upon which the eyes of the two English officers rested when they first entered the cell!

So completely absorbed were the lieutenant and his weeping relatives in their own distress, that at first they took no heed of the appearance of the gaoler and the two visitors.

To gratify the Chilian love of display, the commandant (unknown to Captain Rodman, who, had he been aware of it, would have prevented such an unmeaning and needless theatrical exhibition) had ordered the guard to turn out, and the body of men originally drafted to act as a firing party, to make their appearance in the castle-yard at the hour appointed for the execution, as though no reprieve or pardon had been granted. The ring of the soldiers' muskets, as, at the command of the sergeant, they grounded their arms on the stone pavement, first recalled the unhappy females to a sense of their position. They started, and a thrill of horror ran through their frames, and, turning their heads, they saw that the cell door was open, and that the gaoler had entered, with two officers in uniform.

The wife of the lieutenant was the first to speak. With a sharp cry of agony she started from her recumbent posture, and throwing her arms round her husband's neck, and clinging to him as though she were determined that force alone should sever them, she exclaimed:

"Ha! the wretches! My God, I knew it was false! I feared that they had cruelly deceived us! But they shall *not* part us. Harry, dearest, they will kill you, but I will die with you!"

The mother and sister, equally alarmed at first, had, however, recognized the British naval uniform worn by the two visitors, and had noticed the parchment that Captain Rodman carried, which bore the Chilian Government seal.

Both became paler than before, and shuddered from head to foot, while a gleam of hope came to them still mingled with dread. They knew not what to think or believe, and unable to utter a word, sat gazing upon their visitors.

Lieutenant Fleming, completely engrossed with his care for his young wife, had not even turned his head.

Captain Rodman was the first to speak.

"Harry, my old shipmate," he said, "have you no welcome for me? Do you not know your old messmate, Tom Rodman?"

Fleming started with surprise and amazement. He seemed at first hardly able to believe his own eyes.

"Tom—*you* here!" he cried, at length—"and at such a moment as this?"

"At the best of all moments," replied Captain Rodman, "for I bring you life and liberty."

"The story they told me is true, then?" said Fleming. "I did not believe them. But—that noise in the courtyard! What means that? I thought it was the signal for my execution?"

"Heed not that idle mummery," said Captain Rodman. "See"—holding forth the parchment—"here is your pardon, and the order for your release."

A loud cry from the young wife startled them, and resounded through the cell and the corridors of the prison. The poor young woman had fainted in her husband's arms. The revulsion of feeling from despair to gladness and joy was too much for her. The sister and mother were scarcely less affected, and some time elapsed ere they were restored to consciousness. But it was not until Captain Rodman had explained the part he had played that they were really assured that the beloved husband, son, and brother was free!

"But you must not again serve in the Peruvian navy, Harry," said Captain Rodman, when, everything having been explained, the now happy party were ready to quit the prison, and go down to the boat which was waiting to convey them and the captain on board the frigate.

"I would not do so under any circumstances," replied Fleming. "You know my motives for joining the service; but I have long regretted having done so."

The boat put off to the frigate, and the Chilian colonel was released and sent on shore; the soldier who had fired at Captain Rodman, after being terribly frightened, was forgiven, and released with the colonel; and the same day the Conqueror sailed for Callao, where Fleming and his wife, mother, and sister, wished to be landed, in order that they might settle their affairs in Lima before they embarked for England—it being Lieutenant Fleming's desire, if possible, to re-enter the British naval service.

The Chilian commandant and his officers were right glad when the frigate sailed out of the harbour, and they had seen, as they hoped, the last of such a saucy and unwelcome visitor—though the commandant swore that he would take measures to punish the English captain for the part he had played.

Captain Rodman himself was doubtful of the consequences of his daring action. He knew that he had acted contrary to international law in interfering as he had done, and he expected to be visited with the displeasure of the admiral of the station for acting without consulting *him*. But as his adventure had proved perfectly successful, he did not greatly fear the results.

"If I had failed in my object, Harry," he said one day, as he and Fleming were pacing the frigate's quarter-deck together, "and if they had fired upon us, and perhaps killed some of my men, and compelled us to quit the port, I should feel somewhat uneasy respecting the reception I should meet with on my return to England. As it is, however, I don't think I've much cause to be alarmed."

Captain Rodman was right. The old admiral grumbled, but was secretly pleased with the result of the affair. The Lords of the Admiralty reprimanded him (Captain Rodman) publicly, and privately informed him that he had performed a gallant action. Some grumblers in the House of Commons wished to be informed whether a captain in the British navy was empowered to make war on his own responsibility, and to set at defiance all international laws to suit his own private feelings or interests, and the great body of the members laughed, and said Captain Rodman was a gallant fellow. They wished there were more officers like him. As to the people, they heartily admired his pluck, and declared that it was quite right and proper that England should make her power felt in the remotest quarters of the earth.

So Captain Rodman came out of this scrape with flying colours, as he had come out of so many other scrapes from his schooldays upwards.*

* Although, in relating this adventure, I have, of course, given false names, and have written of a somewhat later period, and, in some slight measure, altered facts to suit my story, it is literally true that the captain of a British man-of-war did, on his own responsibility, blockade a Chilian port, in 184—, and demand and obtain the release of an English officer condemned to be shot, under circumstances generally similar to those I have recorded, and was secretly commended for his promptitude and courage.

CHAPTER XIII.

ON leaving Arica, the Conqueror sailed southward along the coast, it being the desire of Captain Rodman to fall in with the Impregnable (the admiral's ship), and to report the part he had performed at Arica to the admiral (Lord Lintown), before his lordship should hear the story—probably exaggerated, or told falsely —from others. Captain Rodman expected to be blamed. He expected that the admiral would say—"You did wrong, sir, to interfere. It was a breach of international law on your part. I disapprove, like every Englishman, of the bloodthirsty severity of the Spanish-Creole Republicans ; but that neither gives me nor any one else the right, because either I or others may possess the power, to compel other Governments to obey my commands ; and, as you know, Lieutenant Fleming, on entering the Peruvian service, voluntarily surrendered all claim to the protection of his own Government."

This was the nature of the reproof Captain Rodman anticipated ; and, as I stated towards the end of the previous chapter of my story, it was the reproof he met with. He knew himself to be a favourite of the admiral's ; and when his lordship had eased his conscience by expressing his disapprobation of Captain Rodman's conduct, as in duty bound, he added (also as the captain had anticipated) : "However, the job's done, and can't be undone ; and to tell the truth " (with a smile upon his countenance), "I'm glad the young fellow is out of the hands of those bloodthirsty wretches. I hope it will be a lesson to him, and will teach him to remember in future that his services are due to his own king and country. Keep out of such matters hereafter, Rodman ; though I don't know but what, if I had been in your place, and had the opportunity to save the life of a friend, I should have acted in the same way. At all events, you've taught these people that Englishmen are not to be trifled with."

And so the matter ended.

But Captain Rodman did not fall in with the Impregnable so soon as he had anticipated.

The Conqueror had been twelve days from Arica, when, soon after the third lieutenant (Mr. Wilton) had taken charge of the morning watch, one of the forecastle men reported that he thought he saw land ahead.

It was soon after four o'clock a.m., and as yet quite dark. The moon had gone down, and day had not yet begun to dawn, and the faint gleam of light afforded by the few glimmering stars served but to make the darkness visible.

As I have heretofore said, it is only of comparatively late years that correct charts of the vast Pacific Ocean, with its innumerable groups of beautiful islands, have been correctly drawn. At the period of which I write, the position of many groups of islands was laid down falsely, and there are hundreds of islands—some of them of considerable extent—in the Pacific which were then altogether unknown.

"Land, say you, my man ?" said Mr. Wilton. "You must surely be mistaken It must be a cloud-bank you see."

"It do look like land, sir," said the sailor ; "but it's hard to tell what it be. It looks up darkly to the southward there ; though, as your honour says, it may be naught but a cloud-bank."

"Ask the ward-room servant for my night-glass, Mr. Farmer," said the lieutenant to a midshipman, "and bring it to me;" and as he spoke he walked forward to the forecastle.

"It has a *look* of land, certainly," said he, as he stood gazing in the direction the sailors pointed out. "But day will dawn in half an hour, and then we shall be able to see more clearly."

"Your glass, sir," said the midshipman, handing the telescope to the lieutenant, who adjusted it, and looked through it steadily for the space of a minute.

"It *is* land, and high land too, I really believe!" said he, removing the telescope from his eye. "And yet no land is marked down just hereabout on the chart."

The frigate was bearing down before a light breeze right towards the supposed land. The third lieutenant remained on the forecastle, waiting for the appearance of dawn, or until he could satisfy himself whether it *was* land, or a heavy cloud-bank that loomed darkly right ahead.

"Mr. Farmer," said he to the midshipman, "go aft and tell the quartermaster to keep the ship away half a point to the eastward. Should it prove to be land, it will not do to run in too close until we know what we are about."

That it *was* land was, however, soon apparent to the whole watch, even with the naked eye. Very soon day began to dawn, and then it could be seen through the spy-glass that it was a large and apparently very fertile island, with a mountain or a range of high hills crossing its centre. As the sun rose above the horizon, its rays gleamed across the water, and resting upon the land disclosed an abundance of vegetation; and as the ship drew nearer, it could be seen, without the aid of the spy-glass, that tall trees and dense shrubbery grew down close to the water's edge.

The lieutenant ordered the master to be called, and presently that officer appeared upon deck, bringing his chart of the Pacific Ocean with him.

"We've discovered a new island, Mr. Busby," said the lieutenant, smiling, "or come across an old one unawares. You have your chart with you, I see. Just look if there should be any land hereabouts."

"Thirty degrees south latitude, and seventy-nine west longitude!" muttered the sailing master, as he unrolled the large chart, and spread it open upon the ward-room skylight. "That was our reckoning, as near as possible, at noon yesterday; and I reckon we've made a hundred and thirty miles of southing since then."

"So much, think you?" said the lieutenant.

"Yes—fully so much. You see, though the breeze is so light now, we had a spanking breeze all day yesterday, up to midnight—though maybe we haven't made much headway since. But that would bring us to thirty-three south latitude —longitude, I reckon, about the same."

He marked the spot on the chart with the aid of his parallel-rule and compass, and found a blank!

"Strange—very strange!" he muttered. "There's land, for a certainty, and the chart gives clear water! Now what do those fellows who plan such charts deserve? Suppose, in the darkness, the frigate had run on shore, whose fault would it have been? Better have no charts at all than false ones!"

"The surveys of this ocean are very imperfect," said the lieutenant. "It's not the fault of the chart-makers. Still, it shows that one has need to be very careful while navigating these seas. But now that we are sure that we see land, the question is what land can it be?"

This was more than the master, or any one else, could tell. The slight alteration in the frigate's course, caused her, instead of bearing down upon the island, to skirt its eastern shore, sailing along slowly at a distance of about a mile from the beach. When it grew full daylight, the ship was so near, and the scenery of the island was so exceedingly beautiful, that the third lieutenant thought the captain would like to see it.

He went, therefore, himself to the captain's cabin, and told him that the vessel was close to land which had the appearance of being a large island.

"Land—an island!" exclaimed Captain Rodman. "I had no idea that we were within three or four hundred miles of any land. What is it like? Is it inhabited?"

"It appears very fertile and well-wooded, sir," replied the lieutenant, "and there is a mountain apparently in its centre. But, as yet, though we have been sailing along the shore for half an hour, I have seen no inhabitants, nor any signs of human habitations."

"You should have called me as soon as you saw it," said the captain, as he turned out of his cot. "I will be upon deck directly."

The lieutenant retired, and the captain dressed himself hastily and hurried upon deck.

"A lovely spot indeed!" he exclaimed, as soon as his eyes rested on the green sloping shore, thickly lined with trees.

The master stood near, looking at the shore through his telescope.

"Well, Mr. Busby," said the captain, "this is something unexpected. This island is not laid down in the charts?"

"No, sir," was the reply. "Nor can I conceive what land it can be. At all events, beautiful as it appears, I suspect that there are no inhabitants upon it, or we should have seen some signs of their existence ere now."

Captain Rodman had brought his spy-glass upon deck with him. He now gazed through it for some time upon the coast.

"There seems to be several bays and indentations in which a vessel might anchor, tolerably well sheltered, if there is good holding ground in shore," said he, at length. "Mr. Wilton, lower the quarter-boat and put a hand lead-line in it. We'll heave-to, sir, and I'll take the boat and see if I cannot pick out a safe anchorage. If so, we'll carry the ship in, and I'll go on shore, and have a look at this island. Is that a chart of this part of the Pacific, Mr. Busby?"—glancing at the chart spread open on the skylight.

"Yes, sir," replied the master.

Captain Rodman examined the chart for some moments in silence.

"The boat is ready at the gangway, sir," said the third lieutenant, touching his cap.

"Very good, Mr. Wilton. Let the men keep her alongside awhile. Mr. Busby, what do you make the latitude and longitude?"

"Thirty-three and a half by seventy-nine, sir, or thereabouts," replied the master. "That is, allowing for the course shaped and the distance run since yesterday noon."

"Hem! That would place us nearly opposite Valparaiso, and about four hundred miles to the westward?"

"About that, sir."

The captain considered awhile.

Presently he said:

"It strikes me, gentlemen, that we've unexpectedly run across Robinson Crusoe's famous island! The position of Juan Fernandez is not correctly ascertained as yet, and the hydrographers, not knowing exactly where to place it on the charts, have left it out altogether. But only a week or two since I was reading one of the books in my cabin, in which it was stated that the island lay about four hundred miles west from Valparaiso, and in about our present latitude."

"Juan Fernandez!" exclaimed the master.

"Robinson Crusoe's island!" exclaimed the third lieutenant; and the midshipman whose duty it was to be on the quarter-deck started and stared as though he were struck with amazement.

The next moment he descended the after hatchway in such haste that he was in danger of breaking his neck, and on reaching the cockpit, he roared out:

"Turn out there, fellows! Turn out! Make haste upon deck! What do you think? The frigate's off Robinson Crusoe's island!" And awaiting no reply, he hastened upon deck again, shouting in the wardroom as he ascended:

"Gentlemen, Robinson Crusoe's island—Juan Fernandez*—close to us!"

In a few minutes every midshipman, and the two surgeons' assistants, made their appearance upon deck, as eager to behold the far-famed island as a parcel of schoolboys would be. The lieutenants, the doctor, and the purser followed, almost as eager as the youngsters; and some of the watch having spread the news throughout the 'tween-decks, several of the sailors and warrant-officers, whose watch-below it was, turned out of their hammocks, and hurried up to get a glimpse of the island of which they had all heard or read so much.

The frigate was hove-to, and Captain Rodman, taking Lieutenant Peters with him, proceeded in the boat to sound the depth of water near the shore, and look out for a good and safe anchorage.

One was soon found in a wide bay, and the boat returned to the ship.

"Run the ship in shore, sir," said the captain to the first lieutenant. "There's capital anchorage ground just within yonder point—six fathoms water, and smooth as a mill-pond."

"The very spot, I truly believe," said Lieutenant Peters, laughing, "on which the savages landed when Robinson Crusoe saved his Man Friday! Depend upon it, we shall find the cave, in which the dying goat took shelter and frightened Crusoe half out of his wits, and the winter and summer abodes, and the spot on which the print of a naked foot was seen in the sand, and all the famous places spoken of in the story!"

The officers laughed, and looked as if they would like nothing better than a run on shore, during which they could amuse themselves by fancying they had made such discoveries; nor were the sailors a whit behind the officers in their eagerness to tread the shores of the island rendered immortal by the genius of Daniel Defoe.

The sails were clewed up and furled, and under her foretopsail the frigate was run in shore, and in less than a quarter of an hour was snug at anchor in a well-sheltered cove, within a quarter of a mile of a smooth, sloping, sandy beach.

Captain Rodman, the second, third, and fourth lieutenants, the surgeon, the chaplain, the purser, and, in fact, all the ward-room officers except the first lieutenant and the master; some of the midshipmen and one of the assistant surgeons, went immediately on shore, eager as children to visit the spot where Selkirk is supposed to have lived "monarch of all he surveyed" for so many

---

* By some means, the island of Juan Fernandez, in the South Pacific, has come to be generally supposed to be the island on which Alexander Selkirk was left on shore, and on which he lived in solitude for four years. It was from Selkirk's description of his solitary abode that Defoe wrote his glorious and immortal romance of "Robinson Crusoe." But in reality, the island on which Selkirk lived and of which Defoe wrote must have been one of the Bahamas, or of the West India islands—very far distant from Juan Fernandez.

years, and to recall to memory the details of the romantic story they had so often read in their boyhood.

A party of the warrant-officers, and the sailors of the starboard-watch, were also permitted to spend the day on shore—of course carrying food with them, for there were no refreshments to be obtained on the island, save those which Nature provided; neither was there any fear of their going to any excess through drunkenness, unless they could have contrived to get intoxicated on the juice of the wild grapes which grew in great abundance; while those on board comforted themselves by looking forward to the morrow, when it would be their turn to visit the island.

Lieutenant Peters, who was always as ready for fun and frolic as he was when a young midshipman, strolled away by himself a short distance over the sandy beach, when he pulled off one of his shoes and stockings, and made a deep print of his naked foot on the sand, and an hour or two afterwards he contrived, by some means, that one of the midshipmen should pass near the spot.

Presently the youngster gave a loud shout, and was soon seen running back to his party at full speed.

"What's up?" cried one of the party. "Here's Morgan running as if the ghost of Crusoe were in chase of him!"

"Perhaps he has seen some savages. The island may be inhabited, after all," said another.

In a few moments Morgan came up, almost out of breath, and in answer to the questions that were eagerly put to him, declared, as soon as he could find breath to speak, that he had discovered the spot where Robinson Crusoe saw the print of a naked foot in the sand.

"Stuff!" exclaimed the surgeon's mate. "How could you possibly make that discovery?"

"It's there—there now! As plain as it could have been when it was first made," replied the excited youth.

A roar of laughter burst forth from the party—Peters, who, with some other officers, was within hearing of Morgan's declaration, laughing as heartily as the youngsters, at the success of his trick.

"There *now!*" said a master's mate, contemptuously, as soon as the laughter had subsided. "As though a print in the sand could have existed for more than a hundred and fifty years! Why, man, it would have washed out by the next rising tide. What folly will you imagine next?"

"It's *no* folly," replied the youngster. "Perhaps the tide never rises so high. Indeed, one may see that it does not. At all events there it is, plain as possible. I marked the spot with some sea-shells. Mr. Peters sent me to yonder hillock to see whether any of the boats were coming on shore from the frigate, and I saw the print, both going and returning."

There was a general movement towards the spot, and there, sure enough, plain as possible to every eye—even every toe distinctly marked—was the print the young gentleman had spoken of!

It was a source of amazement to all. The lieutenants, the surgeon, purser, chaplain, and even Captain Rodman himself, were equally wonderstruck as the midshipmen; while Peters had great difficulty to conceal his satisfaction at his success in hoodwinking his shipmates.

"It *is* indeed very strange—most remarkable!" said the surgeon. "If there were inhabitants on the island, I should think little of it. And if there were other footprints near, I should be inclined to think that the island *is* inhabited, and that the savages are concealing themselves in the bush. As it is, one would think that the footprint had been providentially preserved intact, for more than a century, in order to furnish proof to future navigators of the veracity of the wonderful narrative which many people, in this age of doubt and scepticism, believe to have been nothing more than a clever fiction."

"You forget, doctor," put in the chaplain, "that, if you study the narrative, there is evident proof that Alexander Selkirk, the Scotch mariner, from whose story of his abode on an uninhabited island Defoe conceived his admirable romance, must have been left on shore on one of the West India or Bahama islands. His ship never visited the Pacific Ocean, though, by some unaccountable means, it has come to be generally believed that the island of Juan Fernandez was the scene of his wonderful adventures. This fact, doctor, upsets your theory at once."

"It does nothing of the kind, sir," replied the surgeon, angrily. (He and the chaplain, though the best friends in the world, were always disputing on some subject or other.) "It only goes to prove beyond doubt that those people who, like yourself, are always ready to find a flaw in everything, and to contradict everybody, are decidedly wrong in denying that Juan Fernandez is Crusoe's island; and for my part I shall believe henceforward, more firmly than ever, that the story of Alexander Selkirk is a *fiction*, and that Robinson Crusoe is *true—literally* true, sir. *There*, what do you say to *that*, sir?"

"That you are a very obstinate, credulous individual, sir," answered the chaplain.

"No more an individual than yourself, sir," cried the irate surgeon. "There's the footprint, sir. Deny *that* if you can, and *one* fact is worth all the humbugging theories in the world, sir."

Lieutenant Peters, after enjoying the joke for a while, had explained the matter to Captain Rodman, who had been as much mystified as were his officers. The captain now stepped forward.

"Pray do not quarrel, gentlemen," said he, smiling. "The print is certainly remarkable; but I think if you examine it narrowly, you will perceive that it is not the footprint of a savage, but rather of a person accustomed to wear boots or shoes. You may see that by the conformation of the toes "——

"Begging your pardon, Captain Rodman," interposed the surgeon. "It is the custom of many savages to wear sandals, and it is apparent "——

"Pray hear me out, doctor, and then I will hearken to your arguments," said the captain, quietly. "I remarked that the footprint was evidently that of a person accustomed to wear some covering for the feet, and I suspect that if Mr. Peters will kindly pull off his right shoe and stocking, it will be seen that *his* foot will exactly fit the print."

This Peters did, and then, greatly to the triumph of the chaplain, and to the equally great vexation of the surgeon, Captain Rodman explained how Mr. Peters had succeeded in mystifying them all.

The laugh was against the doctor, and thereafter, during the remainder of the cruise, whenever the chaplain and the doctor engaged in an argument, and the chaplain thought he was getting the worst of it, he invariably brought up the incident of the footprint in the sand, and by raising a laugh against his opponent, succeeded in gaining his own point.

The trick, however, was explained to the officers alone, and though many of the warrant-officers and seamen heard afterwards how it was effected, they generally chose to disbelieve it, and stuck to the fact that they had beheld the veritable footprint in the sand, which caused Robinson Crusoe so much alarm and dismay.

The Conqueror remained at Juan Fernandez a week, and every day some of the officers and crew went on shore, and amused themselves by pretending to discover signs of the cave in which Crusoe resided, and of his summer-house and garden, and on the spot on which he built his boat, and of all the principal scenes in the famous story, and really derived more pleasure from their visit to the lonely island than they derived from any other place at which the frigate touched during her cruise.

On leaving Juan Fernandez, Captain Rodman, despairing of falling in with the admiral's ship on the open ocean, made sail for Valparaiso, in hope of finding the Redoubtable in that port.

CHAPTER XIV.

THE Conqueror, however, did not reach Valparaiso without an adventure. A strange sail was reported the morning after she sailed from Juan Fernandez.

"Where?" asked the first lieutenant.

"Right under the sun, sir."

"Away aloft with your glass, Mr. Farmer, and see if you can make her out," said the lieutenant.

"I think, sir, she's a brig," cried the midshipman, after a few minutes; "but the sunshine conceals her. Yes, she *is* a brig. Looks like an English vessel lying-to."

"Lying-to in such a spot, and in such weather as this?"

"Yes, sir, that she certainly is—though, now that the sun does not dazzle my eyes so much, it appears that her yards are braced anyhow; and, by George, sir, she's got her colours hoisted union-down."

"Ha! A signal of distress, said the lieutenant. "Are you sure of it?

"Sure, sir. I can see her quite plain now."

"How do we stand towards her?"

"We're bearing right down upon her, sir. She's no distance off. When the sun gets a bit higher, you'll see her plainly from the deck."

"Very good. But remain where you are, Mr. Farmer. Keep your eye upon her until you're called down."

The captain was informed that a strange vessel was in sight, and was soon upon deck. In five minutes the brig could be seen quite clearly from the quarter-deck; and from the disorder of her yards and sails—the former being braced different ways, and some of the latter being half-clewed up, and from the way in which she yaw'd about—it was thought that she had been deserted by her crew; though why she should have been deserted in such fine weather no one could conceive.

In the course of an hour the frigate was close to the stranger. She was a large English brig, so low in the water that she was evidently either too deeply laden, or water-logged; and, as yet, there were no signs that any one was on board of her. Still, there was no appearance that she had suffered from heavy weather; and that she had been on shore was quite out of the question. Indeed she looked as though she had not been many days out of port; her paint was fresh and clean, and, though her canvas was in disorder, nearly all the sails were set, or but partially clewed up.

Captain Rodman had given directions to Mr. Peters to board her. One of the quarter-boats was being lowered, and the first lieutenant was about to heave the frigate to, when suddenly a figure was seen on board, and a handkerchief was waved from her quarter-deck.

"By Jove, she appears to me as if she were settling down!" exclaimed the captain. "And that man, or rather boy, as he seems to be, is the only creature I can see on board. Be careful how you approach her, Mr. Peters, if she *is* sinking. The person on board, whoever he is, can jump overboard, and you can pick him up."

The boat left the ship's side while the captain was speaking, and in a few minutes was alongside the brig. Apparently the second lieutenant saw that there was no danger of the vessel's going down suddenly, if she were sinking; for he not only ran the boat close alongside of her, but went on board himself, with three of his boat's crew. He remained on board nearly a quarter of an hour, and then re-entered the boat, taking on board with him a young man from the brig, besides his own men, and returned to the frigate.

The stranger—a youth about seventeen years of age—ascended the side with the lieutenant, and was brought by him to the quarter-deck to tell his own story. Then Captain Rodman learnt that the brig was the Heron, of Liverpool; that she was loaded with copper ore; and that after filling up with this cargo at Valparaiso, she had sailed to Guyaquil to take on board three hundred thousand dollars in bar silver.

"She was on her way homeward, *via* Cape Horn," continued the youth, "and we had a fine passage so far, and fair weather, till the day before yesterday, when a vessel hove in sight which we took to be a Chilian war-schooner. This vessel came up with us and spoke us. The captain asked where we were from and whither bound; and on being informed, inquired whether we had any specie on board. Our captain by this time began to grow suspicious, and he said we had none. But this did not satisfy the Chilian captain. He told us he was going to send a boat on board, and bade us heave-to.

"To this command, our captain, at first, paid no attention; but the schooner fired a shot across our bows, and her captain said he would fire the next shot on board if we did not obey. We had no alternative. The schooner was full of men, and was heavily armed, while we had a crew of only fourteen, all told, and carried but two small carronades.

"The boat, with the Chilian captain himself in her stern-sheets, and with ten armed men, came alongside, and the captain came on board, and asked to see our papers. Our captain showed him some papers; but he was not satisfied, and declared that we had others. While this talk was going on, two more boats, full of armed seamen, came alongside, and the sailors then came on board, leaving only a man in each boat.

"We knew then that they were pirates, or that the vessel was a Chilian cruiser, and that her captain and crew were ready to act as pirates, now that they had the opportunity. The specie was again asked for; but our captain persisted in denying that there was any silver on board. Perhaps it had been better had he given it up quietly. But no one can say. They might have done the same whatever we did. At any rate, the Chilian captain shot our chief mate, and that was the signal for the rest of the schooner's crew to attack us. The captain was soon struck down, and several of our men were shot or cut down, and then the rest would have given in. But that did not satisfy the pirates. They bound those of the men who were still unhurt, all but myself—I, when the rest of the men gave in, contrived to escape unseen down the fore hatchway and conceal myself—and then they set to work to pillage the ship. I soon heard, from my hiding-place, that they had found the silver, which was stowed in the lazarette beneath the cabin deck; for, though I can't understand Spanish, I heard them laughing and speaking of *plata*, which is, I know, the Spanish for silver; and when they had put the silver in the boat, they plundered the brig of everything that could be easily carried away. They even came into the hold, and I expected every moment to be discovered; for they passed close by the water-casks behind which I was crouching. However, they did not see me, and presently returned to the deck. They remained on board a long time afterwards—to me it seemed hours; but it could not have been so long, for it was still daylight when, after waiting till I heard the boats pull away, I crept cautiously upon deck. Then, to my horror, I found that they had murdered and thrown overboard all our crew. Not one but myself was left! The deck was stained with blood and everything was in confusion, and before long I discovered that they had scuttled the brig before they left her, and that the water was pouring into her hold. The schooner was still in sight, sailing away to the northward, and I dared not show myself, nor hoist any signal of distress, lest they should return, and serve me as they had served my shipmates. I expected that the brig would soon sink, and believed that I must sink with her.

"She remained afloat, however, all night, and when daylight came I found that she was half full of water, and that the water was still coming in, though very slowly.

"Then I hoisted the Union Jack upside down, and soon afterwards I saw a sail bearing down towards the brig. It was this frigate, sir, and your officer soon came on board and took me away from the sinking vessel."

This was the story of the poor lad who had escaped the fate of his shipmates. His appearance told of the terror he had felt, and the second lieutenant corroborated his statement respecting the blood-stained deck, and the plundered cabin, and the confusion on board the brig.

"Will she sink, Mr. Peters, do you think?" asked Captain Rodman.

"Yes, sir," was the reply. "She may float an hour or more yet, but it would be impossible to save her."

The captain then asked the lad to describe the appearance of the schooner. This he did to the best of his ability; and though his description might apply to other vessels of the schooner's character and tonnage, it answered exactly to that of a Chilian schooner that had treacherously cut out a Peruvian vessel during a short stay that the Conqueror had made at Isly (at that period a neutral port) and but for Captain Rodman's intervention would have succeeded in carrying her off.

"And she steered a northerly course, after leaving your vessel?" said the captain.

"Due north north-east, sir. I marked her course by the compass in our binnacle."

Captain Rodman consulted with his officers, and though it was very doubtful whether the frigate would be able to overtake the pirate, he determined, at all events, to go in chase of her.

"It strikes me strongly," he said, "that the schooner is the same vessel whose captain strove in such a treacherous manner to carry off the Peruvian vessel. I have heard, ere now, that the commanders of some of the so-called vessels of war, belonging to the South American Republics, are no better than pirates, and that they are suspected of having plundered and sunk more than one specie-laden vessel that is unaccountably missing. The captain of the Chilian schooner, that lay at Isly, is just the fellow, in my opinion, to enact the pirate, to suit his purposes, and I should like nothing better than to come across him."

The wind blew fresh from the southward. The frigate's yards were squared, and in five minutes she was sailing away to the northward on what certainly appeared to be something like a wild-goose chase.

CHAPTER XV.

To quote an old and well-known proverb, it was something like searching for a needle in a stack of hay to sail over the Pacific—the widest ocean in the world—in search of one particular schooner, among the numerous vessels of that class, which sail out of the ports of the South American Republics, without knowing whither she was bound, nor whether she put into port, or was still at sea.

Nevertheless, Captain Rodman's usual good fortune again attended him. For two days and nights the frigate sailed northward, before a fresh sou'-westerly breeze, without sighting a solitary sail—a case of common occurrence in that vast, and, comparatively speaking, little frequented ocean, over which ships sometimes sail for many weeks without sighting vessel or land.

Then the wind began to die away, and on the morning of the third day the frigate was scarcely making four knots an hour.

Captain Rodman was beginning to suspect that he was engaged in an idle chase. (His officers and crew had held that opinion from the first.) Still, he never liked to give in when he had once decided upon any course of action.

On the morning of the third day, he made his appearance on the quarter-deck after breakfast, together with the chaplain, surgeon, purser, and first lieutenant, who had breakfasted with him.

"Nothing in sight, I suppose, Mr. Wilton?" he said to the third lieutenant, who was the officer on the deck.

"Nothing, sir," replied the lieutenant, somewhat wearily. "The wind is dying away," he added. "I fear it will fall calm before long; and heaven knows, the weather is sufficiently hot and oppressive."

The captain glanced aloft and around him. The sky was cloudless, and not a single object appeared upon the water between the ship and the surrounding, far-distant horizon.

There was a look of indecision in the captain's face.

"If we are caught in a calm in this latitude," he muttered, as if to himself, "we may be detained for days—perhaps for weeks!" He then paced the quarter-deck in silence for some minutes. "Take a cast of the log, Mr. Wilton," he said, presently, suddenly ceasing his walk.

The log was hove over the lee quarter.

"How many knots?" asked the captain, when the line was hauled in.

"Three and a half, sir," replied the lieutenant.

"And when it was hove before?"

"She was making four knots and a quarter, an hour ago, sir."

"Hem! It's annoying to have run all this distance to the northward to no purpose. But I fear that a longer chase would prove equally futile. Brace up the yards, sir. We'll shape our course for Valparaiso again."

The boatswain's whistle sounded. The men were at their several stations. The first lieutenant had raised his trumpet to his lips to give the orders the sailors were anticipating, when something was seen right ahead in the far distance, which had the appearance of a sail.

"Avast there!" shouted Captain Rodman. "Let the yards remain as they are awhile; but do not quit your stations, my lads."

He raised his spy-glass to his eyes, and other officers did the same.

"It's hard to say what it is," said one.

"It looks like a sail, but it may be but a cloud hovering in the horizon," said another.

"Or an albatross on the water," said a third.

However, the object, whatever it was, appeared to remain stationary, and the general opinion was that it was really a distant sail; and this opinion was soon resolved into a certainty.

The men were ordered away from their stations, and the chase was continued, though none could say whether the sail were ship, brig, or schooner; and even if it were a schooner, the chances were two to one against it being the vessel that was sought after, while it was exceedingly doubtful whether the frigate could overhaul the strange sail, or even lessen the distance that existed between the two vessels, if the chase were sailing the same northerly course, as it very soon became apparent that she was. Some hours passed away, the breeze still blowing, though there were signs that it would die away altogether before nightfall.

"We seem to be drawing nearer," observed Captain Rodman, about noonday. "I can make her out to be a topsail schooner now. I suspect that she has the wind lighter than we. We must be carrying the breeze with us."

He had become so anxious that he now went aloft to the topmost crosstrees with his telescope, and remained there some time. When he returned to the deck, he declared the vessel in sight to be a low, rakish, topsail schooner, with black sides. "And from the look of her," he added, "I imagine that she can show a pretty set of teeth. I have no doubt that she is either a Peruvian or Chilian cruiser. Mr. Bowling, or you, Mr. Peters, did you remark any peculiarity about the Chilian or the Peruvian vessels between which the affray took place at Isly?"

"I really did not, sir," replied the first lieutenant. "It was late when we entered the port, and dark when the vessels left. It was almost impossible to remark any peculiarity in either of them. Besides, those vessels are all much alike."

Peters appeared to acquiesce with the remarks of the first lieutenant, though he did not speak.

The frigate was under a perfect cloud of canvas. Every sail was set that could possibly draw, and the sails were all wetted, to cause them to hold the wind.

The log was again hove, and though the breeze had slackened considerably, the ship was still making three and a half knots, good.

Either the people on board the schooner did not yet see the frigate, or they had no desire to avoid her; for it was now clearly manifest that the frigate was rapidly drawing nearer to the chase. And, moreover, it could now be seen that the schooner was jogging along under easy sail, as though she had no occasion for speed.

Some time before it grew dark, the captain again went aloft. The schooner was not now more than four miles distant, at the utmost; and when he again returned to the deck, he said that he could make out, through his glass, that the schooner's foretopmast was scraped and bright-varnished, though her other masts were black, and that there was a large triangular patch of white canvas in her foretopsail. "I can't make out what armament she carries," he added; "but she is certainly heavily-armed for a vessel of her size. However, if the breeze holds, another hour will bring us close up with her, unless she spreads more sail."

"She can have no wish to avoid us, sir," observed the first lieutenant, "or she *would* press on faster. She must have seen us ere now."

"I am not so sure of that," replied the captain. "Not perhaps suspecting to see any vessel near, no one may be looking out for such an object; and we usually see a vessel ahead of us, long before we see one that is astern."

The second lieutenant had been conversing in an undertone with Mr. Wilton and the master. He now came up to the captain and first lieutenant.

"You say, sir," said he, addressing Captain Rodman, "that the schooner has a bright foretopmast?"

"Yes," replied the captain; "and it has rather a strange appearance in contrast with the other black masts and spars."

"I now recollect," continued Mr. Peters, "that the Chilian schooner at Isly had such a peculiarity. I noticed it particularly; though until you spoke just now, it had altogether slipped my memory. Mr. Busby and the doctor noticed it also; but as we did not see her sails set, of course, I cannot say whether or not she had a patch in her foretopsail. I have no doubt it is the same Chilian schooner that is now ahead of us."

"Nor I," replied the captain; "but I do begin to think now that her captain has no cause to avoid us. He must, I should think, see us by this time; and if he had lately been engaged in a brutal act of piracy, he would surely take alarm on seeing a large ship of war bearing down under a crowd of canvas."

The young lad who had been rescued from the plundered and scuttled brig had been standing near the quarter-deck, and had heard the above conversation. He now approached Captain Rodman, and removing his cap from his head, said, in a voice tremulous with excitement:

"The schooner that plundered and scuttled our brig, sir, had a bright-varnished foretopmast, and a triangular patch of white canvas in her brown foretopsail. She was pierced to carry sixteen small carronades, sir, and carried a long-Tom amidships. *That* schooner, sir, is the same vessel."

"Can you be *sure* of that, my lad?"

"Sartin sure, sir; I noticed her partic'larly as she sailed away, arter I came out of the hold."

"Look, sir—look! She sees us now, apparently for the first time. The fellows have been sleeping!" cried Lieutenant Peters at this instant. "There can be no doubt, *now*, that she wishes to avoid us."

It did appear that such was the case. The schooner until now had been jogging along easily under her foretopsail and spanker. Now every stitch of canvas that her spars could carry was crowded upon her. It could be seen through the spy-glasses that her crew were damping her sails, and her course was slightly altered to the eastward, so as to bring the breeze upon her quarter and enable every sail to draw.

"Her guilt is manifest," said Captain Rodman. "Why should an honest vessel of war take to flight as we approach? . . . Oh, that we were a couple of miles nearer!" he presently went on. "The breeze is dying away rapidly, and she will take advantage of the lightest breath of wind when it will no longer avail us!"

This was true. As the sun sank lower in the horizon the wind sank rapidly. The frigate was hardly making two knots an hour, while the light schooner, under a press of sail, was evidently already beginning to gain upon the larger and heavier vessel.

"Oh, that it would at once fall calm, or that it would blow half a gale!" cried Captain Rodman. "The breeze that bears her on scarcely stirs the frigate. I fear she will yet escape us!"

Happily, the captain's first prayer was granted. Ere another half hour was passed, during which period the schooner had gained nearly a mile over the frigate, the wind died away suddenly ; and, before dark, both vessels lay becalmed, distant about three miles and a half from each other.

This was too great a distance to send the boats in the coming darkness, and Captain Rodman was somewhat annoyed and disappointed.

"I hope the calm will continue through the night," he said to the first lieutenant. "Should a breeze spring up, the schooner may escape under cover of the darkness. A very sharp look-out must be kept. I think the night will be sufficiently clear to enable us to keep her in sight by means of the spy-glasses."

Darkness came on rapidly, but the men on the look-out aloft were provided with telescopes, and by this means were enabled to keep the schooner in sight. Captain Rodman remained upon deck until past midnight ; and then, having been awake since an early hour in the morning, he went below to take a few hours' sleep, leaving strict orders that he should be called should a breeze, however light, spring up, or should any material change take place in the relative positions of the two vessels.

The night, however, passed quietly, not a breath of wind rising. At daydawn the captain again appeared upon deck. The calm still continued, and the schooner was still in sight; though she appeared, by some means or other, to have increased her distance from the frigate by half a mile at least, and had drawn somewhat nearer the coast, which was dimly visible to the eastward.

"They must have been towing her during the night with the boats," he observed to the officer of the deck, Mr. Peters, "or else some current must have caught her and increased her distance."

"I suspect that they have had their boats out, sir," was the reply. "I fancied, when I came upon deck at four o'clock, that I could see a boat being hoisted on board. I suppose they tried to tow her so long as they thought they could do so unperceived, and gave over at daybreak, not wishing further to increase our suspicions."

For some minutes Captain Rodman paced the deck in silence, stopping occasionally to gaze intently at the schooner through his telescope.

In a few minutes the first lieutenant appeared upon deck, and was speedily followed by the master. Captain Rodman called the officers together.

"If this calm continues, gentlemen," said he, "our only plan is to attack the schooner in the boats. Still, I am unwilling to risk the lives of my officers and men in such a dangerous conflict. That vessel is heavily armed, and she carries as many or more men than we can send against her in our boats. You may depend upon it that the Creole-Spaniards will fight desperately when they find themselves brought to bay, and they will have every advantage over us."

"If that be the vessel that plundered and scuttled the brig, sir," said the first lieutenant, "her captain and crew may as well fight to the death as be taken ; and it is my opinion that, under the circumstances, they *will* do so."

"Then you think her capture by the force that we can despatch in boats improbable ?"

"Nay, I do not say that ; but it cannot be effected, I believe, without serious loss to ourselves. Still, sir, I am of your opinion, that we ought not to permit her to escape us."

"If we were a mile or two nearer," said the captain, "our shot might take effect. Try a gun, Mr. Bowling."

The frigate had swerved round in the dead calm, and lay broadside on to the schooner. A gun was fired from amidships, and the shot was seen to fall about midway between the two vessels. It *ricochetted* across the water for another half mile, and then disappeared.

The schooner took no further notice of the shot than to hoist the Chilian man-of-war ensign.

"We can do nothing with the frigate while this calm lasts," said Captain Rodman; "and even should a light breeze spring up, she would probably escape us. Let the boats be lowered and manned sir."

The launch, yawl, pinnace, and two cutters were lowered and manned with as many seamen and marines as they could safely carry. Still the captain hesitated for some time to send them away. Neither he nor any of his officers cared to confess their fears; but no doubt they did fear that, urged to desperation, the pirates (for such they were, though the schooner was disguised as a national vessel) might be enabled to sink the boats while the frigate lay helpless, unable to save the men, or to send any additional force to their aid.

It was near noon before it was decided to despatch the boats; but then, perceiving that the chance of a breeze was less than ever, they were sent off, under the command of the four lieutenants and the boatswain.

The orders were to dash in, heedless of the guns which would doubtless be fired with the object of sinking them, and, if possible, carry the schooner by boarding; but this was found to be quite out of the question under the sharp fire that took place. As soon as the boats got within range of the schooner's guns, the Chilians, by means of the long sweeps which they had by this time got out, brought her broadside to bear upon them, and commenced firing so rapidly, and with such precision, that every moment it was expected that the boats would be sunk. The shot *ricochetted* over them, and plunged in the water so near them as to splash the sprays over the crews. The larboard oars of the yawl were carried away by one shot, and the men who pulled them were disabled, though, for-tunately, no shot actually struck the boats. Mr. Bowling pulled in with the first cutter, shouting to the other boats to follow; but the schooner's foretop was crowded with men, who fired their muskets so rapidly, and with such good aim, that nine of the cutter's crew were wounded; and had not she been pulled back, every man on board would have been killed before the vessel's side could have been reached. Seeing the attempt of the first lieutenant thus frustrated, none of the other officers followed his example. It would have been madness to have done so. The frigate would have lost a hundred officers and men to no purpose. Several men in the other boats, however, were wounded by the fierce discharge of musketry, not only from the schooner's foretop, but from her deck likewise; and in the confusion that prevailed another broadside was discharged, one of the shot from which passed through the bows of the pinnace, and, ripping open several of her planks, severely wounded six of her men. The boat, of course, immediately filled, and being heavy with arms and ammunition, sank, carrying down with her two poor fellows who were too much hurt to attempt to save themselves. The other men were picked up by the yawl and second cutter; but while they were being taken on board, the Chilians still kept up their fire, dropping one of the English sailors with almost every shot.

The boats had not been ten minutes within range of the schooner's guns before half their crews were more or less severely wounded, and six men killed.

Still the first lieutenant would not give in. He shouted to the officers of the other boats to return to the frigate, and then, when the Chilians were off their guard, to dash in at a given signal, and board at the schooner's bows, stern, and amidships at the same moment.

This attempt, however, was more disastrous than the former one. The Chilians probably suspected the *ruse*, and directed their fire upon each boat so rapidly and skilfully, that again they were compelled to retreat.

At length the first lieutenant, very wisely, gave the order to return, and at the same moment Captain Rodman, who had been anxiously watching the boats through his spy-glass, ordered a gun to be fired as a signal of recall; for he saw that, as he had feared from the first, it was impossible to board a vessel so numerously manned and so heavily armed, under circumstances so disadvantageous.

The Chilians cheered, and fired a gun in derision as the boats retreated, and in another quarter of an hour they reached the frigate and were hoisted in. The third lieutenant and the boatswain were both wounded, though not very severely. A musket ball had carried away the gold strap on the first lieutenant's shoulder, six seamen and two marines were wounded—nine of them severely—while there was hardly a man who had escaped without some slight scratch.

"This has been sharp work indeed, Mr. Bowling," said the captain, as the wounded men were carried down to the cockpit. "I watched you closely, and I saw that you did all that men could do; but I had a *presentiment* from the first that the attack would prove impracticable. I wish now that I had taken the secret warning, and not sent the boats off. Those rascals fight like demons; but escape us they *shall* not, though I have to follow the schooner into port, and cut her out from under the guns of a Chilian fort!"

"It has been desperate work, indeed, sir," said the lieutenant, glancing over his shoulder. "Had the ball that carried away that strip of gold-lace struck a little lower, I should have lost the number of my mess."

"It is the first time I ever retreated in a boat attack," put in Peters.

"And the first time that any plan of mine has been unsuccessful," replied the captain. "But never mind, gentlemen. We will punish those fellows as they deserve to be punished yet, before I have done with them."

"If I am not greatly mistaken, we shall have a breeze, and a strong one, before long," said the master. "Look at that bank of clouds rising to the westward."

Even while the master was speaking, the frigate's sails filled and flapped, and filled again, and in ten minutes she was gliding through the water before a light but rapidly-increasing breeze.

The frigate had caught the breeze before the schooner; but when the sails of the latter vessel did fill, she had an advantage over the frigate, such as all small vessels have when the wind is light.

The frigate had got almost within range before the schooner stirred, and the guns were being pointed towards her, and every man was at his station ready to fire at the word of command, when she suddenly keeled slightly over, and righting again gracefully, darted ahead, going two feet to the frigate's one.

Captain Rodman ground his teeth with vexation.

"She appears destined to evade us," he muttered; "but, by Jove, she shall feel our power yet, and her captain shall account for his misdeeds!"

In less than an hour the schooner was hull down; but by this time the wind had increased so that it was with difficulty the frigate could carry her royals. In another half hour the royals were taken in, and she was staggering under her topgallant sails, set over single reefed topsails, and rapidly overhauling the schooner, although the latter vessel was almost buried beneath a press of canvas—the sea, which was rapidly rising, constantly sweeping over her deck.

"She's ours at last, thank heaven!" exclaimed Captain Rodman, rubbing his hands with glee, and pacing the quarter-deck with swift steps in his excitement. "She's ours, gentlemen; and, by George, her captain and crew shall pay for the trouble she has given us, as well as for their own misdeeds!"

In another two hours the frigate, as was proved by an observation with the sextants, had neared the schooner by a mile and a quarter. But now her lighter sails were necessarily taken in, or her masts would have gone, and she sailed the better for it. She did not bury herself so deeply in the water, and though the frigate still gained upon her, she did not do so so rapidly as before.

All through the day the chase was kept up. By the time the darkness set in, the sea had risen tremendously; the frigate by this time was running under double-reefed topsails, and the schooner had been compelled to take in everything save her foresail and spanker. The sun went down angry, and fiery red. By midnight it blew a furious gale. The frigate's topsails were close reefed, and her foresail was hauled up and furled. Still she was making full twelve knots an hour; while the schooner bravely held her own, though her foresail and spanker were now both close-reefed. The frigate still gained upon her, but very slightly.

Captain Rodman now began to fear lest the chase should furl her sails and heave-to, in the darkness, and thus allow the frigate to pass her without seeing her. Hitherto she had been kept in sight by constant watchfulness; but as the sea continued to rise, and the gloom became deeper, it was found to be very difficult to keep the glasses fixed upon her.

"By heaven!" exclaimed Captain Rodman, "the captain of that vessel, villain as he is, is a brave fellow. He would do himself credit were he to fight in a better cause."

Throughout the night not a single officer—not even the surgeon or chaplain quitted the deck. All were too highly excited to sleep; and such was the case with many of the sailors, who remained upon deck during the whole of their watch-below.

The captain's fear lest the schooner should furl her sails, and thus evade the frigate, however, proved futile. Either such an idea never entered her captain's head, or, more probably, he knew that it would be dangerous to attempt such a manœuvre in such a tremendous seaway.

When day dawned again, the schooner was standing on under a press of sail that would have been dangerous in a gale of half the force of that which now blew. The seas broke over her constantly, burying her beneath the water till the hull was completely hidden. More than once it was thought on board the frigate that she was about to founder. Still she held bravely on. The chase grew every moment more exciting. Heedless of the seas that broke over them, and wetted them to the skin, the officers stood on the forecastle, clinging to the knight-heads, watching every movement of the schooner, often at the imminent peril of being washed overboard.

The frigate already carried more canvas than she could safely bear. Nevertheless, Captain Rodman ordered a reef to be shaken out of the topsails, and the mainsail to be set.

Not satisfied with this, he set the topgallant sails over the reefed topsails; but almost immediately both topgallant sails were blown clean out of the bolt-ropes, and the fore-topgallant yard was carried away just as the men sent to loose the sail had quitted it—a moment sooner, and they would have fallen into the raging sea!

By noon it blew almost a hurricane. Running dead before the gale, it had been found necessary to relieve the frigate to save her masts, and she was now scudding under a close-reefed maintopsail and reefed foresail. The schooner had close reefed her spanker, but she still carried it; though it was seen that to save themselves from being washed away by the seas that swept over them, every officer and man on board was lashed to the rigging. Three men stood at her helm, and they also were lashed to the wheel. She must either have carried the sail she did, or have taken in sail altogether; and in the latter case, the frigate would soon have run her down, and passed over her. As it was, she was now so pressed down by the great force of the wind, that her speed was greatly lessened, and the frigate was fast gaining upon her; while, to add to the peril in which both vessels stood, land was sighted in the distance, and they were bearing down upon it, nearing it rapidly.

By three o'clock p.m. the frigate had got within range of the schooner; but it would have been highly perilous, in such a sea, to yaw round in such a manner as to bring a broadside to bear upon her, and the bow guns were under water. Marines, therefore, were lashed in the tops, with orders to fire and pick off the men from the schooner's deck, one by one, as soon as they were within musket range; while other marines, lashed in a sitting position, loaded the muskets for the firing parties. The ship was rolling until her yard-arms dipped in the water with every lurch to port or starboard, and it would have been impossible for the men to take aim had they not been lashed to the rigging.

In another half-hour the frigate was within a cable's length of the schooner. The marines had been constantly firing for twenty minutes. A great many of the Chilian's crew had been shot down, and the men at the wheel having at length fallen, the vessel would have broached to and capsized, or foundered, had not the captain and a seaman unloosed themselves and crept aft, at the risk of their lives, and lashed the helm amidships. The marines might have covered them easily; but, struck with their coolness and courage, Captain Rodman ordered his men to spare their lives.

As it was, however, the schooner yawed fearfully, and it was necessary slightly to change the course of the frigate in order to avoid running her down.

Just, however, as the frigate ranged up abreast of the schooner, and was in a position to pour a broadside into her, at two cables' lengths distance, which would have sunk her to a certainty, her captain—who was himself severely wounded, and who had lost, either dead or disabled, two-thirds of his officers and crew, by the sharp fire of musketry—waved his hat in token of surrender.

It was high time to decide upon some course. In another minute, had the frigate's guns been fired, the schooner would have been blown out of the water. Had the guns not been discharged, in another hour at the furthest she would have been driven upon the rocky coast, and dashed to atoms!

Captain Rodman waved his cap in return, and ordered the Chilian captain to heave-to—the frigate being hove-to at the same time.

It blew too hard, and the sea ran too high, to risk the lowering of a boat to board the schooner; and through the remainder of the day, and through the night, the two vessels lay-to, as near to each other as was safe.

At daybreak the gale began to moderate, and by nine o'clock the sea had gone down sufficiently to enable Captain Rodman to lower a boat, without incurring the slightest peril. The first lieutenant was sent on board the schooner, with orders to leave an officer and six men in charge, and to bring the captain of the Chilian vessel on board the frigate.

He came, furiously indignant, averring in Spanish and broken English that he was the commander of a Chilian vessel of war; that Chili was at peace with England, and that the English captain was guilty of piracy in attacking him.

"You give me, senor," he said, "your hospitality in Isly. You take me to your table. Den at sea you attack me wid your boats; you give me chase, you kill and wound my officers and men, you compel me wid your frigate to surrender, and you call me pirate! *Carajo!* Who is de pirate, I say?"

Captain Rodman replied that he (the Chilian captain) had abused his

On a Mission of Mercy.

See page 65.

ospitality while at Isly, by taking advantage thereof, to pretend feelings of friendship towards a Peruvian officer who had been his companion at the inner-table, in order that he might more easily seize his vessel, by means f an act of the basest treachery. Then, calling the youth who had been escued from the scuttled English brig, he charged his captive with having iratically plundered an English merchant ship at the time when—as he himself had said—there was peace between the English and Chilian Governments, and with having—in order to conceal his crime—brutally murdered the English crew with the exception of one lad, who had contrived to conceal himself) and scuttled he vessel.

This the Chilian captain indignantly denied, despite the repeated assertions of the boy that he was confident that the captured schooner was the same vessel that had plundered and scuttled the brig, and that he could almost swear that he recognized his (the captain's) face.

Lieutenant Peters had meanwhile been sent on board the schooner with secret orders. At this moment he returned, and spoke a few words to Captain Rodman, at the same time handing a roll of papers to him.

These Captain Rodman showed to his prisoner. They were the invoice of the brig's cargo, the muster-roll of his crew, and the owner's directions to the murdered captain.

The proof was overwhelming. The Chilian, caught, as it were, red-handed, had not a word to say. He had not time to frame a plausible excuse to account for his possession of the papers, and, trembling with fear, he became silent.

"Holding a commission from your Government, and being bound by that commission, and by the position you hold as commander of a national vessel, to protect, not only your own countrymen, but the people of all nations whom you may meet with in distress at sea, you take advantage of your commission to rob and plunder and murder those whom you fall in with, solely for the sake of gain! Wretched villain that you are, you are worse—ten times worse—than a pirate, and I am sorely tempted to hang you and your surviving officers and crew at the yard-arms of the frigate, and so to carry you into the nearest Chilian port. I shall, however, detain you all as prisoners; and, putting a prize crew on board your schooner—having first removed from it the plunder that you took from the brig—shall carry you into port, and deliver you over to your own Government, at the same time demanding your severe punishment, in the name of my king and country. Thank your stars that you are so distant from England; otherwise, I should feel it my duty to convey you thither, to meet the punishment you so richly deserve."

The prisoner expostulated, and begged for forgiveness; but Captain Rodman regarded him with scorn, and ordered him, and those of his crew who were still living, to be placed in irons on the orlop deck. In this condition they were carried into the port of Coquimbo, and delivered over to the authorities—Captain Rodman at the same time demanding that they should receive the punishment they merited.

This was readily promised. The Government authorities expressed their horror of, and their indignation at the crimes of which the captain and his officers had been guilty, and protested that they had no participation in the plunder, and no idea that it was possible for an officer in Captain Rodriguez's position to commit such crimes.

Compelled to be satisfied with this declaration, and having seen the prisoners sent away, in irons, to Santiago, the capital of the country, Captain Rodman sailed from the port.

He heard some time afterwards that the captain, after having been a short time in prison, was brought to a mock trial, and not only acquitted, but reinstated in his former rank and command !

Of course, his officers and crew, who had survived the conflict, were liberated with him.

The Conqueror sailed from Coquimbo to Valparaiso, and there, at length, fell in with the admiral's ship ; and it was now that Captain Rodman received the nominal reprimand, and the secret praise for his exploit at Arica, which I have recorded in a previous chapter.

Soon after the arrival of the Conqueror at Valparaiso orders were sent out from the Admiralty, directing the admiral of the South Pacific station to despatch two of the frigates of his squadron to the West Indies, to increase the strength of the squadron on that station.   The Acteon was selected as one of the frigates, and as soon as Captain Rodman learnt that Captain Lord Milford—his still unconscious rival for the affections of Lucy Sinclair—was going to be removed to a station so much nearer England, he determined, if possible, to proceed to the West Indies himself.

Captain Rodman, as I have told, sailed under a roving commission.   He was to a certain extent, free to go wheresoever he thought he could do most service with his frigate.   Nevertheless, he was, in a measure, subject to the authority of the admiral, or the senior captain of every station he visited.

However, he was, as I have said, a favourite of the admiral's, who, on being informed of his wish, immediately gratified it by despatching the Conqueror along with the Acteon, and in a few days the two frigates sailed out of the harbour of Valparaiso together ; and thus Captain Rodman took his departure from the Pacific Ocean, greatly to the satisfaction of the Chilian officials, who were as glad to see the last of him and his frigate as they were, a few years later, to see the last of the late gallant Admiral Lord Cochrane—"Ladrone Cochrane" (Thief Cochrane), as that brave officer, who *would* have his own way when he took it into his head to do so, was and is still styled by many of the people of Chili.

CHAPTER XVI.

THE two frigates sailed round the Horn and into the South Atlantic Ocean in company, the Conqueror meeting with much finer weather than when she doubled the Cape eighteen months previous, although it was now July and midwinter in those latitudes, and the temperature of the air was much colder.

She fell in with a gale of wind, of course. I never heard of a vessel doubling either Cape Horn or the Cape of Good Hope without doing so; but it was a mere ordinary gale, which blew itself out in three days, and was not so strong but that she was able to beat against it.

During the passage the Acteon was frequently so near to her consort that the two vessels were able to signal to each other, and sometimes a conversation, by means of flags, was kept up between the two captains for hours together.

Lord Milford was still ignorant of the fact that Captain Rodman was secretly betrothed to Lucy Sinclair—the object of his lordship's affections—and being a good-humoured, kindly fellow, he had formed a friendship for his brother captain which the latter would rather have dispensed with, for it is impossible to the best-hearted man in the world—and there were few better-hearted men than Captain Rodman—to feel otherwise than envious and jealous of the man who is his rival, consciously or unconsciously, especially if he have reason to know or to suspect that the chances of success are in his rival's favour.

However, all went on well, and no incident occurred worth recording until the Conqueror was off the port of Rio Janeiro.

It was early in the morning, and Captain Rodman had just made his appearance upon the quarter-deck, when it was reported that land was in sight.

"Ha!" exclaimed the captain, and then addressing the officer of the deck, he said:

"Has the land been long in sight, Mr. Wilton?"

"But a few minutes, sir, though it is so near," was the reply. "A haze hung over the water until the sun rose, which prevented us from seeing the land sooner."

"It is Cape Frio," said the captain, after having looked at the land through his glass. "I should say that we are not more than ten miles distant. Have you seen anything of the Acteon since sunrise?"

"There is a sail away to windward, sir, which I suppose to be the Acteon. But she is a long way off. I can just make her out with the glass, from the maintop."

"It can hardly be the Acteon, I should say," replied Captain Rodman. "She was nearly hull down to the southward at sunset yesterday, and could scarcely have got so far to windward during the night as the vessel you speak of."

"Sail ho!" cried a sailor from aloft.

"I have seen her, my man," said the lieutenant. "You mean the sail away to windward?"

"No, sir. I bean't speakin' o' she," replied the man. "I see'd *her* afore, sir. There's a sail astarn, pretty near hull down, sir."

"Ha! That will be the Acteon," put in the captain. "How does she bear, my lad?"

"Dead astarn, sir.   But I reckon how she's bringing the breeze up with her. I can see her hull a-risin' while I'm lookin' at her."

"No doubt of that," muttered Captain Rodman, in a tone of vexation. "These southerly winds, hereaway, always freshen at sunrise."

It was a lovely tropical morning. The sky was cloudless, and the waters of the ocean—almost as blue as the sky above—were glittering brightly beneath the beams of the rising sun; the atmosphere was perfectly clear to seaward, while a thin, transparent haze still hung, like a gauze curtain, over the land, through which the varied outline of the coast, extending northward from Cape Frio, could be but indistinctly defined.   The wind had blown from the south for some days past, and what little breeze there was still came from the same quarter; but the wind had died away during the night, and was now scarcely strong enough to fill the frigate's sails, which flapped idly, from time to time, against the masts.

The sailing qualities of the Acteon and the Conqueror were so nearly equal, that Captain Rodman was perfectly well aware that the rapid approach of the former vessel was owing to the fact that she was, as he had said, bringing the freshening morning breeze down with her; and this was the cause of the discontent expressed in his tone.

He would not have cared about the matter had not *another* vessel been in sight; but he wished now to know what this strange vessel *was*, before the Acteon should come up with him.

The stranger was evidently a large ship.   Captain Rodman fancied, from the cut and set of her canvas, as seen through his spy-glass, that she was a ship of war.   If she proved to be an English vessel, well and good.   But if she were an enemy's ship, and a fight ensued, and she were taken, the Acteon being in sight, even though she took no part in the action, would share the honour of the capture, and, as Lord Milford was Captain Rodman's senior officer, would probably receive, if she did not claim, the larger share.

It was for this reason that Captain Rodman, at this moment, wished the Acteon were at Jericho, or anywhere else, than where she was.

However, whether she were friend or foe, the stranger evidently had no wish to make off.   The course of the Conqueror was slightly altered, as also was that of the Acteon, as soon as the stranger was seen by those on board that vessel; and as the strange sail was steering towards the land, the three vessels were by this means soon closing with each other.   In half an hour the hull of the stranger was visible from the Conqueror's quarter-deck, and there was no longer any doubt of her being a man-of-war, and one of large size, too—either a frigate of the largest rating, or a line-of-battle ship.

Captain Rodman gave orders to clear decks for action; and the distant roll of the drum, heard across the water in the clear morning air, told that the same order had been given on board the Acteon.

For some minutes all was bustle and apparent confusion on board the Conqueror; but order was soon restored; dead silence succeeded to the stir and bustle, and every officer and man was at his station, each and all ready and eager for the anticipated affray.

"By George, sir, she's a spanker!" exclaimed the first lieutenant, after intently scanning the strange vessel through his telescope.

"A three-decker, by jingo!" exclaimed the master.

"Can you make out her colours, Mr. Bowling?" asked Captain Rodman.

"No, sir, I cannot," replied the first lieutenant.   "They are concealed by her sails; but to me she appears like a French vessel."

"I should say so too," said the captain. "But we have so many French ships in our navy now, that one cannot always judge from appearances. I don't like her bearing down so steadily towards *two* frigates, big as she is. I should be better satisfied if she were to edge off a little, and show some hesitation—though the French certainly don't fail for lack of courage. See that our flag flies out clear, sir. Confound that Acteon, and the lordling who commands her! I wish she were a thousand miles off just now."

"We should be opposed to great odds if she *were*, sir, and that ship *should* prove to be a foe," said the lieutenant.

"So much the more glory in capturing her, sir," replied Captain Rodman.

"Aye," muttered the lieutenant in the master's ear, but in so low a tone as to be inaudible to the captain, "if we *did* capture her; but she might turn the tables upon us."

"I wouldn't advise you to say that to Captain Rodman," replied the master, laughingly.

"There are her colours now!" exclaimed Captain Rodman, as the stranger's flag was seen to blow out clear of her mizzen-gaff-topsail; and glancing astern, he added, gleefully, "And, thank heaven, the Acteon's a good half league astern yet. We shall have the first innings, gentlemen, at any rate, and *that* is something!" He raised his telescope as he spoke, and peered through it intently.

"English *by* Jove!" he exclaimed, in a tone that contrasted so strangely with . his late gleeful cry, that some of the youngsters who heard him could hardly help laughing, and even the lieutenants, disappointed as they were, would have smiled had they dared.

It was true. The stranger *was* unmistakeably English—his Majesty's line-of-battle ship Majestic, of seventy-four guns, commanded by Captain Wallbrook, the commodore of the West India station.

The Majestic rounded to, the Conqueror doing the same, until the Acteon came up with her, when the two younger captains went on board the seventy-four to pay their respects to their senior officer.

"I had much rather we were going on board that ship to receive the sword of a French captain, Rodman—eh?" called out Lord Milford from his boat.

"Yes, my lord," replied Captain Rodman; and then he muttered to himself: "In such case, though, I shouldn't care to divide the honour of victory with you. If this had been an enemy's ship, I'd rather have grappled her myself, without assistance from any one."

Perhaps, however, Captain Rodman was too confident in his own prowess.

His boat had hardly left the ship, when the master observed to a group of officers standing by:

"It *was* something of a disappointment to see the British ensign flying from the mizzen-gaff of yonder ship; but I can tell you, gentlemen, that had not the Acteon been so close astern of us, I should have been very sorry to have seen the French flag flying in the place of the English ensign. I don't say we couldn't have been the victors, if we had engaged with a ship so much larger than our own; but, for my part, I wouldn't care to attack a seventy-four-gun ship with a frigate."

"Captain Rodman has been hitherto so fortunate," replied the third lieutenant, "that he has no idea of being beaten. I verily believe that he'd attack a whole French squadron single-handed rather than retreat."

"And quite right," put in Mr. Peters, the second lieutenant. "It is in consequence of his pluck that he has been so successful. He'd blow up his ship rather than surrender."

"There, again, I don't agree with him, nor with you, Mr. Peters," said the master, laughing. "I don't think any one can say that he ever saw old Jack Busby flinch or turn tail when it came to fighting. But there's reason in roasting eggs, they say, though I'll be whipped if I know what is meant by the saying; but what *I* mean is that it is foolish to run rashly into danger. And as I've got a wife and children at home, I neither wish to see the inside of a French prison, nor to be blown up because my captain won't surrender. It may be very pleasant to Mr. Peters, but"——

"I didn't say it *was* pleasant," interrupted Peters, angrily; "but I *do* say that I'd perish rather than be beaten"——

"Come, come, gentlemen," interposed the first lieutenant. "Don't let us quarrel. Every man has a right to his own opinion; but as the Majestic is an English ship, it is folly to bandy words about what we *would* have done had she been a French vessel."

"*I* have no wish to quarrel," said the master, offering his hand to the second lieutenant.

"Nor I," said Peters, "and least of all with Mr. Busby." So the two officers shook hands, and the conversation was changed.

Meanwhile Captain Rodman and Lord Milford had arrived alongside the Majestic. Captain Wallbrook, a jovial, hearty seaman of the old school, received the two junior captains at the gangway.

"Welcome on board the Majestic, gentlemen," said he; "though," he added, with a smile, "I suspect, from the appearance of your frigates, that you were preparing to give me a warm reception, and were somewhat disappointed, perhaps, to find me a friend instead of a foe."

Captain Rodman acknowledged that he had at first taken the Majestic for a French ship, and had given orders to prepare for action.

"Well, well, gentlemen," said the old commodore, "perhaps I can make up for your disappointment. I made you both out at sunrise this morning, before either of you, I suspect, sighted the Majestic. I guessed immediately who you were, for I knew your ships were on the way to join the West India fleet, and I assure you I was right glad to fall in with you just in this spot. Let me tell you, gentlemen, that I last night received certain information from the master of an English merchantman, whose vessel I boarded, that there are at this moment five French ships in the harbour of Rio Janeiro. The merchant skipper, who was bound from Liverpool to Rio, saw them just as he was entering the harbour, and very wisely put about and made off as quickly as possible. He told me that he heard from the master of a Portuguese fishing-vessel, whom he fell in with outside the harbour, that these ships, which put in to repair damages after a hard gale of wind, were almost ready for sea, and would *positively* sail to-day.

"Now, gentlemen, *I* happen to know that these French ships are on their way to join Admiral Linois' fleet in the East Indies. They sailed from Cherbourg just six weeks ago, and the ships of my squadron have been on the look-out for them this fortnight past. We missed them, and a few days ago I sent the four vessels that accompanied the Majestic back to the West Indies, and I should have followed them thither myself to-day, had I not heard this news, which somewhat perplexed me. I could do nothing against the squadron with the Majestic alone, and I should have followed them, keeping just out of sight, in the hope that one or two of the ships might drop behind, and give me a chance to cut them off, had I not so happily fallen in with you just in the nick of time. They outnumber us, and the odds are against us in the number of men and the weight of metal. There is one seventy-two-gun ship, and the other four are fifty-gun frigates.

Still, I think we are strong enough to attack them, and I hope we shall be able to give a good account of one or two of them, at least. What say you?"

"*I* shall not be satisfied with one or two, sir," replied Captain Rodman.

"Well, well; we shall see about that. *Your* opinion also is that we ought to attack them, my lord?" said Commodore Wallbrook, addressing Lord Milford.

His lordship bowed.

"Very good! Then we are all agreed on one point. Now, the question is "how to manœuvre so as to get hold of them"——

"If they learn we are in force, they will not come out of the harbour," said Captain Rodman, who was delighted at the idea of a regular naval engagement; for, often as he had been in action, and generally as he had been successful, he had never yet entered into action with more than one or two regular ships of war. He had entered the navy just after the battle of Trafalgar, where the French and Spaniards had received the last of a series of severe lessons, and since that period they had never cared to confront the British in a regular engagement, but had contented themselves with sending single ships to capture merchant vessels, and destroy British commerce. Peace was soon afterwards declared with Spain. But though Captain Rodman had captured many single French ships, and had seen many a French squadron snugly at anchor in port, the Frenchmen had always declined to venture forth and respond to the challenge given by the British squadrons to which he had at different times been attached. Hence his reply to Captain Wallbrook.

"Very probably," said the commodore, in answer to his remark; "but the French commodore cannot yet have obtained any information of our presence in these seas, nor do I intend that he shall obtain such information. My plan is this: I will cruise to and fro with the Majestic in this spot when I am sufficiently distant from the harbour to remain unseen, until the Frenchmen will find it too late to retreat. Captain Milford will steer a few miles to the southward, and lay off and on until the French vessels come forth; and you, Captain Rodman, will keep your ship under the lee of Cape Frio, to the northward. You will see them as soon as they come out of the harbour. It will be your duty *then* to run inside them, and thus cut them off should they attempt to return to port. At the same time you will fire a gun, which will be the signal for the Majestic and the Acteon to close up, and thus we shall *compel* the Frenchmen to come to an action with us. Do you approve of the plan?"

Captain Rodman decidedly approved of the plan, which gave the post of honour to the Conqueror, which vessel, if the French ships showed fight, would have to bear the brunt of the engagement until the Majestic and the Acteon could come to her assistance.

He expressed his satisfaction to the old commodore, and then he and Lord Milford returned to their respective frigates.

Ere another hour had elapsed the Conqueror was lying-to off Cape Frio, and the Majestic and the Acteon were both out of sight, the former cruising to and fro off the harbour of Rio, distant about ten miles, and the latter lying-to at about the same distance to the southward.

Captain Rodman was so anxious that he went aloft to the maintopgallant masthead, and remained there, with his telescope almost constantly at his eye, for four hours. At length his patience was rewarded. He saw a vessel standing out of the distant harbour, which was presently followed by four others. They were too far off to permit him to make out more than that they were large vessels; but from their evident size and number he was satisfied that they were the ships he was waiting for. Keeping in line, and each about a quarter of a mile apart, they steered a westerly course until they were abreast of Cape Frio, when their course was changed a couple of points to the southward.

Captain Rodman now descended from aloft, and made sail on the frigate. For all the master and Lieutenant Peters had said, he was not so foolish as to oppose his ship to five ships of the enemy if he could help it, and his object was to get between the French ships and the harbour without being seen, if it were possible, until he could make sure of the prompt support of the Majestic and the Acteon. He sailed, therefore, warily along the coast, just keeping the French ships in sight from the masthead until the Conqueror was off the harbour, when he changed his course, and followed after the enemy, who as yet appeared to have no suspicion that they were watched. He had again gone aloft when the Conqueror stood out to sea, and anxiously watching the motions of the French ships, he felt confident before long that they had sighted the Majestic, and judged, from their closing with one another, and from the interchange of signals which took place, that they had discovered that she was a ship of war, and were doubtful whether or not she was alone.

Careless now about being seen by them, he again descended to the deck, and ordered a gun to be fired, that being the signal agreed upon for the English ships to close up.

Hardly had the gun been fired before the Acteon hove in sight to the southward, and the Frenchmen evidently saw the three English vessels, and discovered that there had been a preconcerted arrangement to trap them, and bring them to an engagement.

To this, indeed, they appeared nothing loth, and with the rapidity that the French have always shown in manœuvring, they took in all their loftier canvas, and, forming into line, awaited the conflict. In another half hour the Conqueror was almost within range of the nearest French vessel, the Majestic could be seen about the same distance to leeward of the Frenchman, and the Acteon was coming up rapidly.

The Frenchmen backed their mainyards, and quietly awaited the onset; but not a gun was fired until the Conqueror, which was the nearest vessel to the enemy, ran in between the two central French ships, discharging both broadsides as she passed through. The fire was returned, but hardly quick enough, or the Conqueror would have suffered severely. As it was, several of the shot struck her, and four of her men were killed and seven wounded, though the damage had been greater had not the Frenchmen followed their usual practice of firing high, by which means her foretopmast was carried away, and much injury was done to her rigging; but most of the shot passed over her or fell astern.

This act of daring on the part of Captain Rodman, who had thus gained his end, and been the first to open the ball, was heartily cheered on board the Majestic and the Acteon, both of which ships now opened fire, and the Frenchmen, having discovered their mistake, lowered the muzzles of their guns, and the fight became general.

The damage done to the Conqueror's rigging compelled her to run some distance to leeward, in order to clear away the wreck; but this was soon done, and then, wearing round, she bore up again, and with the wind abeam, ranged up on the weather quarter of the French line-of-battle ship.

For some time the firing was kept up incessantly, and the smoke was so dense that it was impossible to see what was going on. At length an explosion took place on board one of the French ships; there was a temporary cessation of the rapid firing, and, the smoke slightly lifting, Captain Rodman saw the Majestic slowly passing him to leeward. Captain Wallbrook hailed him as he passed by:

"Sharp work this, Rodman!" said he. "How are you getting on on board the Conqueror?"

"I have lost several men, and more are disabled," was Captain Rodman's reply; "but we shall win through it. What was that explosion just now?"

"A blow-up on board one of the frigates with which I was engaged," replied the commodore. "The frigate is sinking, and the other ships are taking the men on board. That has caused the cessation in the firing, and given us breathing time. But we are terribly overmatched. Three of the frigates are larger than they were reported to be. I suspect we shall have to carry one or two of them by boarding, if we hope to succeed."

"I have been thinking so myself," answered Captain Rodman. "However, we have got rid of one of the enemy, as you tell me."

"Yes; but her crew go to strengthen the rest. Hark! They are at it again!"

The firing had recommenced. The Majestic passed on, wore round, and in a few minutes was in the hottest of the engagement again, as also was the Conqueror.

For another half hour the roar of the guns and the discharge of musketry from the vessels' tops was incessant. Then again the firing became less heavy, and as the smoke lifted, Captain Rodman saw a large dark object looming up on his weather quarter, within two cables' lengths of the Conqueror.

It was the French line-of-battle ship, with her foresail hauled up, and her lower rigging filled with armed men, ready to board as soon as the vessels should close.

"Ha! ha! The fellows are before us with the game we intended to play," said Captain Rodman to his first lieutenant. "But, no matter, we won't baulk them; though, maybe, we'll give them a surprise. Are the men all ready?"

"All ready, sir," replied the lieutenant.

"Don't let them show themselves till I give the word then, sir. We'll allow the Frenchmen to close with us; but be prepared to meet them."

The lieutenant nodded, and the two ships slowly drifted towards each other, the French ship, from her greater height out of the water, appearing as though she must crush or sink the frigate in the collision.

To make what followed comprehensible, I must explain that Captain Rodman had already got together and armed two bodies of boarders, one of which was to be led by Mr. Peters, who during the engagement had commanded on the lower deck, and the other by himself. It had been his purpose, as soon as the firing should slacken, to watch his opportunity, and, if possible, run between two French vessels and board both at the same moment.

The appearance of the French line-of-battle ship so close to him had, however, compelled him to alter his plan. He, therefore, allowed the French ship to close with the frigate, as if he had been taken by surprise, but as the two vessels came together with a terrific shock, he shouted the command:

"Boarders away!" And instantly, as if they had sprung out of the decks, a large party of men, led by Lieutenant Peters, sprang into the French ship's fore-rigging, and as the Frenchmen struggled to repel the unexpected assault, Captain Rodman, at the head of another party, sprung into the main and mizzen shrouds, amidst loud shouts and yells of fury and vengeance. The Frenchmen, not anticipating such an attack, were taken by surprise. Nevertheless they fought with savage desperation. A great number of men on both sides fell, and were crushed to death between the ships' sides. The rigging was cut and hacked to pieces, and for some time the conflict seemed doubtful.

Mr. Bowling, however, ordered a large force of marines to ascend to the

Conqueror's fore, main, and mizzen tops, and fire down upon the Frenchmen, who, thus attacked by a third party, at length partially gave way, and the Englishmen gained a footing on the French ship's decks. There the conflict, for some minutes, was awful. Men met, breast to breast, and foot to foot. They seized one another by the throat, and hurled each other to the deck, or into the sea, sometimes falling together, and still grappling and fighting until the waters closed over them. The decks were slippery with carnage, and encumbered with the bodies of the slain and wounded, who lay in heaps, one on the top of another. At length the French flag was hauled down, and there was a cry that the ship had surrendered. Afterwards it was discovered that an English midshipman had hauled down the tricolour, and run up in its place an English Union Jack, which he had brought on board the French ship with him. But the Frenchmen, seeing their flag hauled down, believed that their own captain had surrendered. They gave way, and the English had possession of the ship.

While this deadly conflict was progressing, the heavy firing had almost ceased. In fact, it was only kept up by one of the French ships, which had hauled off, and hove-to at a short distance, just within range, whence she, from time to time, fired a broadside at one or other of the English vessels, though with but little effect.

The Acteon had been boarded and nearly carried by the French frigate which had received on board the crew of the sinking ship, and being thus doubly manned, was enabled to pass fresh relays of boarders upon the English frigate's decks. Indeed, Lord Milford must have surrendered, had not Captain Wallbrook, after the Majestic had carried the remaining French ship by boarding, come to his assistance.

The appearance, however, of the Majestic's crew on the Acteon's decks, compelled the Frenchmen to give way, and the day was won!

One French line-of-battle ship, the *Timolean*, of seventy-two guns, and two frigates, the *Diane* and the *Mercure*, each of sixty guns, remained in the hands of the English.

The *Guerrier*, of forty-eight guns, was partially blown-up, and sank at an early period of the engagement, and the *Spartiate*, of sixty guns—the vessel which had hauled off when it was apparent that the French were losing the day, and had tried to annoy the English by firing upon them at intervals—set sail, and made off when she saw that all hope was lost, and succeeded in effecting her escape.

The engagement, however, had been a most terrific one. The English and French ships alike were, to appearance, mere wrecks, and the loss on both sides was frightful.

Commodore Wallbrook was severely wounded by a splinter, and having been carried below, was confined to his cot. The first lieutenant of the Majestic was killed, and the third and fourth lieutenants were badly wounded. She had lost several of her warrant officers, and ninety-six seamen and marines were slain or desperately wounded. The loss on board the Acteon was equally great, though Captain Lord Milford had fortunately escaped unhurt.

On board the Conqueror, Captain Rodman had been wounded in the shoulder by a cutlass, while in the act of leading the boarders. Mr. Wilton, the third lieutenant, was killed, as also were two of her midshipmen, and her boatswain and gunner. She had lost sixty seamen and marines, and twenty-six more were severely wounded.

The loss on board the French ships was greater still, though it was impossible to ascertain the number of the slain. Two of the French captains were killed, and one went down with the frigate that partially blew up and afterwards sank. Still, notwithstanding the severe loss of the Frenchmen, seven hundred and eighty prisoners—officers, seamen, and marines, many of them seriously wounded— remained in the hands of the English.

The engagement was reported in the English newspapers to have been the most severe—considering the small number of ships engaged—of any that had taken place during the whole of the long war. Captain Rodman at last had it in his power to say that he had fought and conquered in a general engagement!

For several days, however, his wound confined him to his cabin.

The English ships, with their prizes, put into Rio Janeiro to refit, and there remained for three weeks, when they again sailed for the West Indies. Most of the wounded men and officers had, by this time, sufficiently recovered to be able to return to their duty. Captain Rodman and Commodore Wallbrook were again able to assume the command of their ships, though the former still suffered from the wound in his shoulder, which the surgeon feared, at one time, would cause the loss of his left arm. There was, however, no fear of this now, and it was hoped that, in a few weeks, he would be perfectly recovered.

The number of men killed in the engagement, and the necessity that existed of sending officers and men from the English vessels to navigate the three French ships, reduced the crews so seriously that, taking this fact into consideration together with the condition of the English ships themselves—which could only be partially and temporarily refitted at Rio—they were none of them in a fit condition to meet an enemy, and it was thought desirable that they should keep as close together as possible during the passage, so that they might be able to support one another in case of attack. However, they arrived safely at Port Royal, Jamaica, without accident, and without having sighted any suspicious looking vessel. Here the captains were relieved of the weight of anxiety attendant upon the charge of so many prisoners of war, and they and their officers and crews received the hearty congratulations of the Governor-General, the admiral, the authorities, and all the white inhabitants of the island, for their gallant and successful attack on a French squadron so greatly superior to their own force in men and guns, as well as in the number of ships engaged, the news of which had preceded their arrival.

CHAPTER XVII.

As I have said heretofore, Captain Rodman's chief object in changing his cruising-ground from the South Pacific Ocean to the Carribean Seas was that he might bear the Acteon company. He did not like the idea of his rival, Captain Lord Milford, being so comparatively near to England and Lucy Sinclair, while he remained so far distant from both; but had he known when he was at Valparaiso that which he learnt on his arrival at Port Royal, he would have been tenfold more anxious to sail for the West Indies than he really had been.

Letters awaited both him and Captain Milford at Port Royal, which informed them that Captain Sinclair and his wife and daughter were on a visit to St. Kitts, and that the captain and the ladies would be delighted to see them, should the duties of the service lead either the Conqueror or the Acteon to visit that island.

This was news indeed! Captain Rodman was aware that Captain Sinclair derived a considerable portion of his wealth from the large estates he possessed in the island of St. Kitts and others of the West India islands; but he had no idea that the captain intended to visit these estates, and even had such an idea entered his mind, he would have thought it very improbable that Captain Sinclair would bring his wife and daughter with him.

It appeared, however, from the letters, that Mrs. Sinclair had lately suffered from severe illness, and though she was nearly recovered, the doctors had strongly recommended her to take up her abode for a few months in a tropical climate, and had especially mentioned St. Kitts, as one of the most healthful of the West India islands, and Captain Sinclair had immediately embarked for St. Kitts, thus seizing an opportunity to visit the estates which he had not seen for many years, while he at the same time followed up the doctor's recommendations.

Lord Milford's letter was from Captain Sinclair himself; but *two* letters awaited Captain Rodman—one from Captain Sinclair, and one, which had been despatched secretly, from his daughter Lucy.

Now, it chanced that Captain Milford's servant, on going to the post-office at Port Royal, to inquire whether there were any letters for his master, was told that there was one letter for Captain Lord Milford, of the Acteon, and several others for officers and seamen belonging to the men-of-war in the port.

"Let me see," said the postmaster—"here are two letters, among the rest, for Captain Rodman, of his Majesty's ship Conqueror. One of them appears to be addressed in the same handwriting as that addressed to Lord Milford; the other appears to be addressed in a lady's hand. I guess I ought to send *that* letter on board the Conqueror," he added, with a smile. "Perhaps Captain Rodman—who, I hear, is quite a young man—will be expecting it."

"*I'll* take both letters with me, if you like," said the servant. "I know that Lord Milford will be goin' aboard the Conqueror on my return, to arx how Captain Rodman's wownded shoulder gets on. I heerd him say how he should."

"Then you may take them with you," replied the postmaster; "only be sure that you deliver them safely to your master. And here's a letter for the second lieutenant of the Acteon, and one for the boatswain, and one for the sail-maker. Perhaps you'd best take 'em all."

This the servant did, and on his return to the frigate, handed the letters to

Lord Milford, that his lordship might give them to the persons to whom they were addressed.

Lord Milford glanced at the superscriptions.

"You'd better give these letters to the people they belong to, Watson," said he, handing back the letters directed to persons on board his own frigate. "Those two for Captain Rodman *I'll* take charge of. I'm going on board the Conqueror directly after breakfast."

He then opened his letter, and read it with evident surprise and satisfaction.

"Well, well," he muttered, "I little thought that I should meet with Sinclair out here. I must find out some excuse for sailing for St. Kitts, as soon as possible. Miss Lucy might as well have written herself, though, if it had been but a line; but I suppose she's too bashful."

He then glanced again at the superscriptions of Captain Rodman's letters.

"That's from Captain Sinclair—I'd know his handwriting wherever I saw it," he muttered; and this—God bless me! that's Lucy's handwriting!" he exclaimed, as he examined the second letter more narrowly. He looked at the postmark. "Yes," he went on, "it *is* from St. Kitts. It's strange—very strange—that Lucy Sinclair should find time to write to Rodman, and never send a line to *me*!"

Lord Milford was at once seized with a fit of jealousy. I have stated that he, when he left England, was unaware of the fact that Captain Rodman and Miss Sinclair were secretly engaged to each other. He was aware that Captain Sinclair had a high opinion of Captain Rodman, and that he regarded him with feelings of friendship; but he had no notion that Lucy was attached to the young captain by any stronger tie than that of friendship.

Now, however, all sorts of fancies and suspicions entered his mind.

He recollected how cool Lucy had been in her conduct towards him, although her parents had given their sanction to his courtship. He had set this coolness down as the natural shyness and bashfulness of a young lady; but now he remembered how Lucy had blushed, and how earnest she had become, whenever he spoke to her of Captain Rodman, or whenever she heard Captain Rodman's name mentioned with praise. He recalled to mind also how, whenever he had spoken himself to Captain Rodman of Lucy—which he had very often done—the captain had appeared to be annoyed, and had abruptly changed the topic of conversation; and on more than one occasion, when he (Lord Milford) had alluded to his future marriage with Lucy, Captain Rodman had answered him with something very like a sneer of contempt, and had sometimes actually behaved almost with rudeness towards him.

"I see it all now," he muttered. "There's a secret understanding between the two. Miss Lucy, who would hardly speak to *me* when we were alone together, can *write* to Captain Rodman, and Rodman —— Well, I think it is too bad. It is scandalous on his part that he should conceal his sentiments regarding the young lady from me, though I have spoken to *him* scores of times of *my* attachment to her, and have told him plainly that I have the sanction of her parents to our marriage."

He considered to himself whether or not he should deliver the letter to Captain Rodman, and whether he would not be justified—whether indeed it was not his duty—to send the letter back to St. Kitts, enclosed to Captain Sinclair.

He would gladly have given a thousand pounds to have opened and read the letter; and more than once he fingered the seal, as though his fingers itched to break it open.

A sense of honour, however, forbade him to do otherwise than to deliver the letter intact to him to whom it was addressed; and leaving the breakfast, to which he had seated himself with a good appetite, almost untasted, he hastened upon deck, ordered his gig to be lowered, and went off on board the Conqueror, possessed with anything but his usual friendly feelings for his brother officer, Captain Rodman.

On his arrival on board the frigate, he was invited, as usual, to the captain's cabin; and after a few remarks of an ordinary nature, he presented Captain Rodman with the letters he had received from the post-office, keenly watching the effect they produced.

Captain Rodman started with surprise.

"From St. Kitts," he exclaimed. "I know that handwriting well. It is Captain Sinclair's; but I am greatly surprised to find that *he* is in the West Indies."

He had opened Captain Sinclair's letter while he was speaking; but his eyes at this moment fell upon the second letter, and with another start, and with flushed cheeks, he laid Captain Sinclair's letter aside while he read that which he had received from Lucy.

Lord Milford watched him keenly. He remarked the indignation, mingled with satisfaction, manifest in the expression of his features; until having read Lucy's letter twice over, he folded it up and placed it in his pocket, and then proceeded to read the letter he had first opened.

"This is indeed a surprise," he said, at length. "Captain Sinclair and his wife and daughter are at St. Kitts. I was aware that the captain possessed property in the West India islands; but I little expected to hear that he was in the West Indies. I presume, however, that he has written to you as well as to me?"

"He has," replied Lord Milford; "but *I* have not been favoured with a letter from Miss Sinclair, as it appears *you* have been."

There was something in the tone of Lord Milford's voice, and in the expression of his countenance while he spoke, which annoyed and offended Captain Rodman far more than the words he had uttered.

"Miss Sinclair, I presume, is at liberty to write to whom she pleases, my lord," he replied.

It required very little to excite Lord Milford's feelings of jealousy into those of anger.

"Yes, I suppose Miss Sinclair may write to whom she pleases," he said; "but I doubt much whether her father would be well pleased if he knew that she had favoured a comparative stranger—a mere friend—with a letter, while she has neglected to write even a line to one who holds very different relations towards her, and who has the consent of her parents to make her his wife on his return to England."

"You allude to yourself, my lord, I presume?" said Captain Rodman.

"Yes, sir," was the reply. "I *do* allude to myself."

"And pray, my lord," said Captain Rodman, "by whose authority do you speak of me as a comparative stranger to —— a mere friend of Miss Sinclair's? I have known the young lady from my early boyhood. And since you have spoken so freely, let me tell you that *I*—before even *you* were personally known to Miss Sinclair—received Captain Sinclair's permission to address his daughter as a suitor for her hand; and what is *more* to the purpose, my lord, received his daughter's assurance that my suit was favourably received by her. This letter informs me that the young lady is still of the same mind, and that she regards the vows we interchanged as equally binding to her and to myself; and that being the case, my lord, no one has a right to thrust himself between us, nor is it the part of a gentleman or a man of honour to press his suit when he is well aware that it is distasteful to its object."

Lord Milford retorted sharply. High words ensued, and Lord Milford half an hour afterwards quitted the ship, fuming with anger and jealousy.

That same day he waited upon the admiral, and expressed his desire to visit the island of St. Kitts. Lords and titled personages are often favoured above less fortunate individuals, in the army and navy, as well as on shore. The admiral thought it desirable that a frigate should be immediately despatched to cruise in the vicinity of St. Kitts and the other Leeward islands, and appointed the Acteon to that duty; and Captain Rodman, to his great vexation, saw the frigate sail from Port Royal that same evening, bound for the island at which Lucy Sinclair was then residing with her parents.

As I have said heretofore, Captain Rodman, though he was free to cruise wheresoever he believed his vessel could be of most service, was still subject to the authority of the admiral, or other senior officer, at any station or port he entered.

Moreover, without the admiral's permission he could hardly have taken his frigate to a place whereat a ship of war was already stationed, unless he could have shown satisfactorily that two vessels were needed there.

However, he possessed the peculiar gift of making himself a favourite with almost every person whose favour he sought, or whose friendship was worth having.

The port-admiral at Port Royal was an old acquaintance and friend of his, and, as was the case with most persons who knew him, the old admiral held him in great regard.

Scarcely had the Acteon got clear of the harbour before Captain Rodman made his appearance at the port-admiral's office, and requested to be sent to St. Kitts with his frigate.

"Why, bless my heart!" exclaimed the old gentleman. "Are you fellows gone crazy? What attraction is there at St. Kitts? This very morning Lord Milford called upon me with a similar request to yours, and as I thought it would be as well to have a smart frigate cruising about among the Leeward islands, I sent the Acteon thither, with orders to make St. Kitts her chief station. I'm sorry you did not first make the request, Rodman. I would have given you the preference over Lord Milford. But you're too late, my dear boy. It will never do to send another frigate to the Leeward islands—above all, such a fine ship as the Conqueror, while there's so much work to be done elsewhere in these seas!"

Captain Rodman, however, was unwilling to accept this refusal of his request. He and the old admiral had a long chat together. What was the nature of their conversation was best known to themselves. But some notion of it may be gathered from the fact that when it was ended the admiral said (slapping Captain Rodman familiarly on the shoulder as he spoke):

"Well, then, you *shall* go, my dear boy. I may get a hauling over the coals from my Lords of the Admiralty, but I'll risk it. I don't care about it. I hate double-dealing, and it's a confounded shame for a father—I don't care who the mischief he is—to compel a young girl to accept the addresses of a fellow for whom she don't care a brass farthing. Go, my dear boy. Be off this very night if you like. I see now why that lordling of a captain was so anxious to go to St. Kitts. Lord, how I should like to see his face when he sees the Conqueror entering the harbour, following close at his heels! Not but what Milford's a decent fellow enough, and a thorough seaman—lord as he is, and earl as he will be. But fair play is a jewel the world over. So toss up your caps. Pitch into one another, and let the best man win the prize!"

Captain Rodman quitted the office of the jolly old port-admiral in a much better humour than he was in when he entered it. He expected that Lord Milford would try to influence Captain Sinclair against him, and perhaps would endeavour to urge the father to force the young lady's inclinations, and accept him (Lord Milford) as her husband. But he had Lucy's letter in his pocket, and in that letter Lucy had written:

"My father and mother still urge me to accept the offer of Lord Milford; but, my dear Tom, though I still adhere to my resolve never while my parents live to marry in opposition to their wishes, do not fear that I will ever be induced to wed any one for whom I entertain no affection nor regard. I still look upon the vows we interchanged as binding to us both, and I am still, as ever, yours, and yours only."

He read these lines over again as soon as he got on board. Then he gave orders to the first lieutenant to get the frigate under weigh immediately; and as she sailed out of the harbour, shortly after midnight, he muttered to himself:

"At any rate, I shall be on the spot almost as soon as my rival. 'Fair-play,' as the old port-admiral says, 'is a jewel, the wide world over.' We'll see whether Lord Milford or I will win the prize!"

The Acteon reached St. Kitts but twenty-four hours before the Conqueror appeared off the harbour, greatly to the astonishment, and somewhat to the dismay, of Lord Milford.

As soon as she dropped her anchor, Captain Rodman went on shore, leaving the first lieutenant to furl sails, and make the ship taut and snug.

He easily found his way to the residence of Captain Sinclair; but, greatly to his amazement, he was, for the first time in his life, received very coolly by that gentleman—his first friend and patron. Captain Sinclair even indulged in ill-natured sarcasm.

"It seems to me, Rodman," said he, after having coldly shaken hands with his visitor, and replied briefly and carelessly to the few questions he put, and to his inquiries after Mrs. and Miss Sinclair—"it seems to me that the service has changed greatly since the days when *I* went to sea. Naval captains had something else to do in those days besides dodging one another about from place to place, and giving annoyance to those whom they profess to regard as their friends. It is necessary to have a frigate stationed among these islands; but the admiral should know that *one* vessel like the Acteon is enough to guard our coasts from any enemy that is likely to appear; and surely he might have found employment for the Conqueror elsewhere. Indeed, the days have been, and are not so long gone by, when Captain Rodman would have been more eager to serve his king and country than to idle his time and employ his Majesty's ship that he commands to carry him where his presence is otherwise than agreeable to those upon whom he thrusts himself."

Captain Rodman spoke of Captain Sinclair's former kindness and friendship, and asked to be informed how, or by what means, he had incurred the captain's displeasure.

"You ask, Rodman," replied Captain Sinclair, "to be informed of what you are already aware of;" and then he spoke of his desire that his daughter should give her hand to Lord Milford, who had it in his power to raise her to a proud position. "And you must know, Rodman," he continued, "that your presence here, to counteract my plans and wishes, as well as those of Mrs. Sinclair, is objectionable."

Captain Rodman then urged, in his own behalf, that Captain Sinclair had known of his affection for his (the captain's) daughter; and that, so far from being displeased with that knowledge, he had not only expressed satisfaction there-with, but had given the promise that he would not oppose his (Captain Rodman's) marriage with his daughter at the termination of the present cruise.

This latter assertion, however, Captain Sinclair denied. He acknowledged that he had seen and had offered no opposition to the growing affection of his daughter Lucy and Captain Rodman for each other. But the captain, he said, was then but a young midshipman, and he had looked upon their mutual attachment as but a boy's and girl's fancy; and if he had not subsequently opposed it, it was because he had not then given any serious thought to his daughter's future settlement in life. Nay, more, he acknowledged that had not Lucy received an offer of marriage so very much more advantageous, he might not have refused eventually to accept Captain Rodman as his son-in-law. But such an advantageous offer having been made, he considered it his duty to accept it in his daughter's name, and in her behalf; and, such being the case, he thought that Captain Rodman should, as a gentleman, and a man of honour, think no more of what was, after all, but a mere youthful fancy.

Much more was said on both sides, until at length both the gentlemen grew angry, and Captain Rodman left the house without seeing either Lucy or Mrs. Sinclair. He was satisfied from certain words spoken by Captain Sinclair in his anger, that Lord Milford had, by some means, contrived to set his former friend and patron against him, and he resolved, if he could prove that such were the case, to be revenged upon Lord Milford somehow or other, at whatever cost, or hazard to himself. Lord Milford, however, kept out of his way, though he discovered that his lordship was a constant visitor at Captain Sinclair's house whenever the Acteon was in the harbour. Lucy Sinclair and Captain Rodman did, however, contrive to meet each other occasionally, in secret, despite the strict watch that was kept upon the young lady; and though these interviews were brief, and tearful on Lucy's part, they afforded hope and encouragement to her lover; for the young lady persisted in saying, and called heaven to witness to her truth, that she would never give her hand to Lord Milford, and that though she would never wed without her parents' consent, she would wed no other than the lover to whom she had plighted her troth, and whom she regarded as her affianced husband.

Six months passed away, and the Acteon and the Conqueror still remained upon the station, though they made frequent short cruises among the Leeward islands during this period. Every time the Conqueror came into port, however, Captain Sinclair appeared to grow more and more unfriendly towards Captain Rodman, while the enmity between Captain Rodman and Lord Milford had grown into hatred. They met occasionally, and scowled upon one another, but never spoke, and each appeared to feel that their greatest pleasure would be to hear that some great evil had befallen the other. At length Captain Sinclair decided upon returning to England. He was to embark on the 1st of October—nearly a month distant; and Captain Rodman, who was absent from St. Kitts when Captain Sinclair came to this decision, was informed, when he came into the port a few days afterwards, that Lucy Sinclair was to be married to Lord Milford previous to her father's departure. Another report said that Lord Milford was to follow the family to England, and that the marriage was to take place immediately on his arrival; and this latter seemed to be the most probable report of the two. All agreed, however, that Miss Sinclair had at length been persuaded by her parents to cast off her former lover, and accept the hand of Lord Milford; and while some persons blamed the young lady, others said that she had acted wisely—for, by some means or other, the rivalry that existed between the two captains had become known, the frequent visits of the two frigates to the island being remarked upon. The love affair of their commanders was the common talk of the white inhabitants, and even of the negro slaves; and while some took part with Captain Rodman, others were as strong partisans of Lord Milford.

Captain Rodman was half crazy with rage. It would not have been well for either of them had he and Lord Milford met each other just at this period, in a lonely spot. He could not ascertain whether the report was true or false, nor could he see Lucy Sinclair to make inquiry, and to charge her with falsehood and faithlessness, if she confessed that the report *was* true.

Latterly she had not met him in secret, as she had been wont to do. Either a stricter watch was kept upon her, or conscious of her faithlessness, she dared not meet her lover again.

Captain Rodman naturally believed that the latter was the case, and he determined to write her a letter before she sailed for England, charging her with falsehood and perjury, and casting her off for ever.

This letter he wrote and sent by the hand of a faithful negro, and without awaiting a reply—which he did not believe she would dare to write—he sailed again out of the harbour.

  *   *   *   *   *   *   *

It wanted but a week to the day on which Captain Sinclair was to embark with his family for England. Lucy was not yet married to Lord Milford, nor would she be before she sailed. This fact Captain Rodman had somehow learnt; but he firmly believed that Lord Milford would follow her to England, and that the wedding would take place immediately after his arrival.

The Conqueror lay at anchor in the harbour of Nevis, an island close to St. Kitts, and on the day of her arrival the Acteon also entered the harbour and came to an anchor. Never had Captain Rodman been more eager to engage an enemy's ship than he now was to engage in deadly strife with Lord Milford, and his lordship felt an equal degree of animosity towards him. Willingly would they have met on shore in some secret spot and fought with a stern resolve that but one of them should leave that spot in life.

The two captains had come into the port of Nevis* that they might witness the departure, and see the last of the ship on board of which Captain Sinclair had taken passage for England for himself and his family; though, of course, the object of each was unknown to the other.

At the date of which I am now about to write, there occurred in the West India seas the most terrible cyclone that has ever been experienced within the memory of mankind. Never before had so fearful a visitation been known or heard of—never since has one so terrible been experienced.

It commenced off the coast of Venezuela, and with irresistible force and swiftness swept over the windward and the leeward islands, taking the Bahamas in its destructive track, until, having swept over the Gulf of Mexico, it caught the west extremity of the island of Cuba, passing thence over Jamaica and St. Domingo, until it wore out its fury near the spot where it had its rise.†

The second morning after his arrival at Nevis, Captain Rodman, while

---

* Nevis, the birthplace of the late Empress Josephine, is one of the smallest of the leeward islands of the Antilles. It lies so near to St. Kitts that ships lying at anchor in the harbour of one of these islands can be plainly seen from the harbour of the other.

† A cyclone differs from a hurricane, inasmuch as it is of longer duration, and it sweeps over a much wider space. It is, in fact, a furious rotatory tempest, advancing on a line until it has completed a circle; and while nothing that opposes its course can withstand its fury, it often happens that places or ships in the centre of its rotatory motion feel nothing of it.

standing on the quarter-deck of the Conqueror, saw one of the small schooners that at that period were employed in carrying passengers from one of the West India islands to another, enter the harbour, and lie-to abreast of the Acteon, and shortly afterwards he saw Lord Milford pass in his gig from the Acteon to the schooner. His lordship went on board the beautiful little vessel, and his gig returned to the frigate, while the schooner filled her sails, and went on her passage to Basseterre, the chief town of St. Kitts; and as he watched the schooner's progress, Captain Rodman thought, with feelings of the utmost bitterness, that Lord Milford had gone to take his farewell of Lucy and her parents before they sailed, when he would follow them with his frigate, to England.

For some days past the weather had been strangely dull and brooding, and some people had prophesied that a hurricane was threatening; but on the previous day, while Captain Rodman had been walking on shore near the beach, about a mile distant from the town, he heard a strange rumbling in the air, and then the ground shook so violently beneath his feet that he was thrown down; and while in the act of rising, he beheld the sea suddenly recede, with a frightful roar, leaving a mile of shelving reach, that in ordinary times was always covered with water, perfectly dry. Then, with a rush and roar twice as loud as those with which they receded, the waters turned with inconceivable rapidity, sweeping over beach and meadow land, until they reached half a mile above high water mark, and washed the captain's feet where he stood. Then they returned to their usual bounds, and all was calm and still.

The captain looked towards the town. He knew that there had been an earthquake, and he expected to see that the houses had been shaken to ruins; but all appeared the same as usual, though in walking towards the town, he came every now and then upon some negro hut that had fallen to the ground, or some tree that had been uprooted.

On reaching the town he found the people just recovering from the consternation into which they had been thrown. He was told by them that an earthquake had prevailed, in a greater or lesser degree, throughout the island.

It had been partial in its effects. In some parts of the island it had hardly been felt; in others, villages had been shaken to ruins, and many persons seriously injured, and quantities of cattle killed. It had been the same in the town. Some of the streets were in ruins—others had scarcely suffered at all.

On returning on board his ship, he was told that those on board the frigate had felt a shock as though the keel of the vessel had struck the bottom.

The frigate had rocked violently to and fro, but all was over in a few moments, and nothing extraordinary remained to be seen. The fishermen and the masters of the droghers, that had been out at sea, had a similar story to tell. But they had returned to the harbour unharmed.

Towards evening the dull, brooding weather cleared up, the sky became bright and clear, and those who had dreaded the approach of a hurricane now said that it was the earthquake which had been threatened, and they thanked heaven that it had come and passed away, and done so little mischief after all.

Captain Rodman was still gazing across the bay in no pleasant mood, when his attention was attracted to a vivid green cloud rising from the horizon, to leeward, against the wind, slowly at first, but with ever-increasing rapidity. At the same instant he heard a dull roar in the far distance, which grew upon his ear as he listened. In a moment his decision was formed. That the hurricane *was* coming he felt assured, though he little anticipated what followed. He had had a previous experience of hurricanes, but he had never been in a cyclone.

He ordered the frigate to be got under weigh immediately. He did not wa
to heave up the anchor, but ordered the cable to be slipped, and the end to b
attached to a buoy, so that the cable and anchor could be recovered at any futur
time. Then, under the maintopsail and foresail, he ran out to sea, determined t
get as wide an offing as possible before the tempest should commence.

The wind blew freshly from the land, and, while running before it, he ordere
the topgallant masts to be struck, and everything on deck and aloft to be firml
secured. As soon as he got well clear of the land, he hauled up the maintopsa
and struck the topmasts, allowing the ship still to run out to sea under her fore
course, while she was reduced to her lower masts, which alone remained standing

The harbour of Nevis, as well as that of St. Kitts, contained several merchan
vessels, as well as the Acteon frigate, which still remained at anchor.

As the Conqueror passed the Acteon, Captain Rodman shouted to her officer
to get under weigh directly, if they wished to save the frigate; but they eithe
did not hear, or did not heed him. It was the same with the merchant ships.

"To sea, my men—to sea immediately, if you would save your ships or you
lives!" he shouted, as he passed them by; but the men were busily occupied i
taking in cargo, in order to be ready to sail with the convoy, and, like those o
board the frigate, they either did not hear, or did not heed him. There was
report that the Acteon was appointed to convoy these ships to England; bu
Captain Rodman did not know whether the report was true or false, for he hel
no communication with the Acteon now.

When well out of the harbour, he looked around him. The little schooner o
board which Lord Milford had taken passage was still in sight; but, to Captai
Rodman's surprise she was not making for Basseterre, in St. Kitts, but wa
standing on along the land, as if bound for St. Eustatius, or some other nea
island.

A glance to seaward showed him the awful livid green cloud, still rising an
spreading against the wind. All around was fair and bright. The sky overhea
was blue and cloudless—the sea sparkled beneath the sun's rays; but the hollov
murmur in the air was now continuous, and louder and nearer, and the ominou
green cloud, which at first appeared little bigger than a man's hand, and ha
risen slowly, had now spread over half the circuit of the horizon, and was rising
with marvellous rapidity, casting a baleful shadow, as it rose, over the sea
Captain Rodman stood watching it for a few moments, and then turned hi
head and gazed aloft. The next instant the wind swept over the ship with
roar like thunder. The foresail was blown clean out of the bolt-ropes, and th
captain and every officer and man on deck was thrown off his feet. The sk
darkened as if a curtain had been suddenly drawn across the sun, and the spra
swept over the ship like rain driven before a furious wind. This first gust was s
violent that it took away the breath of all who strove to face it, and the spra
drops felt like fierce, stinging rain.

The frigate keeled over as if she would go on her beam ends, though no sai
was set, and nothing save the lower masts was standing on board; but in th
brief lull that followed she righted, and was got round head to wind —
tarpauling having been lashed in the foremast shrouds to steady her. Scarcel
was this done before a second gust—violent as the first—swept across the sea
The atmosphere became dark almost as midnight. It was impossible to see th
ship's length ahead, or around her. The only light came from the foaming
water, while a dense fog, caused by the spray, filled the air. Then the officer
and men felt themselves struck and bruised by strange missiles, which came from
they knew not where. Boughs, sticks, stones, shingles, together with clouds o

sand and dust, swept over the ship—or, striking violently against the lower masts, the shingles and sticks and stones fell upon the decks, which were strewn with them, until they were again lifted by the wind, and borne on till they fell into the sea.

These materials had been carried off from the shores of the surrounding islands, and had been borne many miles through the air on the wings of the hurricane.

Then the heavens opened, and flashes of fiery, forked lightning darted forth, the thunder rolled, mingling its sound with the howling of the wind, and rain fell in torrents—or rather, was borne by the fury of the tempest, mingled with showers of salt spray, horizontally across the decks of the frigate. And thus at noonday—surrounded by the darkness of midnight. and assailed on every hand by the fierce warring elements that seemed in their savage, unrelenting fury, to be endowed with sentient power, and to rejoice in wild delight over the destruction they wrought—the Conqueror lay utterly helpless, drifting before the hurricane, none knew whither. All hands were on deck, for it was no time now, when, as some fancied and whispered with awe, that the judgment day had surely come, to take shelter below. Yet no one dared stir from the spot where he stood—lashed firmly, or clinging with both hands, to rails or bulwarks—for the furious gusts that burst forth at quickly recurring intervals, as if to add new strength to the hurricane, would have instantly carried any man who had dared to let go his hold into the foaming sea, as if he were a mere featherweight!

It is utterly impossible for those who live in temperate climes even to conceive an idea of the fierce fury of the elements when they rise in their irresistible force to sweep the shores and seas of the tropics!

And yet, for the time being, at least, those on board the Conqueror were probably in a condition of greater comfort and security than were their fellow-creatures on shore or in harbour for a hundred miles around them; and Captain Rodman, as he stood on the frigate's quarter-deck, clinging to a rope wound round the taffrail, thought with bitter grief of the probable fate of Lucy Sinclair and her father and mother, and of those he had lately left on board their ships, snug in harbour, who had declined to accept his warning. The ships, he felt assured, could never have withstood for a moment the first furious gust that heralded the tempest. Ere now they had gone on shore, and most likely all on board had perished. Nor could he hope for a better fate for those on shore. He knew from what he had heard and read, as well as from his own experience, that the strongest dwelling affords no security against the hurricane in its might, nor the densest forest no shelter. Towns and villages, mansions and cottages, are sometimes swept away as if they were towns and houses of cardboard, and forest trees are often uprooted as though they were mere twigs. Ere now, he thought, the islands of St. Kitts and Nevis, he had so lately left, smiling in sunshine, and the abodes of wealth and plenty, were in all probability in ruin and desolation. So far, he and those with him were safe; but he knew not what might be his own and their fate ere another hour, perhaps ere another minute, had passed away. He and they could only wait!

CHAPTER XVIII.

LORD MILFORD, when he embarked on board the Ariel—the beautiful little passenger schooner which had sailed from Nevis shortly before the cyclone commenced—was not bound to Basseterre, St. Kitts, as Captain Rodman had suspected. Unknown to him (Captain Rodman), Captain Sinclair and his wife and daughter had gone on a visit to the little island of St. Eustatius, a few days previous to the arrival of the Conqueror at Nevis, to spend the last few days of his sojourn in the West Indies with an old friend who resided on that island. Lord Milford, better informed than his rival, was aware of this, and he had taken the opportunity Captain Sinclair's visit to St. Eustatius afforded to pay his addresses to, or rather to force his attentions upon, Lucy Sinclair, safe from any intrusion on the part of Captain Rodman—a mischance he was always anticipating when he visited the young lady at her father's residence in Basseterre.

At the same moment that Captain Rodman was sailing out of the harbour of Nevis to obtain an offing before the hurricane that he knew was threatened should commence, Captain Sinclair, his friend, Colonel Daintree, and his daughter Lucy were strolling together in Colonel Daintree's grounds, from which there was a delightful view of the ocean.

The two gentlemen were in earnest conversation, hardly taking notice of anything around them. Lucy had been for some time gazing across the sea.

"Papa," she said presently, "look at the sky! See yonder cloud! I think I never saw anything so strange and beautiful. It is of the colour of an emerald. And yet there is something awful in its aspect. I have been watching it for some minutes. At first it was a mere brilliant green speck in the horizon, and it rose and spread slowly; but see now. It covers half the sky, and appears to be rushing towards us swiftly, as I speak!"

Captain Sinclair gazed in the direction his daughter pointed out.

"If my old West India experience is not forgotten," he said, gravely, "that cloud, and the general and unusual aspect of the sky, portend a hurricane."

"Something worse than an ordinary hurricane, and heaven knows *that* is bad enough," said Colonel Daintree, in a tone of evident alarm and anxiety. "But *once* before—many years ago—I saw such signs in the heavens. A cyclone then swept over these seas. Hundreds of vessels of different sizes were wrecked, hundreds of human lives were lost, the loss of cattle was estimated by thousands, and the crops on almost every island from Barbadoes to New Providence were utterly destroyed. In one short hour I was a poorer man by five thousand pounds. Towns and villages were laid in ruins throughout the Antilles,* and many years elapsed ere the islands recovered from the effects of that terrible tempest. . . . Good heaven!" he continued—"how swiftly that cloud approaches! There is no time to be lost, Captain Sinclair. My dear young lady, you had better seek shelter immediately. Not that a dwelling-house is always the safest place in these dreadful convulsions of the elements; but if any place on the island can withstand the shock of the tempest, I think my house will."

* The correct name of what are commonly called the West India islands.

Coming to the rescue.

See page 9J.

Lucy turned pale, and took her father's arm. Captain Sinclair hastened with her towards the house.

"I *was* in hope," the colonel went on, "that the partial earthquake that was felt a couple of days ago explained the strange brooding weather we have had of late, especially when the weather cleared up after the shock; but "——

"Good heaven! is the man mad?" he suddenly exclaimed.

This last expression was spoken in such a tone of alarm that, anxious as they were to gain shelter, both Lucy and her father stooped and looked at their companion.

The colonel was gazing seaward.

He now pointed to a small vessel that was steering for the island.

"It is the Ariel," he went on. "The tempest will be upon us before she can make the harbour; and if she *should* do so, this harbour affords no safe shelter to shipping of any description, even in an ordinary gale of wind. Captain Barton must be mad not to gain an offing while he has the chance!"

"Ha! there she goes round! He is going to stand out to sea. That is his only chance!"

"Dear papa," exclaimed Lucy, "I do hope that the Conqueror is somewhere safe in port."

"And the Acteon, girl—have you no thought for her?" said Captain Sinclair.

"Y-y-es, papa," stammered Lucy; "but Captain Rodman is so old a friend."

"I should be sorry if harm were to befall either ship, or their officers and crews," went on Captain Sinclair. "But Rodman and Milford are both skilful seamen, and if any one can keep a ship clear of danger in a storm, they can "——

"Do not wish them in harbour, my dear Miss Sinclair," put in Colonel Daintree. "If they are wise they will have foreseen this coming cyclone, and will have put to sea, and run out clear of the islands."

The above conversation had occupied scarcely a minute, while the speakers were hurrying through the grounds which surrounded the colonel's one-storeyed, but large and beautiful dwelling.

They had entered the wide, airy apartment on the lower floor, which was used as a sitting-room, and, with alarm depicted on their features, were looking through the window towards the sea, ere the dull roar which had sounded in their ears as they hastened towards the house, suddenly increased, with a deafening noise more resembling thunder than wind, and yet not exactly resembling either. At the end of the grounds, fronting the beach, stood a strong, wooden, barn-like edifice, used as a storehouse. This house, which was the first to feel the force of the tempest, fell crashing into ruins after hardly half a minute's resistance. Its shingles and weather-boards were seen flying before the wind like chips of cardboard, or shavings, though the weather-boards were of the stoutest and weightiest timber. Some negroes who were hastening to shelter were thrown headlong to the ground, and blown along as though they had no power to help themselves. The earth and sand were torn up by the blast, and, mingled with stones, were hurled alone at the height of six or eight feet from the ground, as if cast from some powerful projectile. The atmosphere was so suddenly filled with a swift-drifting fog (as it appeared) of sand, earth, stones, and shells, that the sea was hidden from view, and everything was enveloped in darkness. The house rocked and shook and trembled; but having, as the colonel had intimated, been especially constructed to withstand the hurricanes with which, from time to time, the West India islands are visited, it did not fall; and presently, in the brief lull between the blasts, faint, half-stifled cries were heard from persons injured by the falling ruins, or terrified, and calling for aid.

Leaving Lucy to the care of half a dozen negro servants, who appeared to be even more frightened than she, Captain Sinclair and Colonel Daintree essayed to go forth to render such aid as might be in their power. Rain and hail were now mingled with the dense earthy fog, and the salt spray of the sea, half a mile distant, was blown inland with such force that it stung and pricked the skin, wherever exposed, most painfully. Thunder rolled overhead, and lightning, red and blue, darted forth from the dense black clouds which now overhung the island, in zig-zag lines, and sent forth a hissing sound like that made by serpents, as it glided, as if endued with life, and eager for mischief, over the ground.

Amidst this wild turmoil of the elements, amidst Cimmerian darkness, which the lightning only made visible, causing the objects seen dimly through the strange earthy fog to appear like moving shadows, and increasing the awful aspect of the scene, the two gentlemen strove to force their way onward, guided only by the half-stifled cries of distress, faintly audible in the pauses of the wind, which seemed to rest for an instant only to gather fresh force for mischief.

It was what sailors aptly style a "living tempest." Each element in fierce commotion seemed to be conscious of its might, and—as if in scorn of the puny efforts of man—to be eager to do all the mischief in its power.

Through this wild, savage tumult, soaked to the skin, the water pouring in streams from their saturated clothing—now twirled swiftly round, now blown off their feet, now striking against some ruined wall, or stump of a tree, now struck and bruised themselves by some missile flying swiftly through the air, the two gentlemen passed on, not knowing whither they were going, nor where they were, save when some vivid flash dimly revealed the house they had quitted, and the ruins that surrounded them.

At length, the loose earth and sand having blown away, the atmosphere partially cleared. Then they saw that, like men wandering in a forest, they had moved in a circle, and though half an hour had elapsed since they had left their shelter, they were not two hundred yards from the colonel's dwelling.

They now made their way somewhat faster towards the town, still blown wildly about—now up, now down, now falling headlong over a heap of ruins, now stumbling amidst a whirlwind of choking sand. People passed them by, or were rudely driven against them—white men and negroes, men, women, and children intermingled—some crying for help—help for the love of God! Some half-stunned, bruised and bleeding, gazing stupidly around them, stretching forth their arms, like blind men feeling in the dark. Captain Sinclair had seen many a hurricane, both in the East and West Indies, in the course of his earlier naval career; but he acknowledged to himself that he had never seen aught like this, which was, as I have said, the most terrific cyclone ever known, a wild witch-Sabbath of the elements, such as the earth has probably seldom witnessed.

As the atmosphere still lightened, the two gentlemen perceived that the island, so far as they could see around them, was one heap of chaos—one mass of ruins. In the town, not half a dozen dwellings—and these were one-storeyed houses, built, like that of Colonel Daintree's, expressly to withstand the hurricanes—remained standing. Dead and mangled bodies lay around them, some crushed beneath the ruins; men and animals lay struggling, or crushed to death together!

The two gentlemen, and others on the same errand of mercy, led some of the women and children, or some old feeble men, to such shelter as they could find, and then went back to seek for more. But now the power to render aid was arrested. All the elements, save fire, had hitherto been at work: fire now united its terrors to the rest. The houses were chiefly built of wood. The fierce heats had rendered them dry and inflammable as tinder. The flying rain had for some time prevented the disaster which, but for it, had sooner occurred; but at length the smouldering flames burst forth into a blaze, and henceforward the rain was powerless to check the conflagration for one instant. For the space of half a square mile the ruins burst forth into one fierce flame. Those who had found shelter in the towns were compelled to fly. Borne onward by the wind, the sparks and flaming brands flew over the whole island. The flames seized upon the forests and plantations, and the entire country blazed as one vast bonfire, the wind carrying the black smoke far over the sea. Only a house here and there, out of the course of the wind, escaped the flames. One of these was that of Colonel Daintree, and that was soon crowded from cellar to roof with hapless, maimed wretches, who had lost all else, but who still clung to life.

Throughout the greater portion of the day the storm raged, then it gradually subsided, and those who had preserved their lives wailed and mourned over the friends they had lost, or the property which had been swept from them. The flames burnt brightly through the night, and, when daybreak came again, the island was one smouldering ruin. During the next day a few small vessels which happily weathered the storm, came in, and those on board brought dreadful reports of the ruin which had befallen the surrounding islands, and of the vessels that had gone ashore or foundered at sea. The coasts of all the neighbouring islands were strewn with wrecks; except their own, they did not believe one vessel, large or small, was saved. The Acteon, it was known, had gone on shore at Nevis, and every soul on board had perished.

Lucy Sinclair heard this report, and turned pale and trembled. Her father caught her in his arms; but she did not faint, as he had expected her to do.

"Poor Milford—poor, poor fellow!" exclaimed the captain.

"And the Conqueror, dear papa!" faintly murmured Lucy. "Where is the Conqueror? and Captain Rodman? He is a skilful seaman, papa. _You_ said so. He will have saved _his_ ship. Oh, tell me, dear papa, that Tom Rodman has saved _his_ frigate!"

"I said the same of Lord Milford, my child," replied the captain; "but no human skill can avail in such tempests as this we have experienced. Heaven grant that the report of the loss of the Acteon be false! Let us hope yet that Milford is safe, and——poor Tom. He was—_is_, I trust—a noble young fellow. Let us hope while we may, Lucy. Pray heaven that _both_ are saved!"

But Lucy was not comforted by these words. Neither she nor her father knew that Lord Milford had quitted his ship to come on a visit to them, just before the cyclone burst forth. If the Acteon were gone, they thought he had gone with her. They had no idea that his lordship was on board the Ariel at the time when—to the great relief of Colonel Daintree—she put about to gain a good offing. And, moreover, to tell the truth, though Lucy, on an ordinary occasion, would have grieved over the loss of Lord Milford as over the loss of a friend, and would have sorrowed at the thought that so many brave officers and seamen had perished in the frigate, her fears for the Acteon and her commander and crew were swallowed up in fears for the safety of Captain Rodman—so selfish are the kindest-hearted among us when we, or those whom we best love, are in peril! Poor Lucy hardly gave a thought to Lord Milford or the Acteon now. She kept her thoughts secret in her own bosom; but they dwelt constantly upon Tom Rodman. No one yet had brought any news, good or bad, respecting the Conqueror. Oh, how she longed, yet dreaded, to hear, while hope was mingled with her fears—the report which she knew _must_ soon arrive!"

After the tempest, the sea still retained an angry look; but the sky was clear and the air balmy, and a bright sun shone down upon the black desolation of the islands, and upon the hundreds of ruined families.

And now people began to wonder how far the cyclone had extended—whether it had reached Cuba or Jamaica, or whether its fury had been concentrated upon the windward and leeward islands.

At St. Eustatius there lived a negro slave, said to be more than a hundred years of age, but still hale, active, and erect, and venerable-looking with his snow-white, crispy, woolly hair, whiskers, and beard. The old man, in consideration of his extreme age, was much respected, and was accustomed—as he basked idly in the hot sunshine—to converse freely with the white men who stood near him, as well as with those of his own colour and class. This old man, whose name was Brutus, heard Captain Sinclair and Colonel Daintree conversing, with other gentlemen, relative to the extent and force of the cyclone.

"I hardly think," said a planter, "that it has extended so far as Jamaica; or if it have, its force will have diminished considerably before it reached that island."

The old negro shook his head solemnly.

"You don't agree with me, Brutus?" said the planter.

"Massa, *no*," replied the old man. "Twice I see cyclone—yerie? (you hear me?) Twice, sah. One time me not long come from Afriky—mos' a hundred years ago. Once more, after fifty years gone by. But bo'f of *dem* was not so bad as dis! *Dem* time it catch Jamaica, massa, an' Cuby, an' de Bahamas too. Go bring ruin eberywhere. An' massa, yerie? de *tail* ob dem not *las'* so long, fo' true, but fo' de *time* it las', it was wuss den de fust blow."

"But see how clear the sky is, Brutus!" observed another gentleman.

"Dat nuffin, massa," replied the old negro. "De *tail* come, fo' sure!"

"And how long will it be, do you think, before it comes, old man?" asked Captain Sinclair.

"Dat depen', massa," replied the negro. "See—de sea angry! Dat tell dat de tail *mus'* come. De wind not shift, I tink, massa?"

"No, Brutus; it continues to blow from the same quarter, and that surprises me."

"S'pose de wind shift when de blow was over, den, massa, de tail come quick. S'pose no shift, den he long time before he come—tree, four day, week, maybe; but when de sea keep angry, dat a sign dat de tail *will* come. Yerie, massa? Dem cap'en dat go to sea for tree or four day after is 'toopid fools. Dem not know what dey doin', sah."

The old negro, though he had not expressed himself very clearly, had spoken truly, and predicted the course of storms, which, until the scientific discoveries made of late years by Lieutenant Maury, of the United States navy, Captain, subsequently the late Admiral Fitzroy, of the British navy, and others, was little known, even to the most skilful navigators. One of these discoveries was that if, after a severe cyclone or rotatory hurricane, the wind suddenly shifts after the first fury of the hurricane has subsided, the diameter of the storm is small, and it may be expected to return speedily after completing its lineal course; but if the wind does not shift, the diameter is larger, and sometimes two, three, or even four days elapse before what the old negro called "the tail" of the cyclone—that is, the furious squall with which the tempest ends, near the spot at which it commenced, is felt.

The cyclone which I have feebly attempted to describe extended from the coast of South America, near the Island of Trinidad, to a spot considerably west of the Bahama islands, thus pursuing a slightly curved line of more than eighteen hundred miles in length. Its circumference may be estimated at between four and five thousand miles, and its diameter at more than a thousand miles. Cuba, St. Domingo, and Jamaica, the three largest West India islands, escaped its onward progress altogether; but it swept over Jamaica with terrific force on its return, while the southern portion of Cuba and the island of St. Domingo, lying near its centre, felt it but slightly, and vessels sailing along the north coast of St. Domingo, and being, therefore, exactly in the centre of its diameter, experienced nothing more than an unusually heavy swell of the sea, for which the captains, until they heard of the cyclone, were unable to account.

On the day after the above conversation took place, it became known that the report of the total loss of his Majesty's frigate Acteon, at Nevis, was but too true. The frigate and every other vessel, large or small, that lay in the harbours of St. Kitts or Nevis, had gone ashore, and every soul on board of them had perished. Boats and portions of the wrecks were found afterwards miles inland. But it was also reported that Captain Lord Milford was not on board his frigate when the cyclone commenced. He had just taken passage for St. Eustatius, on board the schooner Ariel. It was also reported that his Majesty's frigate Conqueror, Captain Rodman commander, had sailed out of the harbour of Nevis about half an hour previous to the outbreak of the cyclone. But what had become of the Conqueror, or of the little Ariel, no one could say.

It would be false to state that Lucy Sinclair was sorry when she heard that Lord Milford was not on board his frigate when she went on shore. The young lady really felt glad that there was at least a hope of his lordship's safety. Still, withal, she *did* experience a strange feeling of *uneasiness*, which she would have found it difficult to describe, when she heard the report; and if she longed to hear that Lord Milford was really safe, she longed ten times more to hear of the safety of Captain Rodman, and felt a terrible anxiety, that caused her bosom to ache with pain, while his safety was a matter of doubt.

This anxiety, however, was set at rest on the morning of the third day after the cyclone, for on that morning Captain Rodman made his appearance at St. Eustatius. He certainly *had* proved himself a skilful seaman, or rather, I ought perhaps to say that his usual good fortune had attended him. Running out to sea before the tempest, he had found the wind gradually to subside. He had, in fact, without being conscious of it, run into the centre of the diameter of the cyclone, and had brought his ship to anchor in the harbour of Porto Rico, where she lay perfectly secure from any tempest, however fierce. But dreading lest some evil had befallen the Sinclairs, and especially being anxious to hear tidings of Lucy, he had, immediately on bringing the frigate to an anchor, taken passage on board a fishing vessel bound for St. Eustatius, where he arrived safely, as I have stated, and was kindly welcomed by his former friend and patron, Captain Sinclair, who even permitted him on this occasion to see Lucy in his (Captain Sinclair's) presence. But though Lucy's heart was secretly set at ease, Captain Sinclair, now he knew that Captain Rodman was safe, was tenfold more anxious than ever to hear of the safety of Lord Milford.

Towards noon of that same day a schooner was sighted standing directly for the island, and it was soon known that the schooner was the Ariel, and that she had suffered serious damage during the hurricane. Her mainmast was carried away, also her foretopmast, and she was running in under her foresail. She was on the opposite side of the island to that on which Colonel Daintree resided, and where the town and harbour, such as it is, are situated, her captain probably intending to sail round the island to the harbour.

Hitherto, there had been no signs of the recurrence of the hurricane, except that the sea continued to wear an angry aspect.   The sky was clear and cloudless, the weather fine, and the wind light and steady.   Many people began to laugh at the old negro's prediction; and at the hour in question, a number of men, half fishermen, half sailors, were, together with several negroes, among whom was old Brutus, idly watching the progress of the approaching schooner.

"Ah, you old croaker," said a fisherman to the old negro, "it's not enow that we've lost our boats, and that our dwellings are in ruins, and all our little property gone; but *you* must amuse yourself by prognostifying another gale!"

"An' he *come*, massa, fo' *sure*," said the aged negro.   "He come dis a minit. Golly!   I not gib much, under de sarcumstances, fo' dat schooner, dar.   He! he! he! he!"

"Hold yer jabber, ye black nigger," said another man, "or else "——

"Look!   See *dar!*" interrupted the old negro, pointing his crooked forefinger to seaward.   "He come dis berry minit.   Ha! ha! I tell you fo' true.   No?"

The fishermen gazed in the direction pointed out.   As if by magic, the lately clear sky had become obscured by threatening black clouds, lit up by strange fiery "horse-tails" of all the colours of the rainbow, amidst which leaping flashes of lightning played incessantly.   These clouds were driven onward with more than railroad speed; there was audible the dull rumble in the air which always precedes a hurricane; suddenly the clouds opened, the leaping lightning darted forth in fiery zig-zag lines, the thunder roared, the rain fell in torrents, the atmosphere darkened, and the schooner, which had been running before the wind, was taken aback.   For an instant she appeared as if she were going down stern foremost.   Then she was, apparently, lifted half out of the foaming water, and hurled onward hopelessly and helplessly towards the reef that girdled the island on this shore.

"Dere I *tol'* you.   He! he! he!   De *tail* come now!" exclaimed the old negro; and even while he was speaking, the hapless vessel was tossed bodily on to the reef, where she fell over on her side, amidst the sharp rocks, and instantly went to pieces, leaving her crew and passengers struggling hopelessly for life among the breakers.

Captain Rodman, hurt by the comparative coolness with which he had been received on his visit to St. Eustatius by Captain Sinclair, who had only permitted him to see Lucy in his presence, had that morning strolled across the small island, full of bitter feeling towards everybody, and thinking how different would have been the reception of his hated rival had *he* returned unexpectedly to the island. At this moment the captain came to the beach, and mingled with the crowd of fishermen and negroes, who, as he was clothed in rough sailor attire, had no idea of his rank, and supposed him to be the master or mate of one or other of the merchant ships that had been wrecked in the cyclone.

Some of the unfortunate crew and passengers of the Ariel were still struggling amidst the breakers, close to the shore, yet none of the lookers-on dared offer to aid them.   It would have been almost certain death to have attempted to assist them.

Captain Rodman asked the name of the wrecked vessel.

"The Ariel," was the reply.

Then it recurred to his memory that Lord Milford had taken passage on board that vessel; and looking upon the few unfortunate wretches who were still struggling vainly and hopelessly for life, his eyes fell upon Lord Milford, who, stripped to his trousers, and almost exhausted, bruised, bleeding, and helpless, was still faintly struggling to gain the shore.

There was his hated rival—the man who had blighted the dearest hope of his life—about to perish! For him to gain the shore without help was impossible, and to offer to help him was apparently to commit self-sacrifice.

For a moment a gleam of savage joy flitted across Captain Rodman's countenance. He had wished to meet this man face to face, and struggle with him to the death of one or the other. Here he was, dying before his eyes, through no act of *his*—apparently beyond the reach of human aid. Soon he would be rid of him for ever. At this instant the eyes of the two captains met. They recognized each other. Lord Milford's features wore an expression of hopeless agony and despair. His strength was exhausted. A few moments more, and he must certainly perish. At the same time, when he saw Captain Rodman on the shore, a look of defiance for a moment crossed his countenance, which seemed to say:

"Fortune has favoured you. You have triumphed; but my hatred of you will linger in my bosom till I draw my last breath. Rejoice over my destruction; but I hate and defy you still."

Captain Rodman could not bear that glance unmoved. He knew that, in all probability, if he attempted to aid his rival, he would perish with him, even if he were possessed of his usual strength and activity, and that, suffering as he still was from the effects of the wound in his shoulder, there was still less chance that he could render any service to his brother officer in the present hopeless condition of the latter.

Nevertheless, actuated by a sudden impulse of humanity and generosity, he prepared to plunge into the midst of the foaming breakers. He did not expect to return, but he thought to himself:

"I care little for life—we shall probably both perish. But if I *can* I will save that man, for Lucy's sake, at my own desperate peril. If I save him, and perish in the attempt, I shall at least win Lucy's gratitude, and she will ever respect my memory."

Pieces of rope and timber—the remnants of the wrecks that strewed the coast—lay about the beach. Fastening a rope round his body he gave the end to one of the fishermen, and bade him hold it firmly, and drag him back if he should succeed in rescuing the man he wished to save, or if it were apparent that his efforts were vain.

"I will fasten the rope round his body if I can," he added. "If I succeed, haul *him* on shore. Take no heed of *me*."

"Hold back, you fool!" cried several of the men on the beach, supposing him, as I have said, to be the mate of some lost vessel. "Is it not enough that you have lost your ship? Would you recklessly throw away your life as well?"

These remonstrances, however, were uttered in vain. Captain Rodman plunged into the breakers, and the men, seeing his determination, caught hold of the end of the line.

Lord Milford was already insensible before Captain Rodman reached him. As the latter endeavoured to wade and swim out towards the drowning man, he was thrown again and again upon the sharp-pointed rocks. His legs were entangled with seaweed; once or twice he was almost stunned. Once he gave himself up for lost, as did the people on shore. At length he succeeded in reaching the spot where Lord Milford lay insensible. He grasped him firmly in a death-like grip, and signed to the people on shore to haul in the rope. It was his last effort. The next moment he, too, became insensible.

The hauling in of the rope was a difficult and dangerous task. The surf several times dashed the two men violently against the rocks, and it was feared that the rope would be severed by their sharp edges. Captain Rodman, however, clung unconsciously with his death-like grip to Lord Milford, and at length both were hauled to the beach, though it was thought that both were dead. Soon, however, they showed signs of life; but Captain Rodman was the first to revive. He recovered consciousness, but felt himself in dreadful pain. The wound on his shoulder had reopened in his struggles, and his left arm was broken; but it was feared that though Lord Milford breathed, *he* was too far gone to recover.

"Leave *me*," said Captain Rodman to the men. "I shall do well enough alone; but take him to the nearest shelter, and if a surgeon can be found, send for one."

A couple of guineas which he handed to the men quickened their efforts and stimulated their humanity. They bore Lord Milford to a ruined negro hut, near by; and Captain Rodman, crawling with difficulty to a flat rock on the edge of the beach, threw himself upon it, and again became almost unconscious through the agonizing pain he suffered.

Meanwhile, the squall had passed on and the sky had become clear again. The "tail" of the cyclone had been fierce but brief, and had quickly done its work, for not a vestige of the wrecked schooner was now to be seen.

An hour passed away. A surgeon had been sent for to the town on the opposite shore of the island; and during this period, though Lord Milford continued to show signs of life, he had not recovered consciousness. The fishermen and negroes stood around the rude pallet on which he lay, and though none of them knew his rank nor had any idea who he was, they paid him all the attention in their power, while they left Captain Rodman, who it was supposed was not near so seriously injured as was really the case, to bear his sufferings alone.

A report had reached the town that the Ariel had been driven on the reef by the squall, and had become a wreck, and that all on board had perished. It was by this time known to Captain Sinclair that Lord Milford had sailed in the Ariel from Nevis, and in a state of great alarm the captain set forth for the spot at which the wreck had occurred, taking his daughter Lucy with him; and the only medical man on the island accompanied them, to give his attention to the as yet unknown rescued man.

A great number of people of every class, white men and negroes, most of whom were now houseless and ruined, came over also to see the wreck.

Captain Sinclair, with his daughter clinging, pale and trembling, to his arm, walked down to the beach, where the doctor left them and entered the hut into which Lord Milford had been carried.

"Are *none* saved but the poor fellow in the hut?" asked the captain of the crowd.

"None, yer honour," replied the fisherman. "Nobody, massa," cried the negroes.

"Captain Milford—is *he* on board? Are you sure that *he* is lost?"

The people, who knew nothing of Captain Lord Milford, naturally supposed that Captain Sinclair spoke of the captain of the schooner, whose name was unknown to them.

"Yes, massa, *he* on board fo' sure," answered a negro. "Me see him at de helm. He *gone*, massa—gone fo' sartin!"

Captain Sinclair now caught sight of Captain Rodman, who had raised himself up on the appearance of Lucy and her father, the latter of whom did not, in his excitement and grief, notice the deathly pallor of Captain Rodman's countenance, nor the expression of intense pain that his features wore. He imagined that Captain Rodman had come to the spot to witness the wreck.

"And *you* were here, Rodman," he said, in a tone of scorn and indignation.

" *You*, sir, who glory in your daring courage, and your carelessness in the face of danger. And yet, sir, you witnessed the loss of the schooner, and the dreadful death of a brother officer, and made no attempt to save him! Your motive for this callousness is plain enough to *me*. You believe, sir, that a rival has been removed from your path. But mark me, sir, it will not serve *you*. Had anybody told me you could act thus, I would not have believed them. Our friendship, sir, is dissolved from this time forward, for ever!"

And Lucy gazed with a strange expression upon her lover. Her looks seemed to say, as plainly as if the words were spoken :

"Captain Rodman, until now I believed you worthy of my affection. I believed that, regardless whether he were friend or foe, your courage and humanity would urge you, even at the imminent risk of life, to do your utmost to rescue a fellow creature whom you beheld struggling amid deadly peril ; and yet you have sat and looked coldly, perhaps exultingly, on, while one whom you deemed your rival perished before your eyes!"

So Captain Rodman read the young lady's looks. He had paid little heed to the taunts of her father, but had returned scorn for scorn. But now he rose and staggered to his feet, and with a degree of strength that a few moments before he did not possess, he stepped forward and took Lucy's hand, and led her towards the hut. His steps were uneven, and his broken arm hung listlessly at his side ; and now Lucy, and her father too, remarked his livid complexion, the distortion of his features with pain, and his feeble steps, and the latter felt some compunction for the language he had used, while Lucy regarded him with pity. Tears rose to her eyes, as she said :

"Tom, you are ill—suffering! I am *very* sorry that my father spoke as he did. He was excited. He did not mean what he said ; and *I* too, dear Tom, for the moment, forgot that your wounded shoulder renders you unable to act as you would act otherwise. But where are you leading me ?"

Captain Rodman made no reply. He compressed his lips to conceal the physical pain he suffered, and the mental agony he was silently enduring. But he still retained his hold of Lucy's hand with his own right hand, while his left arm hung listlessly at his side. Captain Sinclair followed after the pair, wondering whither Captain Rodman was conducting his daughter.

At length they reached and entered the hut. Lord Milford was, by this time, partially restored to consciousness, though he still appeared to be bewildered, and looked as though he wondered where he was, and what was the matter with him. The doctor was administering restoratives to his patient, who presented a ghastly spectacle. His face was cut, bruised, and swollen, and stained with blood ; and his lips were drawn aside with pain, as he gazed wildly around him. It was barely possible for his visitors to recognize his features. Still, they knew him ; and Lucy, starting with surprise, turned towards Captain Rodman to ask for an explanation of this shocking scene. And now, for the first time, she perceived that Captain Rodman's hands were bleeding, and that *his* garments were torn and stained with blood.

"Lord Milford here, and thus!" exclaimed Captain Sinclair ; and Lucy, again turning to Captain Rodman, murmured, in a voice tremulous with emotion :

"Tom—*dear* Tom—tell me—what is the meaning of this ?"

"That I *have* saved him—my rival, for whom you wantonly cast aside, as worthless, the love I bore towards you," answered Captain Rodman, in a hollow tone of voice, and in tremulous accents. He paused, as if to gather strength. His lips moved silently, but at length he again gasped forth : " Ay, saved him, at the peril of my own life—saved him, that you, Lucy, might be happy "——

He strove to speak further, but he had taxed his strength too much; and stretching forth his right arm, he grasped for a moment wildly at the air, and fell heavily to the earthen floor of the hut, with his broken arm beneath his body.

*   *   *   *   *   *

When Captain Rodman again awoke to consciousness he found himself with his head resting upon Lucy's shoulder, while she was supporting him with her arm. The hut had been cleared of all save the doctor, Captain Sinclair, and his daughter, and the two wounded officers. Lord Milford still lay on the rude wooden pallet, but he now seemed to be aware of all that was passing around him. During the period that Captain Rodman had lain insensible, the discovery had been made that his left arm was broken, and the doctor had set the bone as well as he could under the circumstances, and had temporarily bandaged the arm, as well as the wounded shoulder. Captain Rodman now started with surprise, and feebly endeavoured to detach himself from his fair supporter.

He thought to have seen Lucy in anxious attendance upon his rival, and he gazed upon her with a strange, wondering look.

Lucy understood the look, and whispered softly in his ear.

What she whispered was known only to themselves; but the words brought a flush to Captain Rodman's pallid cheek, and his eyes lighted up, while an expression of affection and gratitude and glad surprise overspread his countenance. He made no further attempt to detach himself from her; but again, overpowered by suffering, he let his head fall upon her shoulder, and closed his eyes, while she retained possession of his hand.

"Leave me, papa—leave me," she replied, in answer to some remark gently urged by her father. "It is no time now for false shame. I have whispered the truth in Tom's ear!"

Colonel Daintree's carriage was sent for, and Lord Milford and Captain Rodman were carefully lifted into the vehicle—Lucy also entering, and supporting the latter, who was much the most seriously injured of the two officers—Lord Milford's injuries being merely slight cuts and bruises, his insensibility having been caused solely by his frequent long submersions beneath the water. Captain Sinclair and the doctor followed the carriage on foot to Colonel Daintree's residence.

*   *   *   *   *   *

Several weeks elapsed ere Captain Rodman was sufficiently recovered to be able to leave his room; but as soon as he was able to sit up, Lucy was in constant attendance upon him, endeavouring in every way to amuse him in his weary, enforced idleness. During his illness, the Conqueror had been brought round by her first lieutenant, from Porto Rico to St. Kitts, where she now lay at anchor; and as soon as Captain Rodman was in a condition to bear removal, he went with the Sinclairs to St. Kitts, and at Captain Sinclair's request, took up his abode with the family. All was arranged satisfactorily between him and Lucy now.

Lord Milford, deeply and sincerely grateful for the great service Captain Rodman had rendered him, and convinced at length that it was vain for him to strive to gain Lucy's affections, had voluntarily surrendered the young lady to his younger and more fortunate rival; and Captain Sinclair, seeing clearly that the marriage he had opposed, in his foolish ambition to see his daughter a countess, was essential to her happiness, had freely given his consent to her union with Captain Rodman.

Captain Sinclair had deferred his departure for England until December, and before that month came round, Lucy and Captain Rodman were wedded by the

Captain Rodman boarding a French line-of-battle ship.

See page 119.

chaplain of the Conqueror, and Captain and Mrs. Sinclair, and Lucy—now Mrs Rodman—eventually embarked on board the frigate for England, as the *guests* of her commander, ships of war not being allowed to carry passengers.

Lord Milford, who came so near suffering death by drowning, heard on his recovery, for the first time, of the loss of the Acteon. His lordship embarked as soon as possible for England, to take his trial by court-martial for losing his frigate, in accordance with the rules of the service. But as it was known that so many vessels had been wrecked in the cyclone, he was honourably acquitted, and his sword was returned to him. His lordship, however, did not again go to sea. During his absence from England his father had died, and he was now Earl of Camden. Soon after his accession to his title, he married a young lady who was more eager than Lucy Sinclair to style herself a countess; but to the end of his life he remained a staunch friend of Captain Rodman's.

During the passage of the Conqueror to England, Lucy had an opportunity to witness—or rather, I should say, to hear—a naval engagement; for previous to the engagement she was conveyed below by her husband, and placed in the most safe position that could be found on board the frigate.

Off Cape Finisterre the Conqueror fell in with two French ships—a corvette and a gun-brig. These vessels endeavoured to run for a French port; but a chase ensued, and, finding it impossible to escape, they gave battle, and after a short but sharp conflict, were compelled to surrender, and, four days afterwards, were carried, as the prizes of the English frigate, into Plymouth.

Captain Sinclair volunteered to command on the forecastle during the action, and fought bravely, fortunately escaping, as did his son-in-law, without a wound; but, after the battle was won, he declared that it had reminded him of former days, when he had command of a ship-of-war, and had made him feel quite young again.

The Conqueror made a triumphant entry into Plymouth, followed by her two prizes, and Lucy had the proud satisfaction of landing with her husband and parents amidst the enthusiastic greetings of the populace, who made the atmosphere ring with their hearty cheers for Captain Rodman.

Captain Rodman remained six months on shore. He then again sailed in command of the Conqueror, on board which vessel he served with honour and credit until the end of the war, when he retired from the service with the rank of Vice-Admiral. At the same time he was created a baronet, and a Commander of the Bath, as a reward for his distinguished services.

Vice-Admiral Sir T. Rodman, Bart, C.B., removed, on the death of his father-in-law (about five years after his marriage), to the Grange, in Cambridgeshire, which demesne his wife inherited from her father, Captain Sinclair, and there for many years he lived the quiet life of an English country gentleman.

When Captain Rodman quitted the service he took with him, his faithful companion in so many perils, Pat Hennessy, who thenceforward resided at the Grange in the capacity of a servant—though it would be hard to say what were Pat's especial duties. In fact, the honest Irishman was left to do pretty much what he pleased.

Lieutenant Peters was promoted to the rank of captain shortly before Captain Rodman retired, and appointed to the command of the Druid frigate, in which he sailed to the East Indies. On his return to England at the expiration of three years, he brought home with him in the Druid, from India, Colonel Charles Morton, his and Captain Rodman's former schoolfellow, and on their arrival at Portsmouth, Captain Peters and Colonel Morton paid a visit to the Grange, where they found Admiral Sir Richard Blakeley, Rear-Admiral Sandstone, Captain Thompson, Lieutenant Fleming—who had been permitted to re-enter the British naval service, after his fortunate escape from the castle at Arica—and several other guests, all of whom had been schoolfellows together when boys, with whom they spent several pleasant weeks; and the acquaintanceship thus renewed was kept up until, one after another, they passed away to the grave.

Vice-Admiral Sir Tom Rodman, C.B., lived to a good old age; and though he has now been dead many years, he still lives in the memory of several aged officers who served under him when youths as midshipmen, and his name is still honoured in the service as that of a brave, generous, and distinguished officer and seaman.

The son of an honest retail tradesman, whose integrity and industry had enabled him to realize a moderate independence, Tom Rodman rose from the lowly condition in which he was born, to rank, fame, and fortune, and eventually to become the master and owner of the estate upon which he first set foot by accident, while a truant schoolboy, solely through his own exertions, and his earnest resolve, even from his early boyhood, to *adhere to the truth,* and, under all circumstances, though it might bring him into temporary trouble, *to do what he believed to be his duty.* His acts of boyish frolic and mischief were numerous, for he never pretended to be better than his companions, nor set himself up as an example to his fellows, as is the case with many who too frequently but play the hypocrite in so doing; but these frolics did him no harm, for the reason that they were simply the outbursts of youthful spirit, and were free from meanness, falsehood, or evil purpose of any kind. It is true that Tom found influential friends who helped him forward on his path to fame and fortune; but he would not have *found* those friends had he not been *deserving* of them, nor would he have retained their friendship had he sacrificed his own sense of independence to them, or had he subsequently proved false to them, or otherwise unworthy of their support. All boys or young men—even among those who strive to the utmost—will not be so successful as Tom Rodman, whose tact and abilities rendered him what is commonly termed a favourite of Fortune; but all who choose, and adhere to the maxims which guided Tom's adventurous career, may reasonably hope to climb some steps of the ladder, on the top of which Tom at length took his proud and well-earned position, amidst the applause of his admiring countrymen.

THE END OF " CAPTAIN RODMAN."